EVIL IS A DISEASE. THEY ARE THE CURE.

THE SUPREMACY

The Wehtiko Influence

Eric Peter Brown

authorHOUSE®

Contents

Acknowledgments

I would first like to thank my mother, Peggy Ann Brown, for her love and willingness to let her children be who they wanted to be. To my grandfather, Oscar E. Hawkins, who believed there was nothing I could not do and who inspired me to use his surname. To my oldest brother, Kent D. Brown, who took it upon himself to educate me in all the cool things on television that he watched back when I was a kid, and that I still watch today. Genres like science fiction, action, adventure, and fantasy. Thank you very much, Bro. To my nephew, Rodney A. Sadberry, who was my sounding board, even though he may not have known it, and a muse just by listening to an idea I was trying out. I would also like to thank family and friends for their support. And lastly but certainly not least, I would like to thank the team at AuthorHouse. If not for their dedication, professionalism and proficiency in their crafts, my book might still be shelved. Thank you all.

Qi-Tahh

I

Murder, sabotage, and treason are just a few of the crimes I am guilty of, though from what I was told, the list of charges and violations are much longer. Currently under Habitat confinement, I lay in my king-size, mahogany bed, stretched out my arms, and yawned deeply. I looked toward the window and saw it was approximately five in the morning.

My mind raced, and I was unable to sleep. I had not done much of that ever since I was arrested five days before. Not wishing to simply lie in bed, I got up—naked as a newborn baby—I walked over to the blue wingback chair in the corner and retrieved my black shorts.

I found it unnecessary to be properly dressed while awaiting word on my execution, but having visitors drop by unexpectedly at all hours was the norm. So for my benefit as well as theirs, I forwent the nudity I had become so accustomed to, but not the public display.

Smiling, I chuckled at the thought of my being nude around others. Anyone visiting me or seeing me unclothed in the corridors would pay me no mind and talk to me as though I were fully dressed. Here, nakedness meant nothing to my Pride. In fact, some of my Pridesmen were naked all the time. There were no hypocrisies around it—or around sex for that matter—and I found that refreshingly mature and open-minded. It was a shame so many humans practiced these opposites.

Heading to the kitchen to make a cup tea, the automatic lighting provided the correct illumination. I made a fresh pot and retrieved my favorite mug. Studying it as I have done many times before, the cup was covered with different designs, pictographs, and languages—flat and raised—and it kept the temperature of what was placed in it. The mug and teas were gifts from U'kristu, my Ket-sho. It was a peace offering on her part after she fucked me on Volaris Engrom–and not in a good way.

I chuckled and grinned while shaking my head. "Volaris Engrom. Now that's a nightmare I'm never going to forget, fasbi U'kristu," I said to myself aloud.

The tea was soon ready. Sipping the hot beverage, I scrunched my face. The taste of the tisane, normally delicious, had an opposite effect, so I set the mug down and went into the living room barefoot, wearing only my shorts. Looking at the large, white claw marks printed on my clothing, I shook my head. By now, I thought I would be accustomed to having all my clothing looking like I was wearing some new-age design fashion; but in truth, these were symbols of honor—and the claw marks of my Elphah.

Considered to be of average height my brown definition was anything but—Buffed and beautiful—I had a very fit physique that mirrored serious dedication to going to the gym, but in actuality, this was but a minor benefit to being a Human-Augment.

Pacing the living room, I began thinking about a great many things, one of which was finally adjusting to these thirty-six-hour days. I did not know why that particular thought crossed my mind. It was trivial compared to everything else I was facing. I thought of Joryd, who tried to warn me that there were consequences for my actions. But at the time I could not hear him, and later, I did not think. At least not clearly and not when it came to Angela. Because of the three major offenses, the Council assembled to decide how they should proceed.

Scratching at the claw marks crossing my heart, I took notice of the alien works of art and artifacts, both bought and gifted from planets my new family had taken me to. I ceased rubbing and stopped to look at the painting of lupine creatures called Krankas.

Hanging on the wall above the gray sofa, the family resembled the Alaskan timber wolves on Earth, except these dogs were twice their size. They had dark gray fur with large white spots and six legs with five-toe paws, and their ears were pointed. They looked beautiful, and the bold, pure whiteness of their eyes, which matched their spots and six-inch fangs, were enchanting. And then there were their pups. They were adorable, especially at play. The artist truly captured the family well.

Gathered under a large tree, the male lay sphinx-like next to his mate, head raised high as he looked off protectively. The mother watched one pair of pups chase each other and allowed the two youngest to climb on her as though she were a rock for them to wrestle on, while the oldest pup sat beside his father and helped keep watch.

I purchased the artwork while visiting Emiyku II with Antonio, Torr, and Syn'nar during my first year in this galaxy. I looked at it for a few moments longer before resuming my pacing, and smiled while recalling the fun time we had that trip.

Looking at the sculptures and other alien artifacts staged throughout the living room, I passed the mirror on the wall and suddenly stopped. Backing up I examined my personal claw marks, which I was still getting used to.

Gliding my fingertips lightly over them, my mind flashed to the day I was marked. Though painful, the memory of how it made me feel cut deeper than Joryd's claws ever could. I felt he was being made my master, and the marks I would bear for all to see were his signature informing other Elphahs and their servants who my master was.

My direct ancestry to those who lived and died during Earth's barbaric times of slavery, and a family history that went back a thousand years had contributed to the creation of my prejudicial viewpoint. The stories of my ancestors' struggles were passed down through every generation, so we never forgot our heritage or their enslavement.

As it happened, I was partially right but for the wrong reasons. An Elphah's clawing was not a marking of ownership as much as a symbol of integrity and respect. Yes, they were used to identify those within the Supremacy, but the true meaning behind being clawed was about family. It was about bearing the insignia of the inductee's Pride.

Walking with my head dropped, I became lost in a pool of memories and emotions and realized I needed to talk about this, about everything. Perhaps I would learn where it all went wrong. But so much had happened in the two years that I had been here and more so in this past year—my first encounter with those Influenced by the Wehtiko, my battle against the mad Sorcerer Telus, and then, of course, the incidents involving Angela, which added to the hot water I was already in.

"But where should I start?" I asked myself. Stopping abruptly, I raised my head as a voice inside said, "From the beginning." It would probably be my last entry anyway, so I cleared my throat.

"Momja, Chronicle Entry 2-2-5-6. Start record," I said loud and clear.

A calming female voice replied, "One moment, Marc," and then paused. "Jamonaka proceed."

I started to pace once more. Two years ago, an alien delegation visited my wife, Angela, and me and told us that I had been selectively chosen by the Ohdens to join their cause. Their leader, Kerebrol, insisted all was explained to us and that I understood exactly what would happen should I accept their offer. They would alter the time line and erase my existence on Earth before taking me to their galaxy.

I was speechless, and more so to learn I would have to submit to some sort of medical procedure. By the time I found my voice, Kerebrol was telling Angela and me that I would be placed with a Pride who was to be my new family and with whom I was to live and fight alongside for the next eight of my planet's years. And if I survived this Tour of Duty, they would send me back home and everything would be as it was before I had left. But if I died, this new time line they created would remain, and on Earth it would be as if I never existed.

I was blown away, to say the least. I mean, before they came, I was an entrepreneur with several successful businesses. I was happily married to Angela, who had just started her third trimester, and we were enjoying the good life living between Chicago and San Francisco. I was no soldier. I was a nervous first-time dad. A warrior? Who? Me? Are you kidding? The only battle that lay ahead for me was diaper duty and my dedication to raising my child right.

I suddenly became joyfully tearful and smiled at the thoughts of my life as a dad. Shoot. I was busy trying to have everything ready by the time Angela was due. I had neither the time nor the desire to fly off to some unknown galaxy and play Flash Gordon. Our lives together were good and were about to get better, so why would I choose to join some alien war that had been waging for thousands of years, claimed countless lives, and that I had nothing to do with?

Kerebrol told me the choice was mine and that I could refuse if I so wished. However, I would also be responsible for what may befall all of humanity if I did. That stopped me and got me thinking. What if this possible cataclysmic event turned out to be the death of my family? How would I feel then, knowing I had the power to stop it and did not? I was filled with heartache.

"Some choice. It sounded more like an ultimatum. Sacrifice my life here on Earth and join their war, or refuse and one day sacrifice all of mankind, including my family? Now I ask you—was there really ever a choice? Of course I accepted the alien proposal despite my being very much against it. What choice did I have? Which life would you have chosen?"

Tired of pacing, I walked to the sofa and dropped onto it. I moved about, looking for that comfortable spot until I found one. I continued, and thought about this military corp.

"They call themselves Qi-Tahh, the Qi-Tahh Supremacy. A bit too audacious and arrogant for my taste. At least that was what I thought before serving with them. And though it may appear my tour of duty was over, it was also an eye-opener into who these creatures are and why they were so badly needed in this galaxy. The Supremacy are the Prides, the Life Protectors, and the first line of defense against threats like the Wehtiko, a diabolical disease capable of unleashing one's darkest nature, and this was only one of the battles the Qi-Tahh fought in their galaxy. They also coped with would-be invaders like the Tukylis, a terrifying intelligent plant species, and were also responsible for stopping warring planets. The Supremacy defended various species against whatever dangers threatened this galaxy."

For thousands of years, the Ohdens, the Governing Council Authority, had been selectively choosing and recruiting humans so that we could aid them in their wars.

I lay there, chuckling. My voice was light because I knew what I just said sounded like a theme for a Saturday morning cartoon, and I wished to God it was. However, that was simply not the case, for despite all its strangeness and differences, life in this galaxy was just as real as life was on Earth, only for me, it had become far more deadly. I learned a Linksys Cleansing was the catalyst for my being recruited, and then I was taught what a Linksys was.

Taking in a deep breath, I exhaled hard and rubbed my hands over my brown face, feeling its stubby roughness from days of not shaving.

"In Jhanctum, a galaxy twice removed from ours, in the Oria star system, the fifth planet was named Seregaia, a word meaning tranquility, and it was dawn there. The planet's twin suns and three moons were described to me as amazing. Its lavender skies and soft red clouds were breathtakingly beautiful, and the lush green landscape below was gorgeous. A setting as picturesque as it was peaceful. At least it used to be." I sprung up from the sofa, planting my feet firmly and clenching my fists.

On the other side of the hills, death as far as the eye could see. Gibbon-like creatures littered the ground, slaughtered in some of the most horrific ways. Their bodies were ripped apart, some were disemboweled while others were decapitated. These were only a few of the atrocities committed by the Linksys.

My pulse raced at the thought of those monsters and of what they represented, and I wished to repay them for their crimes. I clenched my fist even tighter, but then I quickly lessened my grip. My current predicament made vengeance unrealistic as my mind catapulted me back to my present, where I fought against thinking about the Council and dwelling on an outcome I had no say in. I concentrated hard on my entry.

Though try as I did, it still was not easy to calm myself as thoughts of the Linksys now filled my mind. The stories my Pridesmen shared with me about those mechanical monsters and their experiments, their interrogation practices, and their insane Cleansing Prime Directive made my blood boil.

"The Linksys are sentient, highly evolved, artificial life-forms, geniuses who possess morphogenic and regenerative capabilities. Self-aware of their own existence, the Linksys hate all sentient species and will not stop until every man, woman, and child have been wiped out of existence and they are the only remaining intelligence in the galaxy." I took in a deep breath and exhaled hard.

The Gibbon-like creatures are called Seagues. Still in their primal stage of evolution, they walked predominantly hunched over and looked as though they were handicapped while their primordial features reflected an unintelligible race. I have seen photos of these creatures. Their face, hands, feet, and long tail has an olive complexion, and their bodies are covered in red fur. The young ones looked adorable, almost like stuffed animals. Thinking of them made me smile. But my grin faded when I thought of them being hunted by the Linksys. My head dropped, my heart sank, and my pulse raced once more. I felt a deep sadness for them as my rage started to flare, so I lay back down and tried to calm myself once more.

"A lone Seague had survived the massacre, injured. His head wound leaked purple blood, and the lacerations across his chest and arms were deep. Gripping the metal whip wound about his throat, the creature fought to free himself, but his efforts were in vain, for the whip was the arm of a Bio-Drone, the Linksys version of an android. They were silvery grey and had black visors in place of eyes and no mouth."

The Seague ceased his struggles. "Why?" he asked with a raspy voice in his native language.

"You know why," it replied in the same idiom. "Now tell us. Where is your secret hideout? Its voice spiked as its black visor intensified with energy. "The place the Council had built for your people should we Linksys ever visit your planet."

"You will kill them if I say."

Towering over him at six-foot-four, the armored-plated Alpha unexpectedly tugged hard on the whip and lurched the creature forward, causing him to nearly fall. Recoiling its arm/whip, the mechanical monster lifted the creature off his feet.

"You should be more worried about what we will do to you if you do not speak."

Suspending him made reply impossible as the Gibbon-like creature gasped for air and again fought to break the Drone's grip. Clawing at its hold, his struggles were in vain and soon his hands fell to his sides, and he passed out from lack of air. Paused, the Alpha finally relinquished its hold and allowed him to crumble to the ground. Lessening its grip slightly, the Linksys leader delivered a strong electrical charge that painfully revived the Seague.

"You do not die yet, Seague. You still possess information we require."

"Your insurrection will fail, Linksys," he replied, weakly.

"Who can stop us?" the Alpha-Drone asked as it once again constricted its grip tightly around the Gibbon's neck, and lifted him to his feet.

"Qi-Tahh," he said as best he could.

"Your Life Protectors are not here. We are."

Raspy, he continued, "All that means is I will not be alive to see them destroy you and free my people." He smirked.

The black visor of the Alpha again flared as its anger grew. Growing a set of arms from its sides, the Linksys seized the helpless creature, and held him firmly, as it ripped off one of his hands. The Seague cried out horribly as purple blood squirted from his splintered stump. Thrashing about from the pain, the creature remained steadfast in the grip of the Bio-Drone.

"You assume we will kill you quickly. You are mistaken."

The Seague continued to cry out in agony as the Alpha-Drone grabbed the Gibbon by his hair and yanked his head back. It forced him to look at his severed hand and damaged stump.

It carelessly discarded the hand and again asked, "Where are your people hiding?"

Weeping over his lost appendage, the Seague was kept from coddling his stump. But soon his pain turned to anger, and he spat purple blood in the Drone's face, cursed it and its kind, and spat again.

The Alpha transformed its hand into a serrated double-edged dagger, showed it to the red-haired creature, and stabbed him with it. Suddenly, a horrible sounding shrill echoed across the plains as the poor, tortured creature screamed out in agony. Mercilessly the Drone slowly twisted the knife and dug the dagger deeper into his stomach. Purple plasma poured onto the ground and saturated the once lush green lawn. Removing its fiendish-looking dagger/hand, the Bio-Drone reinserted its dagger/hand and started to dig a new hole. It burrowed slower and deeper than before, ensuring the torture was all the more agonizing.

"Are you ready to talk?" the Linksys asked, suspending the infliction.

The Seague remained strong and silent.

"The silent treatment, huh?"

The Linksys leader shoved its dagger/hand into his side, not caring what damage it caused, and then removed its dagger/hand with the same careless malice. The Alpha transformed its blood-coated dagger into a sword of the same design and showed it to the helpless creature.

"We do not do silence," the Alpha-Drone shouted as its black visor flared a dark coldness.

The Linksys sliced off his leg and unleashed a series of howling cries as the poor creature again thrashed about in unimaginable pain but remained held in place in the grip of the Alpha, which still held him firmly. Showing him its bloodied blade, its sword reverted back to a hand coated with the Seague's purple blood. Extending its arm, the Alpha picked up the severed leg and showed it to him.

"We will take a piece of you each time you refuse to cooperate," it said and tossed the leg away as carelessly as it did with the creature's hand. "Are you ready to talk?"

The Seague's body had begun to shake, and his eyes fluttered upward. He could no longer speak, he was having a seizure and going into shock. The Alpha-Drone fired an energy pulse and cauterize the limb. It produced a thick syringe and injected the creature with something that immediately stabilized his condition, and the Gibbon snapped to consciousness, screaming.

The Linksys leader slapped the Seague hard across the face to stop his yelling, and then transformed the whip into its hand and grabbed the Seague tightly by the throat. "As we have told you, Seague, you do not die yet. Now tell us. Where do your people hide?"

His mouth bloodied from the slap, he remained strong despite the tears of agony that poured down his face. "I'll never tell you! Never!" he shouted.

"Never?" the Alpha asked with a calm even tone.

Grasping his arm, the Drone pulled hard and separated the creature's arm from his elbow. The tortured being again cried out, but he was helpless to do anything except endure, for there was no way to end his suffering without sacrificing his people. "Where are they hiding?" the Alpha asked angrily as its visor intensified once more.

"Go to starros," he shouted back. "I'll never betray my people" Then he spat at the Drone.

"I believe you," it replied with an even tone.

Transmuting its hand to whip, the Alpha-Drone coiled its grip tightly around the creature's neck, and constricted its grasp until the pressure blew the Seague's eyes out of their sockets. The Alpha then ripped his head off and tossed it with the same attitude it did with the Gibbon's hand and leg. It released the creature and allowed the headless body of the Seague to crumble into a pile of lifeless junk.

"Then we will do it the hard way." It activated its com system. "Omegus Pryme, Alpha-Drone 206BD-32 progress report." It paused briefly. "No change. We suggest not bothering with interrogating anymore Seagues. They will not divulge their secret location. They are not like the species we Cleansed on Zantlyn C. However there is a possibility of Qi-Tahh interference. We recommend we continue with our Cleansing and kill all who intervene with our Prime Directive."

"Agreed. Carry on and keep me informed. I want the Seague population eradicated by the time the planet's second moon rises."

"It will be done. Out."

Elsewhere on Seregaia, the male Seagues fought back, unifying themselves. They distracted and challenged the giant Linksys Orbs, which shared the same coloring as the androids that were killing their people. In an attempt to slow them down long enough for the females, children, and the old to make their escape, the males lured the Drones into traps already in place as part of their defenses.

Ensnaring them in vines to bind them up, quicksand pits where the wet sand clogged their systems, and primitive traps that damaged them, the Gibbons seemed to hold their own. Unfortunately, the damage was not enough to shut down the Orb-Drones, and the Seagues' countermeasures proved to be more of an annoyance than a threat. The Linksys quickly regenerated, divided their forces, and continued their killing spree. Five male Seagues gave their lives so that the women and children could escape, and those who survived fled.

In the open fields some distance away, scared, scattered, and running for their lives, a group of females raced to the sanctity of their secret hiding place. With small children on their backs and babies in their arms, they yelled to the older children to keep up as they ran faster. One of the females clinging tightly to her baby suddenly welled up with fear when she saw the giant Orbs moving to cut them off. Although the Seagues were fast on three limbs, the Drones were also fast. The color drained from her olive complexion, and she soon found herself and her child corralled and lined up along with the others in their group.

"Drones, exterminate the vermin," the Alpha-Orb commanded.

Lining up in front of them, the Orb-Drones prepared to fire. Some of the adults pushed the young behind them, and others turned their heads or covered their faces. A few faced the Linksys bravely. A series of weapons blasts and screams suddenly echoed across the land, and then there was silence with only the icy cold sting of death remaining.

Near the Seague Village, a Hexagyn, a hexagon-shaped Portal quietly appeared and opened with a sound no louder than a whisper. A female sukai, a humanoid resembling a Hindu woman, exited first. She was a tiny thing, five feet tall and little more than a hundred pounds. She flipped the lock of her brown and white hair to the side while wearing the long single braid as a choker. She palmed the half opal at her side in her yellowish brown hand. Dressed in loose fitting brown and white clothing, she carried a pouch on her hip. Briefly surveying the area, she completed her check and signaled to the others to follow.

A female Black Panther/sukai hybrid exited next. Tall and athletic, she walked upright. Fitted in tight spandex-like shorts with a port for her long sleek tail, a sports bra of sorts, and leather gloves and footwear that exposed her clawed fingers and toes, she also wore a Gauntlet, her weapon of choice. The cat hybrid breathed in the air around them, and crouching down close to the ground, she again took in scents near and far. She visually checked the area for nearby threats.

Standing beside her, a large reptilian biped seven feet tall with a long, powerful tail trailing behind him. Outfitted with a black leather vest and belt, the XXXL build creature palmed a larger version of the half opal at his side. He too sniffed the air, but he also tasted it. His tongue slithered between his slightly parted lips, and his jaws tightened.

The Black Panther looked to him, "What is it?"

"Linksys," he said, growling.

"How close?" the small female asked.

Again, his forked tongue slipped between his lips, tasting scents both near and far. "Close enough to be a threat."

Last to exit the Hexagyn was an amphibious sukai hybrid. She slithered out into the open. Her lower half was that of a giant snake, and her upper half was humanoid, a contortionist who moved gracefully. She wore a jeweled pendant around her neck, and a brown vest that did nothing to conceal her small breasts. Possessing no eyes to speak of, this creature's sonar-like senses enabled her to see far better than many sighted species. She too was armed. The Gauntlet covered one of her webbed hands as she also was vigilant in surveying their surroundings. The Portal closed and vanished.

Each Qi-Tahh wore an emblem that was lit. The badges, their Life Support Device or LSDs, were active, which signified that the planet's atmosphere was not breathable to them.

"Avedia, take your brother and secure the Village. We may need it as our fallback, so you and Talon check for Seagues who may not have made it to the hiding place and rid it of any Linksys. U'kristu and I will Hexagyn over shortly, but there is something we need to investigate first."

"Yes, Tas'r," she replied. Coiling her tail around Talon's waist, Avedia flicked her wrist, and they vanished.

"What is it, Z'yenn?"

"There are Seagues nearby. I can smell their fear."

The news surprised U'kristu. "What? Talon made no mention of Seagues."

"He knew I would insist on handling this one personally."

"I will have to talk with him later about that. This is not the Juardian way of doing things. Are their scents fresh?"

"Yes." Again Z'yenn crouched down and sniffed the ground and started moving like a jungle predator stalking its prey. Sniffing the air, Z'yenn's tail rose as she stealthily led, and her black coat and white markings glistened under the red sun of the approaching day. U'kristu swiftly moved ahead of her and suddenly stopped.

"I am sorry, Z'yenn. I know you wish to lead this hunt, but under the circumstances as Juardian-Elphah I must take the lead; Juardian regulations."

"You do not know where they are. I do. I've got their scents," Z'yenn said, crossing her arms.

U'kristu stepped in close, looking her in the eye. "Sister, we have been through this many times before, and it always ends the same way—my way. We can discuss this further once the Linksys incursion has been squashed, but for now Omegah we do not have the time–I lead," she said adamantly.

"Fine," Z'yenn replied angrily. "Next time," and took off on all fours, forcing U'kristu to follow in whatever direction her Omegah's scents pulled her.

Elsewhere, Linksys-Androids had captured another group of Gibbons, and were lining them up to be killed.

"Drones, prepare to fire," ordered the Alpha-Drone.

In orbit near the planet, a high-stakes battle was taking place between machines programmed to eradicate the inhabitants and the strange creatures not of this world who challenged their dominion and fought hard to keep them from annihilating yet another sentient species.

Flying ships, weapons blasts, and explosions lit up the black tapestry of space and dwarfed the brightest stars as the two opposing forces engaged. Qi-Tahh fighters attached to the backs of creatures called Xentous, greenish-grey life-forms that exist in the icy cold of outer space, gave Pylot and Creature the capacity to fight as one.

The hordes of Linksys Attack Drones had scattered the fighters in and around Seregaia and its three moons. Near the planet's third moon, three LADs pursued a Creature-Ship with the lead Drone closing in on them. The Xentou Ja-Challah, turned about and she and her Pylot Syn'nar both deployed their offensive weapons. However, neither the creature's powerful electrical charges nor the ship's destructive armaments could penetrate the Drone's shielding.

Charging the lead Linksys, the greenish-grey life-form ducked and dodged its attacker while the lavender-skinned beauty inside the fighter returned fire. Matching the LADs speed, the Xentou dove, evading weapons fire, and then maneuvered underneath the Drone. Sprouting two large wisps that were long, thick, and shaped like broomsticks, Ja-Challah forcibly penetrated its shields, coiled her tentacles around the Linksys, and crushed it. Shutting down its energy field, its systems exploded, and its weapons deactivated. The Xentou hurled the LAD at the two Drones approaching fast.

The redheaded sukai fired all weapons at the damaged Drone

as it collided with the Linksys's shields, and destroyed the LAD, permanently shutting it down. The other Drones were damaged but not enough to stop them, so they returned fire and continued their pursuit while they regenerated. Again, Syn'nar fired weapons, but one LAD had already repaired its shields and protected them from her attack.

The Pylot's control panel began bleeping and informing her that psionics had detected something headed their way, but before she could confirm it, the Xentou telepathically told her that her mind's eye had detected two more LADs heading their way.

Suspending her attack, Ja-Challah turned about and fled, while Syn'nar continued to fire all armaments in an attempt to slow down the war machines that had now fully regenerated themselves. Joined by the other two LADs and now outnumbered four to one, the Xentou broadcasted a telepathic distress call to any brothers or sisters nearby.

Near the fifth planet and positioned between Seregaia and the invading force, the Qi-Tahh Mothership battled two Linksys Base Destroyers, enormous battle fortresses each capable of housing thousands of Drones. Aboard ship in Throne Pryme, the Command Center of the vessel, a collection of creatures dressed to the individual's style all wore insignias, but only a few were lit. Manning their stations, a plant/sukai hybrid sat in the Command chair and telepathically directed them in their duties.

"L'Pom, reroute power and return fire," she commanded telepathically.

"Acknowledged," the Black Panther weapons specialyst replied.

Occupying the Acquil-Throne, a Marten life-form, short arboreal creature with the body of a wombat, was also issuing orders. "Grayel, evasive maneuver SC-4,"

"Acknowledged, Kileo, but they are still trying to flank us and draw us away from Seregaia," the insect Pylot replied.

"Disallow it," bellowed the Marsupial.

"Sythean, ship's armor is losing its integrity! Armor collapse in sixteen et'nims," shouted L'Pom.

"Reinitialize the gravimetric field and send a pulse to stabilize the collapse," the telepathic plant hybrid commanded.

"I've tried that. Negative."

Kileo intervened, "Sythean, what about shutting down—"

The next assault rocked the ship, and weakening its defenses, their shields dropped and left them only with their armor to safeguard them. Suddenly, Bio-Drones and Orbs appeared in Throne Pryme.

"L'Pom, get our defenses back up," Sythean stood, shouting.

Momja, the ship's computer system, sounded an intruder alert and notified the Pride that Linksys had boarded Arjenadann and that she was initiating protocols for this eventuality. However, upon boarding, an Orb disabled the intruder defenses before Momja could activate them. Then she reported that their internal defenses were offline.

A Bio-Drone destroyed internal communications to cease all further use, even though the warning was redundant. In Ashanti, a group of Spider-Drones were attacking the Engineering Pack while one attempted to shut down the Prysm, their power source. In Throne Encyllari, Bio-Drones battled the Pack as one tried to gain access to the vessel's auxiliary controls, and in Arjai Quoni, giant flying Insec-Drones attempted to take the Medical Pack hostage.

Aboard the Linksys Command Fortress, in an unpopulated area, a single Hexagyn quietly appeared, and a young adult human female, a Hindu with brown skin and short black hair, exited cautiously and briefly checked the area. Cleared, she singled to her Pack to follow. A large reddish orange lion-like creature with a red mane stepped out. A wolf-bird hybrid with reddish brown fur instead of feathers followed as did a multi-colored granite sukai male and a sukai male of average height with orange-colored skin and long brown hair. Last to exit the Portal was a species that resembled a large gecko, especially when he moistened his eyes with his tongue. All of their badges were lit, for the Linksys did not breathe and therefore required no life support.

No sooner had the Hexagyn closed and vanished than the Pack detected a patrol of Linksys androids heading their way. Their heavy footsteps and smell of synthetic parts was unmistakable and always sickened the hybrid whenever he first caught their scent.

Arriving in their area, the mechanical men looked around and checked thoroughly for intruders. Not finding anyone, they were about to move on when one Drone looked up and saw the lupine-fowl flapping his large wings straining to keep him and the big cat airborne.

Back on the planet outside the Seague Village, a half opal was stuck to a wooden post by a glob of webbing, and Avedia had become translucent. As the Spiders' web attacks passed through her, the sticky globs broke brick, chipped rocks, and left holes in everything wooden. Well aware of their impact strength, the hybrid maintained her defensive posture as the giant Drones' attack again passed through her, adding to what was already damaged.

Using her Mystik powers to keep herself translucent, Avedia was safe until she could no longer maintain the spell, and returned to her solid state. Though solid, Avedia was also agile and quick. Twisting and dodging, she avoided the onslaught of web globs. However, despite her ability to move nearly three times the speed of an Earth viper, it eventually proved not fast enough.

Struck, two shots anchored her serpent body to the ground, and the three that followed pinned and secured her tail. Striking her in the torso, a glob of webbing spread across Avedia's chest and shoulders and bound her tightly. Hurt and off balance, the amphibious creature tried steadying herself when a second web glob struck her in the stomach and knocked the wind out her. She doubled over, and the glob of webbing wrapped around her like sticky dough, binding her arms tightly to her sides. She nearly dropped to the ground, and she would have if not for the restraints already in place.

The Spider-Drones moved in, marching in unison as they approached their captive. The Alpha-Spider fired a web ball and struck Avedia in the jaw. Her head darted to the side as she sprayed green blood. This assault was nothing more than a show of its dominance, and she responded with a look of anger.

Avedia did not fear them and spat a glob of green at the Alpha. Struggling valiantly to free herself, the hybrid found she could not break the synthetic silk. It was too strong, and so she remained bound.

"You do not die yet, Qi-Tahh. First, you will watch as a species you claim to protect are eradicated in front of you," the Alpha said.

Looking toward the Village, many Spider-Drones moved on it. The structure was of primitive design made out of stone blocks and wood, though it was well-constructed–and wrapped in giant glowing red bands.

Inside the Village, Insec-Drones, aerial robots had pierced the inhabitants' minimal defenses before Avedia and Talon arrived. Flying throughout the primitive metropolis, the marauders blasted buildings, set structures on fire, and reduced homes to rubble, while in their search for Seagues.

Sent into the Village to search for inhabitants, the large reptilian biped had found a group of Seagues being terrorized by the giant metal bugs. Talon intervened. Moving similar to the raptors of prehistoric Earth except with much greater coordination and agility, he was soon between the Seagues and the Linksys. Spinning around, he smashed two Drones with his tail, backhanded another, and catching a fourth, he crushed it, and hurled it at the small swarm. Talon had destroyed three more.

Suddenly caught in a hail of metal disks, Talon was struck across the face by the razor-sharp instrument. Then his arm, his leg, and his face again were cut. Black blood leaked from his wounds. Roaring like an angry T-rex, he looked to his enemy, but before he could act, metal spikes rained down on the Juardian-Omegah, piercing his chest, shoulder, leg, and tail. They had pinned him down.

Not far from the Seague Village, Z'yenn was fighting to get a Linksys Spider- Drone off her back. Her Kaja, a device that looked like a half opal stone, was out of reach, and in its neutral stasis as she struggled to reach it. Webbing her arms to her side and her legs together and tail to her back, the Spider-Drone forced them forward. Z'yenn hit the ground hard but she did not stop trying to free herself.

The artificial arachnid reared back its head, showing its two fangs, and springing forward, it bit Z'yenn in the neck and injected her with its deadly venom. Crying out, she felt the burning of the poison course through her system as the metallic monster grew a black tipped long silvery serrated tail. The Spider held it to her throat, and Z'yenn stopped struggling. Slowly, the Drone began gliding its tail along her throat and caressing her jawline.

"Your Pride will die for their interference, Omegah," it said, and then moved its sharp curved end down her neck. "Fortunately, you will not live to see it." The Linksys moved its serrated tail down underneath her breasts. "Or the niya—" It caressed one. "We finally exterminate your entire species, Zahnobein."

It pulled its black-tipped tail back sharply, cutting her across her chest and staining her black coat and white markings with her own blue blood. "Worry not, the venom coursing through your bloodstream will not be the death of you either." The Spider-Drone poised its tail to strike. "Oh no…you die now, Qi-Tahh."

Supremacy

II

Elsewhere on Seregaia, a Portal suddenly appeared between the captured Seagues and the Linksys. The Hexagyn opened, and a dozen Life Protectors poured out and stood between the Gibbons and the Drones, forming a defensive line. Their hands were poised to touch the half opal device they each carried. The Hexagyn quietly closed and vanished.

"Fire," ordered the Alpha-Orb.

"Kaja-Shields," shouted the Black Panther male version of the Omegah.

Touching their Kajas as the Linksys fired, the devices morphed into full-length shields, and the laser beams bounced off. Again, the Linksys leader ordered them to fire, and again, their beams were ineffective against their armor.

Not waiting to see the outcome of these two powerful forces, the Seagues resumed their race to safety, while the tall, muscular black jungle cat addressed the Alpha.

"Linksys, the Seagues have fled and are no longer in imminent danger of you. Qi-Tahh," he shouted, looking to the life-forms at his side and faced the Drones with a narrowed, cold gaze. "Shut them down."

Uniformed only as a Pack, the assortment of creatures transformed their shields into a variety of weapons and charged.

Not far from the Village, before the lethal instrument of the Spider-Drone could punch a hole through the back of Z'yenn's skull, its deadly head was sheared off. Running toward them, U'kristu leapt up and caught her Kaja-Dysk as it boomeranged back to her and morphed it into a Kaja-Blade, a sword fashioned to the individual's style and virtually indestructible. "Get off my sister," the Juardian-Elphah shouted angrily as she came down and took off another portion of its tail.

Within moments the amputated extension had begun growing back, and U'kristu sliced off the Spider-Drone's appendages, changed her sword to a Kaja-Gauntlet, and fired an energy pulse that knocked the artificial arachnid off Z'yenn. Rolling along the ground, the

Drone landed on its back and at once worked to flip itself over. Firing twice more, the Juardian-Elphah destroyed the Linksys' weapon's system and damaged more of its critical systems.

Morphing her Kaja back to Blade mode, U'kristu noticed Z'yenn's bite mark and hurried to free her of her web bindings. Once freed, the Zahnobein started to stand but found herself off balance and feeling dizzy. She fell back on the ground, and begun convulsing as her temperature rapidly rose. Painful red spider veins covered her face and body. U'kristu worked quickly to remove the poison that would soon kill her sister.

Reaching into her pouch, U'kristu pulled out a needle, turned Z'yenn's head to the side and inserted it into a nerve on her neck. She immediately stopped convulsing. Reaching back into her pouch, the sukai Hindu extracted some greenish brown moss, popped it into her mouth, and commenced to chewing it up while looking to the Linksys, which was still on its back, regenerating. Spitting the moss back into her hands, U'kristu fed it to Z'yenn.

"Eat," was all she said.

She did so. Within moments both the pain and red veins had started to recede as the poison was neutralized. Checking the Zahnobein's pupils, pulse, and heartbeat, and satisfied with her findings, the Juardian-Elphah removed the needle and helped Z'yenn sit up.

"Fasbi," the Omegah offered weakly.

"Wurz kuyo. How do you feel?"

"Well, I'm not dead," she said, looking to her. "Pief Quino?" Z'yenn asked pulling a piece of moss out of her mouth.

"Nature's cure for Linksys Spider venom, provided it is administered in time."

Turning her attention back to the Drone, U'kristu stood and approached the unit. Forming her Blade just as it flipped over, the Juardian-Elphah drove her Blade deep into the Drone's critical systems twisting her sword until the Drone permanently shut down. Removing it, she rejoined Z'yenn. "Are fully recovered?"

"Yes, your dremas works fast."

Digging into her small bag once more, U'kristu retrieved a

medicinal remedy she had prepared, ripped a long strip of cloth from her clothing, and coated it with the Sab and wrapped Z'yenn's wounds with it. Removing a smaller piece of clothing, U'kristu also covered her bite. "These wraps will clean the wound, prevent infection and numb the pain."

Just as she finished, the two were suddenly facing six Bio-Drones. "Bring me the heads of the Zahnobein and Sk'tier," the Alpha-Drone commanded.

Forming swords from their wrists, the Drones' black visors intensified, and they charged Z'yenn and U'kristu.

In orbit on the dark side of the planet, Ja-Challah and Syn'nar had finally managed to disable one of the pursuing Linksys Attack Drones, but they still had three to contend with, so the Xentou repeated her telepathic distress call while they fled, knowing it was only a matter of time before the LADs wore her down and kill them both. Diving, looping, and rolling did not matter. Regardless of the evasive action she took, Ja-Challah could not shake them, and though Syn'nar continued to fire, it did little to deter them. Closing in, the Drones acquired a weapons lock and were about to fire.

Back in Throne Pryme, with her Kaja drawn, Sythean fired at the Alpha intruder, while the Pack fought to defeat its minions. Having only damaged it, she mentally raised the Gauntlet's yield, but before she could follow through, she was struck by a laser beam.

"Illogical. You should have been destroyed," the Alpha retorted, surprised.

The vegetative life-form had duplicated, and touching her plant-like tendrils to the original Sythean's Gauntlet, the primary had created another gloved weapon. Turning to shoot the sniper, they stopped and watched as half of the Bio-Drone slid onto the floor and shut down. Behind it stood a dark blue man-sized grasshopper-like insect holding his strangely configured Blade.

An Orb fired a plasma grenade at both Sytheans, resulting in a blast that rocked the Command Center, but luckily it caused no serious damage to the systems. The Drone waited to see what effect its assault had, but once the smoke cleared, two more plant hybrids stood beside the others.

Throwing a tendril out to her side, the original's Gauntlet flew off, morphed into a Dysk that missed the giant Orb, boomeranged back around, changed into a javelin, and plowed through the back of the Drone's head and into its brain center. It destroyed the crystal inside. Exiting, the spear transmuted back to Dysk and returned to the Sythean original where it became a Gauntlet once more. The newly created Sytheans touched tendrils to the original's Kaja, which caused Gauntlets to appear on their wisps.

"Parthenogenesis capability," the Alpha said. "You are Syth."

They smirked and engaged the invaders.

Aboard the Command Fortress, a Bio-Drone alerted the others to the intruders raised its arms to fire on them when one of its appendage instantly froze up to its elbow in ice. With the next slightest vibration, it cracked, crumbled, and fell to the floor, shattering. It raised the other arm which melted up to its shoulder, and a diamond-crusted fist punched through the back of its skull and through its face before it could take any further action. Withdrawing the jewel fist, the mechanism collapsed onto the floor and permanently shut down as the hand returned to its original granite form.

"You will not harm my family," he said, looking down at the deactivated droid.

Still hovering, the lion leader commanded, "Laisere, drop me."

"Joryd, we're eight meters high," the wolf/bird countered.

"Now!"

Complying, Laisere at once released Joryd, who was twice the size of a full grown lion, and watched as he fell, roaring fearsomely. The last thing the Drone aiming its arms at him saw was his large white teeth.

Racing toward the Android firing on her, the Hindu Human-Augment evaded the assault, moved in and swept the Drone's legs from underneath it. She jumped on top of it, grabbed its wrists, and forced its palms against its face as it fired–she looked away and it destroyed itself.

Spotting a sniper about to fire at Joryd, the granite man raced toward him, changing compositions with each step, he moved in front of his lion leader in diamond form, and took the blast himself. Unaffected, the Linksys fired again as Laisere swooped down, picked it up and threw it at an attacking Drone.

"Starone, now," the winged hybrid shouted.

Retaliating, the granite man doused the Drones with molecular acid that ate through their plating and destroyed them both.

Finishing off the last of the sentries, Joryd partially crushed the severed head of the Bio-Drone he battled and blew the skull from his jaws.

"Let's go," was all he said.

Outside the Village entrance, many Spider-Drones raced toward the gates, and touching the giant crimson bands that enclosed the community, they vanished in a flash of light. The others fired on the barrier, however, their lasers were ineffective and the structure remained undamaged. The Alpha looked to Avedia, and its eight black eyes glowed with anger.

"The Rubicund Ribbons of Diakleze cannot be breached or destroyed unless I so will it."

"You have only delayed the inevitable, Mystik. Kill you, and your spell will cease."

"Many have tried, and I am still here."

"You believe you are unstoppable, that your mystikism will somehow protect you from death, but you are mistaken, and majikal beings such as yourself can die."

"Enough," Avedia angrily shouted. Then yelled venomously, "Pagafatu!"

Spoken in her native language, a single mystikal word caused her web bindings to glow brightly, they turned brittle, and the Mystik was free.

"My turn," Avedia said raising her arms. "Sarkoe Binea!"

Reciting words known only to her Sect, the Mystik formed bubbles underneath all the Drones at the Village's entrance, trapping them inside the effervescences. "S'yun Cooo," she said, and the bubbles filled with white smoke. The Linksys inside and outside the bubbles fired but could not damage them. Once filled, the Mystik snapped her fingers, the bubbles popped, and all that remained of the Drones were a collection of smoldering melted metal.

The Alpha was not impressed. "Your Mystik Arts will not stop us, Avedia of Oolong."

"You Linksys said the same thing when first we met eight meads ago on Karphortyn II in the Sueng Zhal star system." She maintained her defensive posture. "You were using the inhabitants in one of your mad experiments to change a planet's atmosphere. If successful, you would have had the means to asphyxiate all life in the universe. My Pride and I stopped you."

"A most regrettable outcome. Your Pride destroyed the only known piece of Luthium in existence–the key element needed for the process to work."

"Correction, Drone. It was I who destroyed the Luthium."

"Then it will give Omegus Pryme great pleasure in knowing the one who destroyed the Luthium is dead. Kill her."

Inside the Village, Talon was again roaring like a dinosaur as he angrily ripped out the spikes. His black blood coated them and sprayed everywhere. Removing the last two spikes, he roared and threw them back at the Linksys. Striking his targets, it was not enough to shut them down, and the hovering Insec-Drones regenerated before his eyes.

Showering him with discs and spikes, the reptilian touched his Kaja, forming a large shield that deflected the deadly hail. They paused their attack, and the enraged Scorpilyn hurled his shield at them. Morphing it into a large Dysk, it divided into three Dysks and sliced through the bugs. Reforming as one Dysk, the Kaja returned to its master. Again the Juardian-Omegah split his concentration and fashioned a large broad sword to go with his shield. Talon then raced to meet their next descent.

Blocking and slicing through the mechanical bugs, the Scorpilyn moved incredibly fast, and littered the ground with their remains while avoiding their metal projectiles and laser beams. The Insec-Drones retreated to the skies where they regrouped and hovered out of reach. Watching them coldly, the solid blackness of Talon's eyes and his chilling glare never wavered. His forked tongue slipped between his parted lips while the metallic bugs formed long lances from their mouths, readied their weapons, and moved in for the kill. Talon roared in anger like a Tyrannosaurus rex charged the Drones.

Back in space, before the Linksys Attack Drones could fire on Ja-Challah, it was encased in a cloud of corrosive enzymes that destroyed its systems and shut it down. The arriving Xentou expanded a portion of his body and pelted another LAD with a series of grotesque pink and blue pus projectiles that grew like a living fungus, quickly enveloping the Drone. It too shut down. Pressing their advantage, both Xentous and Pylots fired on the last war machine, overwhelmed its defenses and permanently deactivated it. The larger Xentou went to his sisters.

"Ja-Challah, Syn'nar, are you both alright?" a male voice inquired telepathically.

"We are safe Renn. Fasbi to you and Te'lar," Ja-Challah replied using her telepathic device.

The Xentous exposed their tendrils and began brushing the other lightly until Renn noticed Ja-Challah's burned tentacles, *"Sister?"* he said, gently holding up her wisps.

"I am fine."

"No, you are not. You have third-degree burns."

"That's just what I told her," Syn'nar said, adding herself to the telepathic conversation.

Ja-Challah attempted to convince her brother that she was all right and that Torr or the Arjai Pack would heal her when they returned to the ship. However, Renn knew their mother would kill them both if she discovered Ja-Challah was this injured and they put off healing. But Renn knew he could not force his sister to accept treatment.

"I know I need arjai, Renn, but our Pride need us more, as do the Seagues. I will go get arjai when our assignment is finished. I promise."

Ja-Challah's logic was inescapable. In a show of affection and relieved he and his Pylot Te'lar arrived in time, the Xentous gently touched appendages, reabsorbed them and rejoined the battle. This time Renn and Te'lar would keep their sisters close and safe.

Back aboard Ship-Arjenadann, the Throne Pack continued to battle the Drones, Kileo, the Marten life-form, destroyed one of them attempting to access their systems.

"So you are Syth," the Alpha-Drone said. "We have heard of you. Energy weapons will not be effective against your species. However, you are not invulnerable, Plant."

Transforming its arms into cannon barrels, long and slender with a metallic sheen, the Alpha fired. The new configuration unleashed circular waves of sound that bombarded one of the Sythean duplicates. Within moments the creature's vegetative body vibrated, as she was slowly ripped apart from the inside out. Telepathically crying out, her screams were unintentionally projected out, and her thoughts of aguish were sent crashing into the minds of her fellow Pridesmen aboard ship. Her body continued to be ripped apart until she lied on the floor, sprawled out, looking as though she were put through a shredder. The duplicate was dead.

In shock, Sythean and her duplicates were unable to move. They looked in horror at what remained of their sister. All Syths, whether original or duplicate, shared a psychic link with one another, and so when anything happened to one, it was felt by all. The death of one wrecked them and broke the original Sythean's concentration, inadvertently causing their weapons to vanish and hers to revert to its non-combative stasis. The Alpha-Drone turned and aimed its arms at the original Sythean.

Struggling with a Bio-Drone, Kileo saw what was about to happen, and using his kangaroo-like feet, he kicked it off of him, and in two powerful leaps he reached the emotionally stunned Sythean original. Touching his Kaja and forming a large shield, Kileo safeguarded them both against the attack. Again the Alpha fired, but could not penetrate the shield. Touching his Kaja-Shield, Kileo split his concentration and formed a Dysk which he hurled at the Linksys Drone. Evading it, the Android formed a more powerful weapon while maintaining its deadly cannon, and aimed them both at Kileo and Sythean.

"If this configuration can tear a Syth apart, Marsupial, imagine what it will do to you. That is of course after… "

Before the Alpha finished its sentence, the Dysk boomeranged back around and sheared off the Drone's head. The Kaja returned to Kileo, and the Linksys managed to squeeze off a shot before shutting down. Morphing his Dysk into a Gauntlet, Kileo mentally chose a setting and fired. The blast neutralized the Linksys' discharged weapon.

"You neutralized the blast with a metallurgy dissection pulse," Sythean said confused. "How did you? Her voice trailed off.

"You can fasbi our brother, Laisere, who knows weapons better than anyone. He taught me. The configuration the Linksys formed originated from the planet Tygiss, and so I took the chance the Drone was going to fire Hona at us, a nano metallurgic dissection beam."

Another Drone was made Alpha.

"Momja, Linksys scenario two. Countermeasure one," the original Sythean commanded having recovered from her trauma.

"Acknowledged Deggzytepol," the computer interface replied.

At once the ship and all its systems powered down. Shields, weapons, and life support were taken offline, and all personal LSDs that were not already active switched on. Emergency lighting came on, and the vessel was no longer protected by energy shields. Rocked by a continual assault by the Destroyers it fought, the Pride were tossed about.

"Momja … now," shouted the vegetative life-form.

"Acknowledged."

The computer blanketed the interior of the ship with electromagnetic sonic vibrations attuned to the frequency of the crystal that all Drones carried in their artificial brains, and they all were shut down.

Stations exploded, fires broke out, and breaches formed in the armored hull. The Pride scrabbled to handle the situation, and hoped their armor would not buckle. However, before they could fully restore their defenses, more Linksys transported into Throne Pryme and attacked the Sytheans. They murdered the duplicates and critically wounded the original before the Pack could destroy them.

"Sythean," Kileo shouted, hopping to her aid. Squatting beside her, they were joined by E'nie.

"E'nie, take care of our sister." Kileo ordered, and took the Throne.

"Arjai Quoni this is Throne Pryme, we have an Arjai emergency, send an Arjai Pack immediately. Deggzytepol Sythean is down," E'nie commanded.

Aboard the Command Fortress in the Plexus, the brain center of the enormous destroyer, an Insec-Drone flew to Omegus Pryme and informed it that intruders had boarded the Base and had deactivated several Drones, but they were masking their location and could not be tracked. The giant nine-foot Bio-Drone, sitting in its Command chair, looked to the smaller unit.

"The Supremacy, they do keep showing up in the most unexpected places," it said, leaning back into its seat. "I wonder if our old friend will be leading these fools. After all, it has been awhile since last we saw him." The giant android paused. "Alert our forces. Find them and kill them, and send additional Drones to assist in protecting the Crystal Resonator. Logically that should be their objective."

"Acknowledged," the large mechanical bug replied.

Suddenly, the doors leading to the Plexus exploded, fell inward and hit the floor heavily. Joryd stepped inside and roared loudly, "This Cleansing ends now," he shouted.

The granite man fired a powerful sustained blast, and the Insec-Drone, which was preparing to leave was destroyed. Lowering his smoldering appendage, Starone joined Joryd at his side as his hand returned to its natural composition. In the hallway behind them, the Pack finished off the last of the Drones and joined them.

"Joryd Kenton, I was just talking about you," the Linksys leader said lightheartedly, but its tone quickly turned dark. "It was foolish of you to come aboard my Destroyer, Pantherus. Your Kajas will not function here, and you and your Pack are defenseless. Yield, and I promise you and them a quick death."

"You think we need Kajas to shut you down, Pryme?" Joryd replied and called to the winged hybrid. "Laisere, take the Pack and go find your sister, Meva. Starone and I got this."

The lupine/fowl acknowledged him and flew off with the others in tow while they faced the giant and his Drones.

"You really believe you and the Elemental are a match for us? How interesting."

"Number One, shields and weapons just went down," a Spider-Drone reported.

"Get them back up," Pryme shouted.

"We cannot. The system has been placed in diagnostic mode and authorization to override has been blocked."

The Linksys leader looked to them, "Before you die, Kenton, tell me. How is your cub sister? Oh, that's right...the Linksys used her in one of our experiments. It's a shame the Supremacy shut down that facility and destroyed our research. The results were promising. Then again she was one of the lucky ones. She lived, though it probably would have been better if she had not. Do you not agree?"

Roaring loudly, angrily, Joryd started toward Pryme hastily, but Starone calmed him and reminded him that the Linksys liked to play mind games. The Pantherus stopped himself.

"You seem as eager to destroy us as we are in eradicating you and the rest of the vermin in this galaxy."

"Why this star system? The Seagues are no threat to you. They are peaceful and harmless. Why the attack?" Joryd asked, almost roaring his question.

"They are a plague like all sentient biological beings," it said, leaning forward. Standing, it walked toward them. "One that we Linksys will annihilate."

Joryd looked to Starone. "You take the Drones." Then he faced the approaching giant. "Pryme is mine."

The Elemental at once attacked the amalgamation of Drones, and encased an artificial arachnid in solid ice. Simultaneously he reduced two androids to puddles of liquid hardware while enclosing an Orb within his gaseous body, and using a corrosive vapor, he destroyed the Drone.

The Pantherus continued to stand his ground, unafraid, despite the heavy footsteps of the nine-foot, three-thousand-pound killing machine coming toward him. Pausing in its approach, the giant android glanced over to the Elemental and was unimpressed by the Drones he had already shut down.

"Impudent creatures, you cannot win. With every Drone you destroy and Base you shut down, you only delay the inevitable," Pryme walked toward Joryd once more, its hand forming a fiendishly looking serrated, wavy sword which it slashed at the air. "Despite your pathetic attempts, our numbers continue to grow, and soon we Linksys will be so powerful that not even the Ohdens or their Supremacy will save this galaxy from our Cleansing."

Joryd roared loudly, "The cryda you will."

Lunging as the giant metal man raised its sword hand, the Pantherus kicked the mechanical monster with his four paws hard in the chest before it could strike and propelled the Linksys Commander back against its chair. Advancing, Joryd's claws grew, becoming more visible with each step as he pounced on Pryme and begun clawing it.

He clawed its face. "First, you need to survive me," Joryd said and struck it again, clawing down its chest and giving it another battle scar.

"Worry not, Qi-Tahh," the giant android retorted as the scars faded, and it seized his next two strikes. "For you may be the Elphah of your Pride, but I am an Omegus Pryme."

Sprouting a large fist from its chest, Pryme punched Joryd and knocked him off. Flipping back through the air, the Elphah landed on his paws and slid back along the floor until his digging claws stopped him. The Linksys leader's black visor glowed with anger as the extra fist was reabsorbed, and Omegus had once again moved on Joryd still brandishing its sword.

"We will unleash a carnage upon this galaxy the likes of which none has ever known and purify the star systems of your infestation. We will exterminate every sentient man, woman, and child and become the galaxy's new supremacy."

"The cryda you will," Joryd shouted, readying himself.

Swinging at the Elphah, Pryme tried to hack him to pieces, but Joryd was agile and quick and was no easy prey. He countered, clawed the deadly sword arm and kicked Omegus hard in the chest. It stumbled back. Looking at its exposed hardware, it quickly regenerated, and soon its hand had reformed.

Roaring loudly, angrily, the Elphah again lunged at the nine-foot android, but it caught his front paws and stopped his lunge cold. Holding him fast, Joryd's hind legs dangled and he could neither break Pryme's grip nor maneuver his head around for a good bite.

"As I was saying…the non-sentient species that remain—"

Joryd continued trying to free himself. "You're awfully chatting, koniya. What's wrong? No one to have stimulating conversation with?"

"The non-sentient species will never come to know self-awareness. The age of biological sentience in this galaxy is at an end."

Maintaining its vice-like hold, the giant grew another set of arms and began beating the Elphah with its fist, battering his stomach mercilessly as though he were a punching bag. With every blow to Joryd's body, the sound reverberated, but the Elphah was powerless to stop it. Pausing, Pryme regrew a hand from its chest, and grabbing the bloodied Pantherus by his throat, it looked him over.

"How can you ever hope to save a planet, let alone an entire galaxy when you cannot even save yourself?"

The three thousand pound giant commenced to beating on Joryd once more. Omegus enjoyed itself incredibly. Again, Pryme grabbed Joryd by the throat, but this time it punched him and sent him sailing across the room. Bouncing, rolling, and sliding, the Elphah slammed against the back wall and was down.

On Seregaia outside the Village, with a flick of her wrist, the Mystik displaced herself, giving her room to move and to fight. Caught in a hail of web globs and laser beams, the amphibious creature dodged the assault, and sprouting another set of arms, she caught a glob of the synthetic silk and began weaving an enormous web.

Fashioning the sticky mesh majikally between her and the many Drones approaching, Avedia trapped those who would plow through it.

"Zeh-Tou," the Mystik shouted, and the animated web clogged their systems, restricted their movements, and disabled their weapons. The other Spiders wisely avoided the network, retreated, regrouped, and suspended fire. Avedia reabsorbed her second set of arms.

"Impressive," The Alpha-Spider said. "You destroyed our web capacity when you destroyed the Drones, but this is of no consequence because you cannot win Avedia of Oolong. We can regenerate, but soon you will be exhausted, powerless, and defenseless.

Drones opened fire on the Mystik, who waved a hand across her chest and boomeranged their laser beams back at them. She damaged and destroyed many of them. They again fired. Holding out her scaly webbed hands, she conjured up an auburn cloud between her and the attackers, which absorbed their assault. Avedia was becoming angry.

"Is that what your collective memory has stored about me from our past encounters, Drone? Do you not understand who I am?" Avedia's eyeless orifices and the jeweled center of the pendant she wore about her neck turned red, and the red clouds darkened. "Or what I can do?"

Speaking a mystikal phrase, the clouds burst and showered the

Spiders with corrosive acid that severely damaged them. "And what is a rain storm without lightning?" she asked in her growing anger.

The darkened clouds erupted, and red bolts of highly charged energy rained down on the Drones, leaving many more damaged beyond their ability to regenerate. Those soon shut down.

The storm stopped, and Avedia's eyes, her pendant, and the skies returned to normal.

"You Drones may have butchered majikal beings in the past, but I am not them." She pulled out a butterfly-like insect from her vest pocket. Cupped it, whispered something softly, and then released it. "I am more than Oolong." The butterfly transformed into a flock of tiny alien locusts that flew toward the Linksys and commenced circling overhead. "More than a Mystik. Chu-dylai." The locust attacked, eating the Drones' metal hides. "I am Qi-Tahh, and you are on the wrong side of that protection."

Standing erect and balancing on her tail, the Mystik looked to her Kaja still glued to the post, stretched out her hand and the half orb broke free and flew to Avedia's hand.

"Jook fu Zilp, das-cuet zom ben boi," Avedia said.

A barrier appeared and protected her from any further attacks.

"Rogen poy den yaya," She shouted, and fanned an arm out to the side.

Four replicas of Avedia appeared as the barrier moved to ensure protection of each copy. Moving her other arm out, she repeated the mystikal words with more fury.

"Rogen poy den yaya,"

The Mystik created seven more copies of herself. Dropping her arms, her spell continued to safeguard them all. Two replicas levitated and approached the original, who ordered them to enter the Village and assist Talon.

The two replicas vanished as half of Avedia's forces rose up off the ground and hovered. Looking to what remained of the once formidable threat, the Mystik knew defeating these Spider-Drones would be easy, but not the second wave joining them. The Alpha had called for reinforcements. With her duplicates functioning as individuals, Avedia tapped the barrier, dropped her spell of protection, and she and her legion raced to meet their enemy.

Meanwhile, having finished off the last of the Bio-Drones, Z'yenn spotted a small Seague child in the distance fleeing from three Linksys Orbs. Angered, the Omegah watched as the young Seague ducked and dodged their assault, trying to escape, knowing full well the Drones could easily overtake him or hit him dead-on, but instead they played their sadistic game of cat and mouse.

So preoccupied was the Zahnobein that she did not notice the three androids coming up behind her armed with swords. Nor was she aware when their heads leapt off their bodies and shut down. U'kristu joined Z'yenn shortly thereafter.

"You are usually more careful. What is it?"

"Look," she said, pointing.

The child suddenly tripped and hurt himself. Hearing the approach of more Bio-Drones, they turned about and saw the machines coming for them.

The Juardian looked to her, "Go," she commanded. "I can handle them."

Forming her Kaja-Blade, U'kristu met the mechanical men, while Z'yenn watched as the youngster moved slower than before. The terrified boy spotted the Linksys closing in on him and was running as fast as he could, but now he moved like a four-legged animal with a hurt limb. Slapping her Kaja to her hip, the Black Panther sukai took off on hands and feet running as fast as a leopard. Racing to the Seague, desperate to reach him before the Orbs, the child again tripped and slid across the ground. Holding his injured leg, he lied there, whimpering, even though the Linksys were nearly upon him. Z'yenn ran even faster.

The Orbs, no longer fired at the young one, but instead formed an array of sharp weapons and increased speed. This game was over, and it was now time for him to die.

Hurt, the terrified creature again got up as quickly as he could and began running once more, though he moved even slower than before.

Moving at her top speed, Z'yenn reached the child first, scooped him up in her arms, and fled. Startled, the frightened Seague struggled with all his little might against the Zahnobein.

Seeing the Omegah, the Drones retracted their hardware, implemented their maximum speed and fired on them both. Turning about, the Life Protector drew her Gauntlet and rapidly fired at the ground in front of the Drones, kicking up grass and dirt and temporarily blinded their scanners. She took cover behind a large rock formation, where she could set the struggling child down without being seen. Speaking fluent Seague, Z'yenn spoke to him lovingly.

"No, sweetheart, I'm not going to harm you. My name is Z'yenn, and I am Qi-Tahh."

At once he stopped struggling and began hugging her. She could feel the weight of relief leave him as his body relaxed in her arms. She then comforted him.

"We can stay here only for a short time. The composition of these rocks will make it difficult for the Linksys to find us, but it will not take them long once they recalibrate their psionics." As he listened to her calm tone, she gently coaxed him into releasing her. "What's your name, sweetheart?"

His name was Grohn, which meant "Little Brave" in the language of his people. Smiling, Z'yenn told him that the name fit him, but Grohn shook his head in disbelief.

"I'm scared," he replied, dropping his head in shame.

Z'yenn gently raised his head so that their eyes met. "Everyone is scared sometimes Grohn, but acting even though you are afraid, this is what makes one brave." She paused. "I need your help."

"I want to help."

"Good, and together, we'll stop these monsters. Do not worry. I'll not let them hurt you. I promise." And she took her sleek black tail and pointed the end at the child.

In turn, Grohn took his red-haired tail and did likewise to her. Touching their ends together, the young Seague dropped his tail and embraced her once more. Z'yenn flashed him a smile of reassurance.

Multiple blasts against the rock formation startled the young

Seague, who clung tightly to the Zahnobein. The Linksys had found them. Picking him up, Grohn wrapped his tail around Z'yenn's waist as though she were his mother, and secured his hold. The Zahnobein got on all fours and took off.

Agile and fast, the Black Leopard sukai was difficult to hit as she evaded Linksys fire. With Grohn on her back holding on tightly, Z'yenn ran up a nearby rock formation on all fours, took Grohn into her arms, turned about, and leapt off. Executing a midair somersault, the Omegah threw out an arm and hurled the half opal at the Spheres. Her Kaja transmuted into a solid metal baseball and struck one Drone, ricocheted off, and struck the other after that. Soon the Kaja-Ball was bouncing between the three Orbs, increasing its velocity and force with each strike, denting their bodies and damaging their systems. Explosions rung out as the Ball continued to batter them, and the Drones fell to the ground behind them.

The Omegah landed surefootedly with Grohn, and softly spoke. Z'yenn asked Grohn to uncoil his tail from around her waist, but instead the frightened child maintained his hold. She asked him to trust her. Hesitantly, he complied, and she placed him behind a small outcrop of large rocks for safekeeping.

"Stay here. I will be right back."

Facing the Drones, Z'yenn held out her clawed hand and called the Kaja-Ball to her. Becoming a Gauntlet, she touched her gloved hand together, split her concentration and formed another Gauntlet. Mentally raising their yield, the Omegah stepped forward angry. "Furlonus damn you, he's only a baby," she shouted.

Rapidly firing, the Zahnobein crippled the Orbs beyond their capacity to repair and shut down two Drones. The third, badly damaged, barely maintained its antigravity posture as its systems continued to short-circuit. Disarming, Z'yenn's Kaja returned to one, and she slapped the concave device back to her side as she approached. Ripping the Orb from its wobbly levitating state, Z'yenn rolled onto her back and kicked the six-hundred-pound unit high into the air. It came crashing down on top of a rock formation and exploded violently.

Grohn, who was watching from his hiding place, broke clear and raced to embrace Z'yenn, who knelt and whose smiles and arms welcomed him.

U'kristu finished destroying the Bio-Drones and joined Z'yenn and Grohn.

"Are you all right?" the Black Leopard asked looking down at her five-foot tall sister.

The Sk'tier showed no signs of injury or fatigue. "Yes," she said and looked to the child. "This is the little one the Linksys were toying with?"

"Yes," Z'yenn replied, still angry about it.

"And what is your name, precious?" she asked lovingly in Seague.

"Grohn," he answered.

Seeing him stroking his leg, Z'yenn sat him down and examined it. He flinched when she touched his ankle, and she apologized for causing him pain. She picked him back up. "He sprained his ankle during the chase. It must be worse than I first thought. He needs Arjai."

Noticing the Omegah's second-degree laser burns, which she tried to downplay, the Juardian-Elphah informed her that her injuries were not to be ignored and that she too, was in need of healing.

"My injuries can wait. We have bigger problems to contend with first. No more of Grohn's people will die because of the Linksys. Understood?"

"Yes, Omegah."

At the mere mention of the mechanical monsters, the young Seague rewrapped his tail around the Zahnobein's waist for comfort. Understanding his fright, Z'yenn coaxed him into lessening his grip, and commented him on his strength.

"Force them back. We only need to keep this up until the others complete their assignment."

"We know the strategy."

"Good, then find our family and bring everyone to the Village. We'll make our stand there."

"Yes, Omegah," U'kristu replied, bowing. "But first I must get you and our young Charge to the Village safely," she replied and escorted them without any protest from Z'yenn.

In space, after fierce battle against the Linksys Fortress, the Qi-Tahh, managed to damage one of the Base ships beyond its capacity to regenerate and finally it shut down. The Pride raced to help the Xentouwish, Arejenadann, a creature they called Mother who alone was battling two Linksys Destroyers.

Ignoring their attacks, Arjenadann moved in and deployed a strange gaseous cloud, blinding the Linksys psionics to her presence, and deactivated their shields. Physically taking one of the Bases apart, Arjenadann formed ten tentacles and ripped away large parts of the hull. Wrapping her tendrils around the destroyer, the Xentouwish crushed it and filled its interior with her corrosive enzyme. She made certain neither the Base nor the Drones inside would ever regenerate.

The second Destroyer, now able to detect her, moved on Arjenadann quickly, firing high-yield weapons and blasting off large chucks of her flesh. Though badly wounded, the Xentouwish continued to fight and lashed out. Striking the Base, she knocked them back, but their shields were formidable and their weapon powerful. Undamaged, they fired again and again until they weakened her. No longer able to fight back, the giant creature took the brutal onslaught even though it was evident she would not survive much more. With their next assault, the Mothership appeared between them and took the strike themselves. The ship rocked; however, their defenses held, and they returned fire.

Onboard the Linksys Destroyer, Joryd was still hurting, and bled as he tried to shake off the crippling assault he received by Pryme. Starone maintained his defensive composition, which he was now straining to hold. The giant android crossed two set of arms, activated its communications array with the arm out of its chest, and broadcasted the battle being waged.

"Listen to the songs of death my Drones play," Pryme said, looking to Joryd and Starone. "Is it not virtuoso? A symposium for a galaxy soon be sterilized. We will Cleanse ourselves of your biological filth—a plague that has finally met its cure, an end to a disease that we permitted to exist for far too long. An error of our Creators that we will now correct."

"We're not the plague, Pryme," Joryd said calmly as he spat yellow blood. "You and your kind are." He stood glancing to Starone as he spat more of his pallor plasma and faced the Linksys leader. "We," the Elphah said, licking his lips. "We're the cure."

The Pantherus leapt at it, catching the nine-foot android off guard momentarily diverted the Drones' attention from the Elemental, and inadvertently suspended their assault. Joryd had given Starone the opportunity he needed to change compositions safely. With his structure now many times harder than diamonds, the Elemental retaliated with a vengeance.

In the Crystal Resonator section, the huge gemstone pulsated with top efficiency and maintained the Linksys functions, while those in the area worked like bees in a hive. Several Drones entered the section, and the lead mechanism, a Spider-Drone, approached the area Alpha with the other mechanical creatures in tow.

"In'tru'ders have boar'ded th' Base. Num'ber One has ord'e'red us to ass'ist in prot'ect'ing th' Cr'yst'al Res'ona'tor, and cal'cu'lates a 98.524233 per'cen't pro'bab'ili'ty th'at t'hey will att'empt to sh'ut it down," the artificial arachnid reported.

"What is the matter with your vocalization processor?"

"Da'mag'ed, wor'king to fix."

"Understood. Transmit authorization code."

"Aff'irm'at'ive."

Suddenly, becoming flesh and blood to its metallic counterpart, the illusionary cloak dropped, and revealed a Pack of Qi-Tahh. Webbing the Bio-Drone, Meva secured its arms, binding them to its sides, and then she sprayed its face with a powerful corrosive, destroying the Drone's brain. Aimlessly wandering about, the Linksys android collapsed and hit the floor with a loud clang. The giant arachnid then assumed her true form, a four-foot, furry sandy blond creature.

Speaking in broken words, the way her species communicated with most other races except her own, she ordered the Pack to shut down the Resonator at all cost. Changing into a giant two-headed serpent, Meva swatted the approaching Drones with her tail while the Pack attacked.

Flying in, carrying the Octopi life-form, Laisere plowed through the first attack wave as his Pack joined the fight. Dropping Kahnu in the middle of the Drones, the Velfin swooped down, picked up two Spider-Drones, and threw them at the barrier protecting the Resonator. They vaporized instantly.

Quickly wrapping four tentacles around two Bio-Drones' legs, the aquatic creature yanked them off the floor and threw them into the barrier. Fixating his eight red eyes on an Orb, he lunged at it, and wrapping all ten of its tentacles securely around it, Kahnu used his beak-like mouth, and started jabbing holes in the unit. Wobbly, it lost its anti-grav posture and crashed to the floor. The alien octopus continued his attack until the machine finally and permanently shut down.

Changing species, the Animorph transformed into a gelatinous life-form and shielded the others from the Drones' laser fire. Having no effect on Meva, the Linksys increased their energy yield and fired again, but this life-form was impervious to their weapons. Even though they blasted holes through her, they did not harm her or hurt those she protected. Meva's body reformed as quickly as it was damaged. Attacking and making quick work of the Drones, the morphogenic creature returned to her original form, unaware of the Orb rolling toward her.

The Human-Augment called out to her, and ran toward Meva with the speed of a cheetah. Shoving her out of harm's way, Anishaa fell back and the Drone rolled over her.

"An'is'haa," Meva cried out.

A moment later the six hundred pound sphere rose up, and balanced on the soles of Anishaa's feet, she kicked it up and over into the Resonator's barrier where it disintegrated.

"Yes, Meva?" she said, standing.

The Animorph ran to her and wrapped her arms around her waist. "You sc'ared me, sis'ter. Do n'ot do th'at aga'in." Meva then suddenly morphed into a large Sasquatch-like creature, spun around, and catching an attacking android by the throat, she roared. Crushing its throat, Meva slammed it repeatedly into the floor before throwing it at the barrier. Facing the Augment, she smirked, and they rejoined the fight.

Back in the Plexus, the battle for supremacy continued. Joryd had crushed one of Omegus' arms in his jaws, took it from his mouth, and threw it to the side. "I told you. Do that again, and I'll rip your fucking arm off. Did you think I was joking?"

"It seems we Linksys may have made an error with you so-called Life Protectors. You're more resilient than we first believed. No matter. The problem is academic. The solution is elementary." Pryme's arm completely repaired itself. "Kill you and your Pride first, and then we can continue with pest control unhindered."

"Our deaths will not change anything. The Ohdens are aware of our situation."

"Irrelevant. By the time they dispatch more of your Supremacy, all life in this star system will be extinguished. We will set off a thermite explosion that will blanket the planets with enough hard radiation that it will be uninhabitable even to us Linksys, for the next two thousand years. This will be the price for challenging our dominion and a lesson to all who would dare defy us."

The Elphah gasped, and then roared fearsomely in protest, and charged Omegus, who fired on him. The huge jungle cat pivoted, jumped, and dodged the lethal beams of light that destroyed all they struck. Leaping over the weapon systems' primary controls, the android Alpha inadvertently destroyed them. Coming down, Joryd rolled past the controls to the Resonator's force field generator. An Insec-Drone fired at the Pantherus, missed and destroyed the system, disabling the barrier.

"Defective Drone." Pryme said, and raised its arm and destroyed the unit.

Running pass the Drones attacking Starone, Joryd used Omegus to destroy them, leapt up, and began running along the wall, leaving claw marks in the metal structure as he eluded the giant Bio-Drone. With every move he made, the Elphah advanced closer to Pryme until he was finally within striking range and attacked.

Jumping over the Alpha-Linksys, the Pride Elphah wrapped his tail around its neck as he passed and slammed Pryme hard onto the floor. Continuing to use his tail like a whip, Kenton sent the mechanical monster sliding into a console. The station exploded and damaged Pryme moderately. Lassoing an ankle, Joryd pulled Pryme from the caved-in console and flung it into another station, damaging the Linksys and destroying the instrumentations. The Elphah continued his assault, not wanting to give the Alpha Android time to regenerate. Repeating his action, Joryd slammed its damaged body into what remained of its Command chair. The loud grinding sounds of mashing metal echoed throughout the Plexus.

Pouncing on the Alpha android, the Pantherus began clawing at it again, and ripped through its armored body as though it were made of flesh. But Omegus Prymes were no ordinary Linksys, and the Elphah soon found himself lying on the bottom and being choked. Straining, Joryd could not pry its hands from around his throat, and Pryme, in growing another pair of arms, raised his new set of fists overhead and prepared to kill the Elphah.

At the Resonator, Anishaa raced toward the giant gemstone faster than the Linksys could react and ripped the control panel off, but before she could finish, a metal tentacle quickly wound tightly around her, bound her arms to her side, and yanked her away. The Alpha-Orb lifted her off the floor as she struggled to break its grip.

The barrier protecting the Resonator suddenly deactivated, but the valiant efforts of the Packs were in vain as they were surrounded and captured. The most recent Drone-made-Alpha held Anishaa securely.

"You have failed, Life Protector. Cease your struggles. You cannot break my grip," the giant Orb said with confidence.

"You don't know what I can do," Anishaa replied. "Cover your ears," she shouted in Hindu to her family.

Immediately, they complied as she hit a note to shatter crystal, and held the frequency. The Alpha and other Drones began quivering and wobbling. The unit holding Anishaa hit the floor and shut down after the crystal in its brain exploded. Breaking free of its coil, the Human-Augment ceased her vocal attack, and in one fluid motion, she grabbed one of the Orb's tentacles and began twirling it overhead. "Everyone down," she again shouted in her native language.

The Pack dropped to the floor as she spun around and struck the surrounding Drones, she cleared their way. The other Drones, still recovering from the Juardian's vocal attack, were slow to respond, giving her the opportunity to reach the Resonator's control panel without interference. Looking back, she saw her Pack being retaken, and ripped out a power coupling and a power cable from the Resonator's base. Then she held them in close proximity to each other as she looked to the Drones racing toward her. "Back off, Linksys."

"Stop," ordered the new Alpha.

The Drones complied at once.

"Do not touch those cables together. The power feed is incompatible and will destroy the Resonator."

"Exactly. Now back away and let my family go."

"You do not understand," the Spider-Drone now-in-charge said, moving toward her. "Such an explosion will take out fifteen levels of the Base and will kill you and your Pack in the process."

"I understand perfectly," she said, moving the cables closer together. "Do you?"

"Do as she says," the Alpha commanded.

The Drones backed away.

"Very good. Now release my family."

The Linksys remained where they were.

"That wasn't a request." Anishaa again moved the cables closer. "Now!" she demanded.

"Release them," ordered the Alpha, and the Drones moved further away from them.

"Meva, get our family to safety."

"Sis'ter, we're n'ot le'avin' you."

"This isn't a debate, Meva. As Juardian, you are all my Charges." Anishaa's firm tone softened. "I love you, sister." Then she faced the others. "I love you all—my family–my Pride." She smiled briefly. "Goodbye" And then touched the cables together.

"Anishaa, no!" Laisere shouted as he motioned toward her.

The incompatibility released enormous amounts of energy that was channeled through her. Shaking, she squeezed her eyes tightly and fought to hold back the agonizing torment. Unable to contain the pain any longer, Anishaa began screaming horribly. Shaking and screaming, the Human-Augment struggled to hold the cables together despite her fatal electrocution. Vibrating and unable to move, the Drones were paralyzed, and the Velfin motioned to help his sister once more.

"Lai'sere, no, we g'ot to go."

"What? We cannot leave her."

"Meva, we have to help her," the telepathic octopi added.

"Th'ere is no'thin' we c'an do," she replied solemnly.

Meva raised her arms and created a cloud that enveloped them and whisked them away just as the Resonator exploded.

In the Plexus, Pryme halted his action just as it was going to smash Joryd's head in, and watched as the Drones battling Starone suddenly deactivated, leaving Omegus the only Linksys aboard unaffected. Regardless, the giant android faced the Elphah and was about to resume when tremors from the explosion jerked it back and loosened its grip. Seizing the opportunity, the Pantherus shoved his front claws deep into Pryme's chest plates, and with his hind claws he penetrated its stomach region and kicked the Android off him. Hitting the wall, the metal giant left an impression, and the Elphah quickly moved on it. Jumping up, he impaled Omegus with all his claws, rolled onto his back and threw the android as hard as he could against the Command chair. The Linksys leader worked to free itself. Now significantly damaged, Pryme experienced difficulty in getting up.

With all the other Drones shut down, Starone knelt down, breathed heavily, and looked to Joryd and Omegus. Badly injured, the Elemental bled silvery blood and was unable to help, he remained where he was, trying to catch his breath.

Back on all fours, Joryd roared with anger. “Still think I need a Kaja to shut you down, Pryme?” His mix of green and orange eyes narrowed. “Get up. I’m not finished with you.” And the Elphah lunged at the Linksys giant.

Strange New Life

III

In my Habitat and dressed in something other than a pair of black shorts, I rose from the table after finishing dinner. Now wearing jeans and a black tee shirt, I paid no mind to the white claw marks decorating them and went into the living room. "Momja, jamonaka resume recording."

"One moment, Marc," the computer said and paused. "Jamonaka resume."

"Fasbi."

Somewhere in the Novatne star system deep in the heart of this galaxy, a meeting of the minds was waiting to take place. On the planet Zahnobeia, inside the Council Chamber within the huge three-story structure, the Council leaders were in session. Levitating high above the floor, they had gathered around a large oval table made of crystal that was suspended from the ceiling. With much of its center carved out and left empty, it seemed more like a conversation piece than something of practical use.

Eighteen colored brains of different size and shapes were encased in their own protective bubbles and awaited for the Council Elphah to arrive. The creatures are called Ohdens. Not much is known about them, except they are one of the few ancient races remaining. They possessed superior intellect, have formidable mental abilities and have not had bodies for thousands of years. They are said to be immortal. The Ohdens are the Governing Council Authority of the Jhanctum galaxy, the instillators of the Defense Directories, and the creators of the Qi-Tahh Supremacy.

In a show of respect to the Elphah of the Council, the Ohdens spoke Zahnobein, the Elphah's native language. The vacant seat at the head of the table was soon filled by a blue brain that suddenly appeared. They all welcomed Kerebrol.

Rhetnig-Sux, the beige male brain was first to telepathically give his report. *"The Wernucian Qi-Tahh were successful in stopping the Tukylis on Lyriss III before they could kill the inhabitants, destroy all existing life, and seed the neighboring planets."*

"I always did like our Supremecy's finest," a female voice commented.

"Of course you do, Kaivessh. But is it because they follow orders and seldom ask why, or is it because they are your Qi-Tahh?" Wahn-Jemm inquired, another female brain with an oblong shape and sea foam green hue.

Defending her position, Kaivessh reminded the Council that Kerebrol had first pick and could have chosen them, but Heshe wanted the Zahnobein Qi-Tahh instead. *"What's wrong, Ohden? Can't give up your precious planet Zahnobeia, or do you simply have a weakness for strays?"*

You could hear the discontent in her voice and almost see a smirk form across her lips, or rather you would have if she had a face.

"Kaivessh?" Gy-ew, who was shocked by her disrespectful comment, bellowed.

"It is all right, Gy-ew. Our sister never was very good at hiding her jealousy. We all know the Zahnobein Life Protectors are the elite of the elite, making them the true Qi-Tahh Supreme, but because they do not conform to certain minor regulations, they are not given their proper status. So contrary to our dear sister's delusion regarding our flag ship, though very talented, the Wernucian Qi-Tahh are not better than my Zahnobein Pride, they only have the status of being so. Kaivessh is just upset I chose wiser than she," Heshe countered telepathically in both male and female voices calmly.

"Jealous? Delusion? Qi-Tahh Supreme? Why you egotistical—" she started to retort as the red tinge of her brain flared brightly.

Council member Rhetnig-Sux cautioned her, *"Careful, Council member. I see where this is about to go, and I will remind you that though Heshe is our brother and sister, Kerebrol is also the Council Elphah to whom you are about to insult. I suggest you leave it alone."*

The flaring red of the female brain softened, and she said nothing more on the subject.

"You have been spending time with the Fonchuai and Human again," the small grey brain directed to the Elphah.

"What can I say, they intrigue me." Kerebrol replied to him

directly before addressing the Council. *"Speaking of which, any word from my Qi-Tahh?"* Heshe's twin voices inquired.

The Council Elphah was informed that the Zahnobein Qi-Tahh had not reported in since their last check-in but had confirmed a Linksys incursion of the Oria star system.

Wahn-Jemm added, however, on another subject, they had heard from the Elphah of the Verasce Qi-Tahh who were investigating a situation in the Cesuritas star system. Evidence showed the Pyrites have returned.

"Will they ever learn?" Gy-ew asked frustratingly as his grey tinge flared.

"Speaking of never learning, we have also received a request from their Elphah, Syth-Korm. He wishes to transfer Acquil-Omegah Antonio Franco Battista out of his Pride, and he has sent him to us for reposting," Wahn-Jemm reported telepathically.

"Again?" Kerebrol's twin voices of male and female boomed angrily.

Irritated, Kaivessh's red tinge flared bright as well and she inquired why they continue to tolerate the problematic human and why they do not simply remove his augmentations and send him back to Earth?

"I concur with Kaivessh, Kerebrol. This is the third Pride this Augment has been removed from," Rhetnig-Sux added, his beige color was softer than the others.

Outside the Council Chamber, an Italian man from the seventeenth century sat, his hair cut to the regulations of his former Pride. He waited to be summoned. The Augment was five-foot-eleven with a muscular build, and he weighed approximately 205 pounds. He did not have long to wait. Receiving a loud telepathic message, he entered the Chamber and was levitated through the hole in the table, where he remained suspended.

"This is getting tiresome, Battista," the Elphah Oden said. *"I am fed up with Elphahs sending you back to us for reassignment. Why can you not get along with the Prides like our other Human-Augments?*

You have been a Life Protector for three hundred Earth years, and yet you are only a Deggzytepol–a Acquil-Omegah. What is the problem?"

Suddenly, the pseudo image, a holographic form of a non-descript creature, appeared, interrupting their proceedings, and informed Heshe that the Elphah of the Zahnobein Qi-Tahh was calling and standing by. Kerebrol at once allowed the transmission, and moments later Joryd appeared in pseudo form as well. His injuries were fresh, and still bled. His eyes were closed. The left one was colored and swollen shut, while the right eye had three deep claw marks that dragged down its length. He gave his report while attempting to hide his other injuries.

The Elphah told the Council that the assignment was accomplished, and the Linksys incursion of the Oria star system has been crushed. All invaders had been destroyed and the people of Oria V, also known as Seregaia, were safe. But it cost them dearly. Nineteen members of Joryd's family were killed, including Deggzytepol Sythean and Echelon Juardian Anishaa Dhriti. Who, if not for her personal sacrifice, the Packs would have been killed, and the mission might had failed. Sixty-two Pridesmen were critically wounded, and by the time they arrived, Mother and three of her children would have had major surgery.

"Our condolences to you and your Pride for your loss. We, the Council, are saddened," Heshe replied telepathically.

The Ohdens honored their dead with a few moments of silence as their mental energies radiated soft glows, and the Holo-Form of the Pantherus and live Human respectfully bow their heads.

Joryd raised his head, "On behalf of my Pride, fasbi to you and the Council."

"And what of you, my old opo?" Heshe twin voices compassionately inquired.

"I'm fine. My injuries look worse than they are. Besides, the Pride comes first."

Wahn-Jemm corrected him, informing Kenton that it was the Elphah who came first. However, the Ra-Tuth did not agree, and told them he would have Torr heal him later. Presently, the Pride were busy helping the Seagues restore stability.

"Were any other planets compromised, Ra-Tuth?"

"No, Council member Rhetnig-Sux," Joryd answered painfully. "Seregaia was the only planet in the star system under siege."

"We are dispatching Arjai and Satyre Prides to assist in treating the inhabitants and in the rebuilding of their city. Jamonaka, give the people of Seregaia the Council's deepest condolences on their loss, and let them know that an Ohden representative will visit them before two cycles of their third moon passes."

"It will be done, Elphah Ohden."

The Council Elphah congratulated Kenton and his Pride on a job well done, and though they had all earned a long rest, Heshe needed them here. He would explain once they arrived, and informed Joryd that both he and Z'yenn were needed.

"I understand. We will be on our way as soon as our relief arrives."

"The Unasallo Qi-Tahh will be there in eleven savners," Kerebrol's twin voices replied.

"The Pride will be ready."

Before his image could vanish, a male of average height and muscular build, appeared beside Joryd. Orange skin, long reddish brown hair, and beige eyes the Holo-Form faced him. Pausing briefly, the new arrival looked to Kerebrol.

"I informed Arjai-Elphah Sivgins of our condition just in case your healing needs slipped your mind."

"Hey, Kereebs, fasbi for the heads-up," he said, resting a hand on Joryd's reddish orange fur.

"Wurz kuyo, Torr. Jamonaka, take care of our Elphah," Heshe's twin voices simultaneously countered.

"Will do," he said, grinning broadly.

"Yes, Kereebs, fasbi," Joryd repeated, unamused.

Torr led him away, "You know this is all your fault."

"My fault? How in cryda do you figure this is my fault?"

Their Holo-Forms vanished, and Heshe continued with Battista as if their meeting had never been interrupted. Kerebrol informed

Antonio that against Heshe's bretherns' better judgment, the Council Elphah would give him one more opportunity to prove himself an asset to their cause, and reassigned him to Joryd's Pride as their new Deggzytepol.

"But be warned Acquil-Omegah, if I receive one more incident report concerning your interpersonal behavior with this Pride or any dereliction of your duties, I will personally remove your augmentations, wipe your memory of us, and return you to Earth in the circa where you were found. Am I clear?" Kerebrol asked sternly.

"Not interested in hearing my side, Kereebs?"

"Sarcasm?" Kerebrol's twin voices boomed. *"You are hanging on by a thread as it is...your past behavior with three Prides tells me everything I need to know, and it stops now. This is not a debate, Qi-Tahh. This is how things will be from here on. Do not make me regret this decision."*

Kerebrol told Antonio he was to join Joryd's Pride. Heshe would inform the Elphah and introduce Battista as his new Deggzytepol. Know this, Joryd Kenton is not like your other Elphahs, if he sent him back–it would be on a stretcher.

"Believe it. Am I clear?

"Yes," he said bowing. "Elphah Ohden."

"I better be. Until then, you are confined to the base. Dismissed!"

Hovering, Antonio again bowed deeply to Kerebrol before he was lowered back to the floor. Battista faced the Council and bowed to them before taking his leave. Once gone, the Ohdens continued with their Council business.

"What about the Verasce Qi-Tahh. They still need a Deggzytepol," The small grey Ohden brain asked.

The Elphah Ohden, aware of the two Human-Augments serving aboard the Viraconnus, both pursuing the same Acquil-Omegah position, now that Deggzytepol Battista was no longer the Deggzytepol. Kerebrol gave the posting to Eliana Rosenberg, the senior Echelon, and transferred Katia Yuri to the Verasce as their new Acquil-Omegah.

"I do not agree, Kerebrol. You are removing Katia from her family."

"Correction, Wahn-Jemm. The members of the Supremacy are all family. I am just having her live with the faction she does not yet know."

Other members of the Council also did not agree, especially when Kerebrol announced it was Heshe's turn to select the Human who would replace Anishaa Dhriti.

"But you just assigned an Augment to the Zahnobein Qi-Tahh," I get it, you want Battista to learn discipline, order and structure, so why not place him with the best? Kaivessh said, upset. *"Elphah Chyld T'lok and Omegah Ana Sanchez will both insure he gets in line."*

"That may be the problem." Kerebrol's twin voices replied. *"We are trying too hard to make him into who we believe Antonio Franco Battista should be, instead of who he is. He will learn both with my Pride. And for the record, Kaivessh...I have placed him with the best."*

"This is highly unusual," the brown brain owner of the Viraconnus Qi-Tahh added telepathically.

"Not at all. I am simply rearranging which Pride has two Augments serving aboard the ship. Besides, the young man I have selected shows promise in my opinion," Heshe's twin voices replied.

"With you, they all show promise," Kaivessh retorted as her red tinge brightened once more.

"My decision is final and is not open to debate," the Council Elphah commanded.

The Ohdens acknowledged Kerebrol's authority and submitted while Kaivessh asked in a carless tone about who Heshe had chosen. Allowing them to look into Heshe's mind, they saw the image of Heshe's choice, but concealed the reason for Heshe's adamancy.

"His name is Marc Hawkins."

A dome-shaped brain with a rustic hue inquired, *"Why him?"*

Wahn-Jemm started to ask a question about Hawkins when Kerebrol abruptly cut her off and deflected her inquiry, admitting only that Marc was the one Heshe had chosen. Rhetnig-Sux interjected and wished to know what made this human so special.

"Brothers and sisters, any continuance regarding the Human Marc Hawkins would be premature at best. I do not even know if he will join our cause. My Qi-Tahh and I will be leaving for Earth as soon as the Arjenadanns have been healed and repaired. If Marc Hawkins concurs, then we will revisit this issue at a later time."

Still annoyed, especially with their meeting ending so soon, the red brain of Kaivessh again flared brightly as she spoke out, *"And what of our other Life Protectors, their reports, and of our other Council business? This human is not the only thing on our agenda, Kereebs."* Speaking disrespectfully, she aired her bitter thoughts and could care less that she had referenced the human as something equal to or lesser than an insect.

"I do not understand your attitude toward humans, Kaivessh. You have a human serving onboard the Wernucian with your Elphah Pride. I do not recall you ever being bothered by her. In fact, you have always spoken highly of Omegah Ana Sanchez and have always treated her as all humans with our Supremacy should be treated—as true members of our Prides, and not outcasts we adopted and now must tolerate."

"That is because my human is the exception. Call her a leap in evolutionary development."

Kerebrol's blue brain intensified with annoyance. "*Kaivessh, there are times your irrational attitude wears thin even my vast patience. But since you are in such an irritable mood, you will be our representative to the Seagues. Maybe their beautiful spirit will change your disposition. You are very good at giving when you want to be sister. It would be senseless to waste such compassion, and it is a shame your true goodness is not shown more often. As for the rest of you, our business will reconvene upon my return from Earth, and if anyone ever refers to me as Kereebs again, know that neither of us will be happy. Council dismissed."*

Vanishing, Kerebrol exited the Chamber and left the Council members where they were to ponder what Heshe had said.

It is now two years since that Council meeting, and I was still adapting to my strange new life. I missed my family and friends terribly–and my wife even more. I dreamed of them all often, which made my longing for their company worse, but no reverie was ever more hurtful than the ones I would have of Angela.

Abruptly awakened and drenched in sweat, I jumped. Propping myself up on my elbows, I breathed heavily as the tears still streamed down my face. Falling back, I lay on the coldness of the sweaty sheets. "Fuck," I said aloud.

Angry, I paused to catch my breath and wiped away the tears still clinging to my face. Laying in a bed that was not my own, the phantom memories of another hurtful fantasy slowly started to fade. Suddenly, I felt a different kind of cold wetness, but not the kind produced from perspiration. This was a sticky coldness that I felt on my lower back and ass. Moving to one side, I discovered the area was soaked—the remnants of my wet dream with Angela, which now chilled me and no longer gave me the joy it once had. Covering it up, I moved over to the other side of the bed and soon realized the pillow under my head and the one beside it were both wet and saturated with sweat. I replaced them.

"Another Goddamn dream," I said to myself.

Expelling several breaths of frustration and staring at the ceiling, I lay in the solitude of my brother's divan. Once again, my dreams had turned nightmarish. Pissed, I hit the mattress with the side of my fist, and in pausing, another shadowy memory flared in my mind, and ignited another burst of anger. So I repeated my action.

Yes, it was another dream, one of many that I had had for two years now. But this was one of the worse I had experienced in months, and it hurt more deeply. Tricked, the fantasy was cloaked as something pleasant, something pleasurable, but in the end, it was actually a frighteningly cruel reminder that Angela and I were apart.

Glancing over and seeing my wife's picture on the nightstand beside the bed, I reached to pick it up, but then stopped and looked at my gold wedding band that I had refused to remove. Caressing it with my thumb, I ceased and proceeded to pick up her picture.

Touching the glass, I began recalling our lives together as I glided my fingers along her face. My anger and frustration suddenly changed to sorrow as all of my buried feelings rose to the surface like storm clouds gathering strength to unleash their fury.

In the past I was able to keep the hurt and loneliness at bay, but this time I simply did not have the strength to do so. This time there would be no pushing away the loss and the longing that filled my mind, my heart, and my spirit. This time I would surrender to its inevitable conclusion. Uncertain if my decision not to fight was a result of my most recent dreamscape or if it was fatigue from previous bouts, it simply did not matter anymore. The fact I was not in my own bed did not hold any resolve either, because today I would feel my loss fully, completely, and undiluted. I cried.

I cried aloud, intermittently howling at times from bursts of despair. I held Angela's picture close to my heart and curled up into a fetal position. Two years of despair, heartache, aloneness, and especially regret, all held me in its tight clutches. Captive, the emotions washed over me, ravaging me and trapping me in what felt like an eternity in hell. In fact, it was hell, and I was sentenced the day they came. I was trapped in a turmoil without end, tortured by the memories of a love and a world galaxies away.

Remaining in the fetal position, I continued to cry, and did so until too exhausted to do anymore. Slowly, reluctantly, I got out of bed to answer nature's call. Weary, I walked to use the facilities, rubbing and scratching at the itchy wounds across my heart. I was naked–accustomed to sleeping in the nude–something my wife and I did quite often and never changed.

Cleaning up, I hoped to wash away the emotional wave that now gripped me, I splashed water on my face. Repeating my action, I struggled to shake off the lingering effects from the nightmare. I brushed my teeth and hair, and would shower when I returned from a training which always left me sweaty and hurting. I hoped today's combat session with U'kristu took my mind off Angela.

I stared at the white claw marks on my black cotton sweatpants and matching T-shirt, and was grateful the marks were not on my black sneakers as well. I quickly finished putting on my sneakers. I did a quick check of my appearance in the full-length mirror in the corner of the bedroom, and grabbing my standard equipment, I slapped my Kaja to my right thigh and left.

Down the hall I stopped at Torr's bedroom. I could hear him fucking. Pausing for a brief moment, I banged on the door. "Hey, Tee, you're gonna be late for training. I'll see you there. Good morning Sclee-Tonna." I raced downstairs, I neither waited for, nor expected a reply, they were enjoying their time way too much to stop. The front door opened, and I crossed the threshold of Torr's Habitat into the corridor.

Leaving behind my vernacular. Designed to mimic the environment of its occupants, the Habitats represented what the person was most accustomed to. However, outside of these quarters was the ship we shared as a Pride–a family.

Because I too was running late, I hurried to meet U'kristu for our training. Resembling a woman of Hindu descent, U'kristu Rixx was a sukai female whose species were Sk'tier. She was our Pride's Juardian-Elphah. In human terms, this meant she was the Security Chief, except this position afforded far greater responsibilities and scope of command. Though only five feet tall and about 103 pound, she was highly proficient in her position and formidable in the execution of her duties. U'kristu was also my Ket-sho, a word which translated as mentor or educator, but that did not begin to describe her. Rixx was a mystery shrouded in mystery.

Still adjusting to this new life, it was sometimes difficult to see the multitude of life-forms I passed in the corridors as family. Representatives from more than fifty different planets throughout this galaxy made up my Pride, absolutely bizarre. Regardless of their species, we were of the same Pride, and that made us all family. Some of the creatures I passed could be recognized as cat, reptile, insect, amphibian, and humanoid, though in this galaxy, humans and humanoids alike were referred to as sukais.

Among our Pride, Antonio and I were the only humans on board, and aside from us the percentage of sukais serving with the Supremacy was small. Because of this, most Pridesmen did not share any human physical characteristics other than what we might envision in our most bizarre dreams I have formed friendships with some of them, and could even see a few as my brother and sister, while the others required more time. Regardless of what our relationship may or may not be, we were family now—a concept I had no choice but to accept.

I turned a corridor, and an array of pungent odors filled my nostrils as my enhanced sense of smell caught those of creatures past and present who had been through the hallways. I learned to identify which species produced which odors, but I had yet learned how to cope with the smells that were unpleasant. Thankfully, not all scents were bad, and some I actually enjoyed. Like the smell of a newborn baby, sandalwood, or even the salty air of the ocean. Then there were those smells that simply reeked. But these were the natural scents of my new family, and just another tribulation I would eventually learn to live with. After all, I have been told that my natural scent, regardless of how clean I was, was no bed of roses for them either.

Turning another corner, I noticed small insects crawling along the bulkheads, searching for and feeding on microbes, bacteria, and other parasitical entities. They were called Gauls, harmless to all other species and beneficial in eliminating the microscopic bugs that were no more bothersome than ants crawling on the wall.

Some of the Pride were using the Enac Sus Sols, alcove interface units located on nearly every level, which allowed non-telepaths a means of communicating with the Xentouwish and her children, who were also considered members of our family.

The Xentouwish was an ancient species of space-borne creatures who joined the Supremacy millenniums ago to help battle the Wehtiko and those who threatened our galaxy. This species were intelligent, empathic, and telepathic. Gigantic in size and immense in power. The creatures had no eyes or mouth that I knew of, and their skin was of a greenish-grey. Much about her race and offspring were still a mystery to me and almost indescribable—that is, all except their position among our family–Arjenadann was our Mother, and her children were our brothers and sisters. All Supremacy Motherships carried the name of the Xentouwish they were attached to, as did all of our Xentou and crafts, while the Prides were named by the planet we represented.

I turned the corner, smiled and waved to a male Priccaryan who greeted me. Two-headed, grey, naked, bald and buffed. I smiled and returned the politeness. Except for me, everyone has mind-linked with Arjenadann and her children, which was something I had not been able to bring myself to do. The concept was just too alien to me. She and her offspring understood, and no one among our Pride would ever force me to do so. They believed that something of this nature must be done freely and only when the individuals felt comfortable doing it. I did not know why I was so hesitant. From what I had heard, the experience was not painful. Quite the opposite, in fact. I was told the merging was soothing, relaxing, pleasurable, and very personal. Maybe it was because of my understanding of the process or the lack thereof. Mind-linking was more than a telepathic form of communication. It actually linked you and the creature together on a variety of different levels. You shared not only thoughts but ideas, emotions, and memories. It was a very intimate act, far deeper and far more personal than anything I have ever experienced. Perhaps because it was so intimate and beyond anything I had yet to feel with my own kind, that made me so apprehensive. Then there was the idea that I might actually enjoy it and one day become dependent on what she could give me. It frightened me, and that did not sit well with me, so for the time being, I was allowed to indulge my childish fears and unfounded prejudice.

Reaching the Training Facility, I entered and found U'kristu waiting.

"You are late," she said in Zahnobein.

"Apologies. It will not happen again," I replied in the same language.

Normally, I would simply Hexagyn to where I needed to be, but U'kristu had strict rules about Porting to training. She felt it made us lazy, and she was right.

"Jamonaka, take your place and ready yourself."

I walked to the center as she continued speaking the dialect of our Pride. Every Pride had a different primary language they used among their family, and ours was Zahnobein. Therefore, it was the first alien language they taught to me during my indoctrination.

"Are you ready, Marc?"

"Yes," I replied, touching my Kaja and morphing it into a Blade. The Kaja-Blade was what its user fashioned it to be, and I had created mine to resemble the Japanese katana. The sword's handle was rayskin wrapped in red as opposed to the traditional black. On one side there was my Pride's insignia, and on the other side there was a dragon holding a small yin and yang symbol, and the guard was as strong as the Blade itself. Made from a virtually indestructible metal and laser sharpened to no thicker than a molecule, our Kaja-Blades were capable of slicing through nearly anything.

"Momja, novice program level four. Tukyli scenario one."

The room suddenly transformed into a jungle setting, and though this was only a holographic training program, I have learned the hard way from past experiences that these recreations acted like the real thing—just as pleasant or just as deadly. Treading carefully and looking in all directions, I cautiously walked through the jungle using my enhanced senses to guide me. Spotting a large two-headed snake, I struck before it did and decapitated both heads. I continued and soon came to a clearing.

Passing a variety of plants and flowers, I stopped for a moment and took note of their beauty. I continued and watched for hidden dangers, but I was not as vigilant as I believed when I passed some strange-colored sunflowers. They darted toward me. They were fast, incredibly fast. The Tukyli wrapped their stems about me tightly before I could act, and bound my arms to my side. I was unable to break their grip, nor could I use my Blade. Lifting me off the ground and hanging me upside down like a bunch of bananas, the sunflowers moved toward me. Their faces became mouths with sharp animal teeth, and their petals elongated and changed to thorny feeders moving like fingers.

I struggled to break the vines but could not. I tried again and again with all my might and still I could not break free. These augmentations the Ohdens gave me, had given me mega strength–I could now lift two hundred times my weight, and still I was not strong enough to free myself. The animalistic plants suddenly darted toward me with its mouth opened.

"Momja, halt program."

The image around us froze, and I stopped struggling as U'kristu approached, her head lowered and her arms behind her back. "What did you do wrong?" she asked, standing before me and looking me in the face.

"I got out of bed."

"Not funny. If this scenario were real, that Tukyli would have killed you," she retorted, unamused.

"What'd you mean? I was just about to make my move before you interfered."

"And die. Yes, I know," she said, touching her Kaja. U'kristu cut off the heads of the monster plant with her Blade. "Your mind is elsewhere this suet."

"It's nothing."

"Nothing did not almost kill you," she said, slicing the stem. "What is it?

Still bound, I fell to the ground, but I was now able to free myself and broke loose. U'kristu returned her Blade to its null setting and holstered it to her side.

"Forget it. I'm fine."

U'kristu touched my shoulder gently, "It is the dreams again, is it not?"

There was no use in evading the issue. She knew, and she reminded me again that the option to erase my memories of my life on Earth was still available if I wished. I thought it irrelevant that the Ohdens could restore my memories after my Tour of Duty had ended.

"No," I replied adamantly. "Now are we here to train or what?"

"As you wish. Recall your Juardian training when dealing with the Tukylis. They can mimic any plant life. Large or small, it matters not."

It was then I realized she cheated in the scenario. According to everything I read in the Supremacy reports on the Tukyli, this species did not allow the existence of any species other than its own to occupy any planet they claimed.

"You are correct," she replied as a matter-of-fact.

"And yet there was a two-headed snake in the jungle."

"Yes, there was. You must learn to expect the unexpected, Valim. The Vipera should not have distracted you. You knew you were hunting a deadly adversary. But instead of staying vigilant, you allowed the beauty of your surroundings to distract you, and you dropped your guard."

"I know, but only for a moment."

"A moment was all that was needed to bind you and render you helpless, even though you were never truly helpless. Qi-Tahh are never helpless. Remember, mental discipline is key when using the Kaja."

"But how? I could barely breathe and couldn't break its grip or use my Blade?"

U'kristu reminded me that our Kajas responded to our thoughts and took whatever form we programmed into it. It was true that I could not break the creature's grip. Tukylis may mimic plant life, but they were much stronger than many species. I should have morphed my device into another form, but instead I allowed my emotional state to cloud my mind and hinder my actions. A fatal mistake like this in the field, and U'kristu may not be around to save my ass.

In finishing, she warned me not to permit negative emotions to rule over me.

U'kristu was right. Fear, anger, and pain were distractions that slowed my reflexes and actions.

Still holding my Kaja-Blade, I asked, "Anything else?"

"Yes, you morphed your Kaja before knowing the situation. Do not try to anticipate your opponents' actions. Like most species, they are living beings and therefore unpredictable. Instead of acting, learn to react and match their actions accordingly."

"You've never felt pain or anger or been emotionally preoccupied when you've fought?"

"Of course I have, but my training and mental disciplines keep me focused."

I discontinued the Blade setting, and the Kaja returned to its neutral stasis. I asked what setting she would have chosen. The Gauntlet, if she were to presume. Would have been her choice, it was more of a multi-task solution in these kinds of situations.

"I'll try to remember that."

"Wrong, remembering is what I expect from you." she said, turned about and walked back to her previous spot. "Ready? Momja, continue with Tukyli scenario two. Run program."

The new setting revealed a wide-open lawn, the kind one would find on a golf course. I touched my Kaja but did not activate it, and looked around. Walking cautiously along the prairie, I remained ready to act. Suddenly the grass beneath my feet came alive and attacked.

In Throne Pryme, the Twins, female Priccaryans, two headed species that shared one body, arrived wearing silk scarfs about their necks. One wore lavender and the other wore red, with their Life Support Devices fashionably clipped to them. Wearing a thick gold chain for a belt that draped off their hips, the hairless, naked, and partially wet grey-skinned females approached the Elphah and Omegah and both bowed their heads deeply.

"Apologies," Sclee said.

"For our lateness," Tonna added.

"We were detained," they finished in unison.

"Greetings, Sclee-Tonna." Joryd sniffed twice. "Torr kept you two again, eh?" he asked, grinning.

They both smiled, making their long noses more pronounced against their mouths. Turning around, they continued smiling and wordlessly went to their science station.

"I swear that Fonchuai has got the stamina of a Pantherus when it comes to bodeaco," Joryd commented, sitting sphinx-style on his Throne.

Seated in her Acquil-Throne next to his was Z'yenn's seat. "There should be regulations against having sex right before duty."

"And where would the fun be in that? Are you forgetting Regulus B?" he retorted, now smiling fully.

"Shhhh," she countered, bringing a clawed finger to her lips and returning his glee.

In the corridor, Torr was walking quickly on his way to training. Topless and buffed with a thin leather strip between his teeth, he met up with Antonio.

"Grumbah, Torr."

"Grumbah, Tony," he replied through gritted teeth.

"So tell me, who was the conquest this time?" Antonio asked, grinning and speaking in his thick Sicilian accent.

Slipping on his tee shirt and pulling his uncombed reddish-brown hair back into a ponytail, the orange skinned sukai quickly bound his hair with the leather strip. "The Twins," was all he said.

"That's the third time this verstix."

"Fifth. Remember that emergency I had during combat training four niyas ago?"

"You blew off CT just to have sex?"

"Of course," he retorted grinning broadly.

"And then the other niya I used my allergy flare up to get out of a Health and Safety exercise."

"Damn you're bold. Are you three dating?"

No," he said, shaking his head. "We're—now what was it Marc called us...oh yeah. We're bunk monkeys."

"Bunk monkeys?" Antonio said, repeating the words strangely. He suddenly bursted out and chuckled. "Marc is so funny." Then

Antonio checked Torr out. "I'm impressed. Someone's keeping in shape."

Torr just smiled. Sivgins was a Fonchuai, a sukai male of average height with beige eyes. His race were five times stronger than ordinary humans and nearly three times as fast. Though highly intelligent, this race were also inherently sarcastic, making Torr a wiseass by nature, which annoyed Z'yenn to no end. But for him, not to be sarcastic or to mess with others was seldom within his control. Torr was also a lover–of both sexes from what I have heard, but currently enjoyed fucking females solely. Sivgins was also our resident Arjai–Elphah. In colloquial terms, Torr was Chief Medical Officer, and he and his Pack of healers were proficient in treating a variety of different species both on and off the ship.

As for Antonio Franco Battista, he was a Human-Augment like myself, except Antonio was recruited back near the end of Earth's seventeenth century, and his abilities were far more matured than mine. I only hoped I would be blessed with the same abilities as him once my powers have developed, but for now they were still in their infancy stage. Battista wore his hair naturally–his long, thick, wavy curls laid past his shoulders.

"I wonder what U'kristu has in store for us koniya?" Torr asked.

"With U'kristu, it can be anything, but whatever it is, you can bet it'll be harder on Marc than us."

They turned the corner.

"Hopefully, she won't be too hard on him. I like having him around," Torr replied.

Entering the training facility as the program ended, they found me kneeling, sweating, and breathing heavily. My shirt was torn, and I had bleeding cuts across my cheek, arms, and chest. They both just stared at me.

"What is it your species calls it…wishful thinking?"

"Yeah, pretty much," Antonio replied.

Having entered the facility some time ago, Talon, a reptilian biped from a savage race of warriors called Scorpilyns, possessed a cold nature. They had mega strength, superior speed, and great agility and reflexes. They were intelligent, but had an aggressive nature. This species had an extremely large build, with an average height of seven feet, and weighed around 650 pounds. There were few life-forms that posed a threat or even challenged the Scorpilyn or Talon for that matter. As Juardian-Omegah, he was U'kristu's second.

He uncrossed his arms, approached, and expressed his impatience with me. "Well, it's about time you finished," he said as his forked tongue slipped between his parted lips.

Glancing up at him, I slowly stood as my breathing continued to slow.

"What took you so long? There was only one of them," he asked harshly, towering over me, his tongue again moved in and out of his mouth.

"That was only one?" I answered, surprised in between breaths.

"Yes, and do not make it a habit. In actual battle there is never one, and they must be vanquished quickly. That is what you must do with all your enemies."

"Well, excuse me all over the place. I'm new to the world of plant monsters. Thank you very much."

The seven-foot reptilian looked down at me with his arctic glare and I quickly changed my tone.

"What I meant to say was, sorry. You're absolutely right. I took way too long in mowing that monster lawn and pruning those giant killer weeds. I'll try to be more mindful of my timing in the future." I then chuckled nervously.

"Talon, leave him be. Remember, Marc is only a Betah and he is still learning." U'kristu faced me, "Well done, Va-lim."

"Underling," Talon growled, and walked away.

Antonio and Torr joined U'kristu and I with the Fonchuai smirking as he patted me on the back. Reacting to the pain, I told him to be careful and he looked behind me, and saw my shirt was holey with second-degree chemical burns. They were not serious, but they hurt like hell. Torr looked at me, confused.

"The fucking Tukyli transformed into an Acrolin Apse."

Torr faced U'kristu surprised, "You pit him against a korocing Tukyli?"

"Of course, Marc is a fourth-level novice. Tukyli scenarios are part of his training. And watch the language. You both know I do not approve of your fowl idioms."

"Has she given you that dumb lopsin about not morphing your Kaja until you know the type of danger? Yeah, that's one of my favorites."

Stunned and speechless, all I could do was look at U'kristu. Neither Torr nor I said anything more on the subject.

We instead listened as the Juardian-Elphah who thanked us for coming, and then she explained today's exercise. U'kristu had divided our training into four parts. We were to use acrobatic evasion without the use of Kajas in part one. Where we were only to evade, block if we had to, but not engage. U'kristu looked to our reptilian brother, "Talon."

Giving a low lizard growl, we knew he was not happy with the restrictions placed on him. The Juardian-Elphah started to pace, informing us of part two, which would consist of acrobatic combat, again without the use of our Kajas. Here we were to demonstrate our abilities in mumar combat, alien martial arts coupled with our acrobatic skills. The third would be group Kaja combat.

"In the field we are responsible for one another's safety." U'kristu stated flatly. "And must protect each other and our Charges with unyielding vigilances. "The last part of training will consist of single combat in which you will demonstrate your skills. As a Pride, it is important we know one another's strengths and weaknesses in order to function as a unit. Now let us begin."

In Throne Pryme, the Command Center of the ship, all was normal. Manning their holographic stations, the Pack were engaged in performing their duties. Avedia, the sightless Pylot, navigated while Laisere, the weapons specialyst performed diagnostics on the ship's defenses. With the Twins, Sclee-Tonna engaged in their scientific duties, E'nie, the blue-skinned communications specialyst, monitored his console, while Joryd oversaw operations and conversed with Z'yenn when she was not busy with her responsibilities.

"Excuse me, Joryd. I am receiving a transmission from the Comini Defense Directory," E'nie reported. "They have lost contact with their Defenders in the Grawnsom star system. They were sent to investigate reports of a planetary disturbance. They have not been heard from since."

"Try raising the Comini Defenders," The Elphah commanded facing his Omegah.

"Affirmative, Ra-Tuth."

"What do you think?"

"There could be a number of reasons they're not replying. Their communication array could be damaged," the Omegah speculated.

"Comini Defenders, this is the Zahnobein Qi-Tahh Arjenadann. Jamonaka, respond."

"I don't think their Directory would've asked us to investigate something that simple."

"Purrhaps not. In any case, we're only two savners from the Grawnsom star system." Z'yenn replied.

Back at the training facility, the sessions of our workout rolled by as we completed the courses and demonstrated our skills and abilities. Dodging, flipping, and evading, we fought as a team and survived attacks by creatures with primitive weapons in the first section. We combined acrobatics with martial arts against large hairy beast men in the second, and we ended the third training segment by defeating a variety of known foes using gymnastic abilities, mumar, and Kajas. U'kristu gathered us together so that we could catch our breath.

"You have all done well. Now comes personal combat." Rixx looked to Battista. "Antonio, you will fight Torr."

"Whoa, hold the fuck up!"

U'kristu turned and faced me. "What did I say about your use of profanity?"

"Sorry, but that leaves me sparring with Godzilla," I replied, thumbing him.

"His name is Talon, and yes, that is correct."

I looked to the Scorpilyn up and down and faced my Ket-sho. "What the hell's the matter with your mind? Why can't Torr or Tony fight him," I asked, looking to Talon once more. "They're better trained than I am?"

"Well, I don't know about Antonio, but I like my body the way it is. In one unbroken piece. Besides, if he kills me, who will be there for the Pride when they need arjai?"

"Fuck the Pride."

"Language, jamonaka." U'kristu said becoming annoyed.

"Sorry," I said glancing to my Ket-sho, and looked back to Torr. "I like my body the way it is too. Who's going to heal me?"

Torr slowly raised his hand.

"Oh, that's just wrong in so many ways."

"Torr kasauj, you are not helping. Va-lim, this is only combat training. It is not the real thing. Besides, as I have stated, it is important for us to learn the strengths and weaknesses of our family."

"But I already know my weakness is Talon's strength, and so does he…and so do you." I said whining

"It will be as I have said. And do not make me remind you about your fowl idioms, again. Am I clear?" U'kristu asked looking to me sternfully.

"Yes ma'am."

"Torr, Antonio, jamonaka take your places." The Sk'tier commanded.

They did as U'kristu instructed. This was a freestyle match she explained, and once the two were ready, U'kristu ordered them to begin. Moving around each other, Battista informed Sivgins that he did not stand a chance. Torr countered by saying that he had the same misgivings about him.

"How can you win? I'm faster than you." Antonio moved in quickly and hit Torr with three body shots. "I'm much stronger than you are." He reversed kicked the Fonchuai, knocking him out of the arena.

Groaning, Torr got up and returned to his place.

"And I'm way smarter, not to mention I have been a Life Protector at least a hundred meads longer than you."

"And yet you still can't knock me out."

"As you wish."

Moving toward him, Sivgins evaded Battista's kick, trapped his supporting leg with his own legs, and slammed him onto the floor. On top of him before he could act, Torr applied pressure to some specific points on his neck and immobilized Antonio.

"Now what were you saying? Oh yeah, now I remember."

"Torr?" Antonio said, pausing.

"Yes?" He replied smirking.

"Would you jamonaka release me?"

Torr shook his head, "No."

"Torr, let him up. This is combat training, not—"

"In a hotress," he said, interrupting U'kristu. "So… You have mega strength, super speed, a vast," he said, stretching out the word, "Intellect and maturity, and yet you are powerless, defenseless, and if I were an enemy, you'd be dead." Torr said tapping Antonio on the head.

"Touché. I yield."

"I'm sorry, I didn't quite hear you. Would you repeat that jamonaka?

U'kristu shouted, "Sivgins!"

He looked to her, now grinning, "Hold up. I want to hear this."

Battista chuckled. "I said I surrender. Torr, you win."

Releasing him, Torr eased off Antonio and helped him to his feet.

"What was that you used on me?"

"The Binos nerve block. Depending on what nerve you manipulate, you can paralyze an entire body–as you just experienced."

"Where did you learn that move?"

"Guess," Torr replied looking to U'kristu.

I joined them because I wanted them to teach me how to do that.

Done correctly, the technique was painless, but you could also apply pain if necessary. Done incorrectly, it was just painful, and they thought not to educate me because I might end up hurting Talon unnecessarily. They misunderstood. I did not want Talon to hurt me unnecessarily, and this whole matchup thing was so unnecessary. I knew what it was, they liked seeing me get my ass kicked.

"Va-lim, this is only combat training."

"Yeah, you keep saying that. Like I'm going to believe someone who told me to wait for the danger to present itself to morph my Kaja and then sic a Tukyli on me. And don't try and say you didn't because I've got the acid burns to prove it."

"Enough! Torr, Antonio, jamonaka take your places, and this time, Torr, I want to see you demonstrate your fighting skills and Kaja usage. This is not grapple training."

Battista and Sivgins again took their places in the small arena.

"Begin!" U'kristu commanded.

Following her instructions, Antonio morphed his Kajas into a quarter staff, while Torr formed two batons, and charged each other.

Back in Throne Pryme, E'nie continued his hails, "I repeat, Zahnobein Qi-Tahh Arjenadann to Comini Defenders, jamonaka acknowledge." He faced Joryd and Z'yenn. "I am sorry, but there is no response."

"Inform the Comini Defense Directory that we have received their message and are en route to investigate. We will report when more is known."

"Yes, Ra-Tuth."

"Avedia, Arjenadann, set course for the Grawnsom star system. Light speed seven," ordered the Omegah.

"Acknowledged, Z'yenn. Arjenadann has been informed, and course and speed has been laid in."

"Initiate." Z'yenn commanded.

The ship jumped to seven times the speed of light.

At the training facility, Torr and Antonio were Blade dueling.

Armed with a traditional foil and long knife–typical fencing form for him from his era, the Human-Augment was fast. But so was Torr, who countered Antonio's move and speed.

Watching Torr fight, made me hope I would never have to fight him. Being a Healer, Sivgins' vast medical knowledge aided him well in combat. He knew exactly how to strike you, and depending on the damage he wanted to inflict–whether it be with hand or weapons, Torr was formidable. His Blade was similar to the Ninja straight sword on Earth, except the guard and handle were alien in design instead of its traditional style.

In the end, Torr was forced to surrender after Antonio disarmed him in a great display of skill. Rixx congratulated Battista and told Sivgins the areas she wanted to see improvement. They bowed to each other, they bowed to the Ket-sho, and cleared the arena.

"All right, Va-lim. You and Talon are next. Jamonaka take your places."

I again looked at the massive Scorpilyn, and afterward, I lay down on the floor.

"Va-lim, what are you doing?"

"Saving time…and pain."

"Marc, get up. What would you do if Talon was an enemy instead of family?"

"Cry and then die."

"Can't say I blame him. I mean Talon is–."

U'kristu shot Torr a look, cutting his sentence short. He said nothing more and smiled. Looking back to me, her eyes narrowed, and she spoke slowly and sternly, "Marcus Anthony Hawkins, get off the floor and take your place this instant."

"Yes, ma'am," I replied respectfully. I stood, bowed to her and complied at once.

"Sorry, Hawk. As much as I'd love to stay and watch you get your ass kicked, I'm due in Throne Pryme shortly, and have to leave to shower. I guess I'll just have to be content with reading about it in Torr's Arjai report."

"All right, enough! You," she said, pointing to Antonio. "Go. You are late."

Now grinning broadly, Battista made his farewells, turned, and exited.

"As for you, Sivgins—" U'kristu said, facing him.

"I didn't say anything."

"No, but you were going to. Not another word."

Torr at once zipped his lips shut, lock his mouth, and threw away the imaginary key. He smiled.

Rixx ignored him and faced Talon, reminding him that this was combat training and that I was only a Betah. The fact that she felt it necessary to warn him made my stomach queasy. Talon's species was considered one of the strongest in this galaxy. This did not give me peace of mind.

"Hey brother, you know I was just kidding with that Godzilla crack, right?"

Saying nothing, the lizard biped looked down at me, looked to U'kristu, and readied himself. I looked to her and then back to the Scorpilyn, whose forked tongue slid slowly out of his mouth and back in and caught a slight grin cross his lips. Feeling even more unsettled, I took another good look at the reptilian, checking out his massive size.

"Um, Tee?" I said, looking to him.

Grasping at air, Torr used the imaginary key to unlock his mouth and he unzipped his lips looking to the Ket-sho. "Don't 'Um, Tee' me. This is her doing," he said pointing to Rixx, who gave him a serious glance, forcing him to nervously rezip his lips and relock his mouth. He tossed the imaginary key over his shoulder and grinned.

"Begin!" She commanded.

Back in Throne Pryme, the Elphah feeling uneasy about the Comini Defenders, instructed Avedia and Arjenadann to increase speed to light eleven. The Pylot acknowledged and followed his instructions.

"What is it, Joryd?"

"I'm getting an Elphah Black Alert right here." Joryd pawed the back of his head. "Something's wrong."

"Avedia, plot a course for the nearest Cosmic Corridor."

"Yes Z'yenn–course plotted. The nearest Corridor is five light years away–we will be there in two point six three hotress."

"Arrival time to the Comini star system after entering the Corridor?" The Elphah asked.

"Forty-one hotress and three et'nims." Avedia replied.

At the training facility, I hit the floor hard, rolling backward feet over head, and onto one hand, I pushed off, barely avoiding the momentum of Talon's strike. His metal staff clanged loudly striking the floor. Countering with a backhand swing, my staff caught the reptilian's right cheek. Charging, I rammed him in the stomach and came down on his head. Blocking my strike with his staff, I continued forcing down on him, but with Talon's strength far exceeding my enhanced power, he pushed me back.

Jumping up and spin kicking him twice, he stumbled back as I raced toward him once more. Slamming the Kaja-Staff to the floor, I morphed the base into a tri-leg support, balanced myself and kicked Talon hard in his chest. He again stumbled back.

Roaring like a T-Rex, he angrily threw his Kaja to the side and charged. Again I swung at him, but he blocked my blow, knocked the weapon from my hands and spinning around, the Scorpilyn struck me with his powerful tail. Propelled back, I hit the floor three meters later, bounced off my back and landed on my chest and chin. I did not move.

"Talon kasauj," U'kristu commanded, and he stopped. "Marc, are you all right?" She waited for a reply but heard none. "Va-lim?" she inquired again, filled with concern.

"I hear you." I said finally replying.

"You are–okay? Can you move?"

"I don't know I haven't tried."

Talon's blow had been nothing less than stunning.

She looked to the Fonchuai and told him to check me out.

The Arjai-Elphah ran to me, and upon reaching me, he inquired, "Anything broken?"

"If I say yes, can we call it a draw and not continue?"

Torr helped me slowly turn over, and sat me up. "How do you feel?"

"Like I got hit by a truck doing 30." I wiped blood from my nose and lips. "But I'll feel better once my double vision fades and I wring U'kristu's neck." I looked to Torr. "It's only combat training she says," and I wiped more blood from my mouth. "Does Talon even know the meaning of that?"

Torr checked my eyes. "If he didn't, you'd be dead by now."

"Thank you, I feel so much better."

Checking my eyes, Torr asked how many fingers he was holding up? In looking my vision was blurred, so I shook my head and rubbed my eyes. "Three," I replied uncertain.

Torr reported his findings and told U'kristu there did not seem to be any reticular hemorrhaging, nor could he see any indication of a concussion. He told her that I was fine.

"Good. Then let us continue."

"Do we have to?"

No sooner had Torr return to Rixx's side and I stood, than Talon attacked. Grabbing his wrist and falling back, I kicked him over me landing him on his back a half meter away. Now pissed, the Scorpilyn roared, turned over onto his stomach and started to get up.

Before he could, I charged him, and flipping forward I came down with an axe kick, and landed squatting on all fours. Striking him with a right crescent kick, and a left crescent kick, I reversed spun kicked him twice with the heel of my foot.

On my feet and racing for my Kaja, the reptilian was upon me before I could reach it. He grabbed me, and in one fluid motion picked me up over his head, turned and threw me against the far wall. Bouncing off I hit the floor with a loud thud–my head spun and he was upon me once more. Reaching down to pick me up, I turned over and rolling backwards and kicked him with both feet. Upper cutting him he stumbled back. Back on my feet, I assumed a defensive stance and readied myself for Talon's next attack.

The Scorpilyn charged, and spinning around with his tail, I ducked, leapt up grabbing the back of my knees and reversed spun myself. I uppercutted him with the dorsum of my feet, and coming out of the spin I kicked him hard in his chest. Landing on my back, I roll backwards into another defensive stance as the Scorpilyn hit the floor.

Getting up, Talon smirked and nodded his head as if he approved of my actions, but then his grin faded and he charged me once more. I met him half way. Falling to my knees, I slid at him with my back close to the floor. Plowing his legs, Talon sailed over me and hit the wall, bounced off and hit the floor. Roaring like an angry T-Rex, he no longer found my maneuvers amusing, he got up and charged me as though he were going to kill me. My eyes first went wide, then they narrowed, and finally I ran to meet his advances.

We dueled Martial Arts style. Blocking and evading, I found an opening, and kicked him in the side, then in his stomach and finished him with a forearm strike across his jaw when he doubled over. Talon retaliated and broke two of my ribs. Everyone heard them crack. But before I was able to fully react, he stepped back and spun about with his powerful tail and propelled me to where my Kaja lied.

Holding my side, I picked up my device, changed it into a metal staff and used it as a crutch to help me stand. However there was no time to entertain my injury, the reptilian was upon me once more. Driving the opposing end of my staff into his stomach, I followed through with an upward strike–his head flew up and back. I used the staff and swept his feet from under him. He hit the floor hard and I slammed the staff down, but he moved out of harm's way and broke my leg. I cried out.

Back on his feet and roaring loudly, he was on me. Blocking my weak offensive strike, the Scorpilyn ripped the staff from my hand, dislocated my shoulder, and palm struck me in the chest. I sailed back against the wall and somehow ended up cracking my collar bone. Sitting with the wind knocked out of me, and too injured to move,

I remained where I was as the Scorpilyn raced toward me. Raising his two powerful fists overhead, Talon roared loudly and prepared to bring them down on top of me.

"Talon Kasauj," U'kristu shouted.

However, the Scorpilyn continued in his deliverance.

U'kristu quickly repeated herself, "Talon, I said stop! The match is over. You won!"

This time he obeyed and stopped himself just short of smashing in my skull. Talon looked to Rixx as his tongue slipped between his lips. Looking down at me, he changed his posture and extended a clawed hand to help me to my feet.

"Ow," I said, rubbing my chest. "I think you cracked my sternum."

"Unlikely. I heard nothing break when I hit you. Besides, it was only a light hit."

"A light hit, my ass," I retorted, still rubbing my chest.

"Do not worry, Marc," he said as his tongue again slipped through his lips. "I have never killed a fellow Pridesmen during combat practice." And again his tongue slid in and out.

"No," I said, wiping away blood. "You just made them wish you had."

Talon told me that I was improving and formed a slight grin as U'kristu and Torr joined us. My Ket-sho also concurred because it took him longer to break me. I on the other hand was doubtful. In any case, combat training had concluded for today, and U'kristu faced her Juardian-Omegah and thanked him for his participation.

"What the hell are you thanking Talon for? I was the EverLast," I retorted.

"EverLast?" Torr inquired puzzled.

"Yeah, it's the name of a punching bag back home.

U'kristu ignored my repartee, "Jamonaka, make your rounds once you have cleaned up, while Torr and I escort Marc to Arjai Pryme to have his injuries attended."

"Continue to practice Betah, and I will see you next verstix," Talon added. Bowing to me and then to Rixx, he exited.

He must have been on crack if he thought my sparring with him next week was going to happen. Torr retrieved my Kaja, and he and U'kristu helped me to medical. Though I had become accustomed to feeling sore all over and experienced an occasional broken bone now and then with other members of my Pride, with Talon, there was not a session where he did not break my bone.

At Arjai Pryme, the two help me over to one of the divans.

"Grumbah Nahni."

Nahni's species was Gulapalae. A sukai female with golden yellowish-brown skin, medium length red hair, green eyes and three breasts that spanned her chest.

"Grumbah U'kristu," she said approaching us. "What happen to you?"

"Combat training." I replied.

"With who?"

"You mean with what–guess."

"Talon?" she asked.

"Got it one," I retorted painfully.

I asked Nahni when my enhanced self-healing was going to kick in, and she told me that it already had, or else they would have been operating on me each time I came from training. For faster results, she informed me that my system needed to mature, and no one could predict when that would happen.

Nahni faced Torr. "How could you let this happen?"

"Me?" he shouted back surprised. "How the koroc do you figure this was my idea?"

"I'll get the scanner, and be right back." she said leaving to retrieve the instrument.

"Va-lim, when you are finished here, rest and I will see you later koniya." U'kristu faced Torr. "This is the last time I will warn you about your bad language, Sivgins."

"Hey, this is my Dysunn frum section, I'm Elphah here, so there."

U'kristu approached Torr and got into his personal space. "I do not care if we are in your Habitat, I do not care for that language and you will honor that when around me. Am I clear?"

My Fonchuaiian friend looked to me, "Sorry, but this is on you. I know what I'm going to do, or rather not do around her–you have to make your own decisions."

Sivgins looked down at Rixx who continued to look up at Torr awaiting his reply. He was silent. U'kristu informed Torr she was waiting for his answer, and repeated her question. He finally acknowledged her.

"Yes U'kristu, I understand.

"Make certain you do, Torr, I am not going to ask you again. I have been too patience with you, I will be patience no longer."

Stepping out of his personal space, just as the Arjai-Omegah returned, the Sk'tier said her goodbyes as Nahni began to scan me.

"Marc, what made you want to spar with Talon?"

"I was tired of my pain-free existences. Why not ask your sister, she's the one who chose to match me with Dinosaur Dan."

"Well he certainly did a job on you, that's for sure. Lie back jamonaka."

I informed her painfully that my lying down was not possible, because of the acid rinse I received as part of U'kristu's pre-training.

"An acid rinse?" Nahni asked looking to Torr perplexed.

"He's referring to the Acrolin Apse," the Fonchuai replied.

"U'kristu pitted you against a Tukyli," she asked, surprised. "What's she trying to do kill you?"

"No, that was brother Talon's job. Hers was to take my mind off Angela," I replied grunting.

Shaking her head, Nahni walked over to a tray, removed a small sprayer and pumped a few shots on my back, and explained it would treat my burns and ease the pain. She set down the sprayer, and playfully suggested, that the next time I should see her instead of U'kristu. She was sure she could think of something far less hazardous than sparring with a Scorpilyn. Nahni smiled. I told her that I would hold her to that, and returned her smile.

Nahni faced Torr, "And Torr, you know better…letting Marc fight Talon."

"And this my fault, how? You prefer I fight Talon instead? What are you crazy?"

The Arjai-Omegah faced me, "Just promise me the next time you'll be more careful."

"Don't tell me, talk to our sister, Sargent Slaughter," and looked to Torr, "Why does everyone think this is an experience I want to repeat?"

"I don't know, but better you than me."

"I can heal a great many things, but I can't fix a smashed in skull."

"Funny you should say that." I said.

"What?" And again Nahni looked to Torr who this time looked away.

"Well in any case at least you're improving." She said confidently.

"That's what U'kristu and Talon said, although I still don't see it."

Nahni chuckled, "I'll be right back."

Grunting as I lay on the divan, I wished I had stayed in bed. Though I did not think much for her solution, U'kristu's training had dissipated all thoughts of Angela, and all that remained were thoughts of my new family and this strange new life I now lived.

Elsewhere, unbeknownst to us at the time, we were under covert observation by beings from another galaxy. Aboard her Palace ship, two humanoid creatures faced a large screen with only their backs visible.

"This creature, Marc Hawkins, though unnaturally strong and fast, does not seem to be as well trained as the others, Imperial Empress," the taller, armor-clad woman with long thin braids said, speaking a mixture of Swahili and Mayan.

"No, he does not. Too bad his strength and speed might have been useful had he been better trained. Therefore, I will not include him with the others should it become necessary to follow through with those plans." Facing her, the shorter woman with long brunette hair asked, "Are our warriors ready, Captain?"

"Yes Imperial Empress, though I can't help wondering what

will happen if we need these creatures and they prove not to be as powerful as you believed them to be?"

"No need to wonder, dear sister. If I'm wrong, we will all die screaming, and our galaxy will be ruled by a merciless monster.

The Wehtiko Influence

IV

At Torr's Habitat, I was still resting after coming from medical, where I was treated for my injuries. It was customary for humans to spend time and live with each Pridesmen at three-month intervals, and in that way we not only learned about their species and customs but also taught them about ours. After each cultural exchange, we were permitted to reside in our own dwelling for the next three months. This would continue until we had lived with all of our fellow Pridesmen at least once.

En route to discover what happened to the Comini Defenders after they were sent to investigate a disturbance of a possible Wehtiko outbreak. I found it interesting that the Native Indians on Earth used this term to describe the Europeans. They believed White men suffered from Wetiko. A word meaning "cannibal." It did not literally mean the Europeans actually ate the flesh of others, rather it referenced to one who devours the life of others. Something the Native Indians considered to be a mental illness. However in this galaxy, the word Wehtiko did not invoke interest, but fear. It referred to an insidious disease that unleashed the darkest nature of those who were Influenced–or infected.

Retreating into my thoughts, I rubbed my claw marks and drifting off. I thought of Angela, and recalled our last day together and the day our lives hit a turning point—or more accurately, the day a turning point hit our lives.

In the bathroom at our Chicago home, I splashed water on my face to rinse away the remaining shaving cream. When I opened my eyes and looked in the mirror as the water ran down my face, I saw Angela's reflection standing in the doorway. She was an African-American woman of average height, fit, carmel complexion with brown hair almond colored eyes, and a belly beginning her third trimester.

Sadness and solemnity permeated her demeanor, and I could not blame her because I felt the same way. Dressed in her Fila pink and soft blue sweat suit, not even her two favorite colors could lift the weight pressing down on her heart this morning. She continued to stand in back of me.

"Marc, I've changed my mind. I don't want you to go," she blurted out suddenly.

"Ang, we've been through this. I'm not even sure I'm going," I said, drying my face.

I tossed the hand towel onto the rim of the sink, and then walked past her out of the bathroom. I was wearing my black and white Fila sweat pants, and so I picked up the matching top and put it on before checking myself in our full-length bedroom mirror. There were still questions I needed answered first, but I had also made up my mind that if I agreed with those answers, then I would go. That did not sit well with Angela.

"Just like that? You're going?"

"Listen. They'll be here in about six hours, and I'd really like it if we didn't spend that time arguing. Please don't make this any harder than it already is."

"No, you'd rather I say, 'Go ahead, good luck, and I'll see you in what–eight Earth years?' What the hell did he mean by Earth years anyway?" Angela stood with her arms crossed in front of her. "This is, of course, only contingent on you not being killed before your tour of duty is up. And why recruit humans for their war?"

"Just one of the questions I am looking for answers to."

"Fuck looking for answers, tell them no, and stay."

I could do that, but instead I asked Angela what would happen if I decided to stay. What then? And what if they were right about the consequences they predicted might happen? What then?

"What do we do when this impossible future come to pass and we blew our only chance of preventing it because we were selfish? What would happen to our families, not to mention the one were trying to have? What would we say them?" I started to pace. "Oh, I'm sorry. Angela and I were given the opportunity to stop this shit before it occurred, but we decided that our own personal feelings were far more important than anything else, even though now we can kiss our asses and everything in between good-bye. Is that what you want?"

"You know something, Marc? I really hate it when you act like a sarcastic ass. You know damn well that's not what I'm saying. But even you have to admit that this is crazy, and as you just stated yourself, there are a lot of *ifs* attached." She paused, dropping her head and shaking it. "I just don't know."

"Neither do I–and in case you haven't been paying attention–" My voiced spiked. "I don't want to go either."

"Don't yell at me. Then don't go," Angela screamed back.

I let out a frustrating breath, informed her that I was going to start breakfast and walked out of our bedroom, down the stairs, and into the kitchen to cook. I thought a large meal would be nice since it would be the last one we would share for a while. Angela followed. I knew there were a lot of *ifs* involved, but I also knew that *if* they were right in their plausible prediction, I could not afford to gamble on a wish, a hope, or a prayer that they were wrong.

Ever since they first approached us a week ago, Angela and I have discussed this. I insisted that she have a say in this decision because it affected us both. At the time she agreed that I should go. There simply was nothing more to say.

"But what if?" she started to ask.

Holding up my hand, I stopped her in midsentence and reminded her that we had already been through that and all the possibilities therein. I went to her and took her into my arms. We hugged as though neither of us ever wanted to let go.

Later when breakfast was ready, we found neither of us had any appetite, and we sat in silence, trapped within our own thoughts, our own pain. Periodically, we would glance out the window into our backyard, although we were oblivious as to its beauty. Though our argument flared brightly, it also died quickly, and now only the heavy weight of hurt filled the air.

"I'm sorry," Angela said with sadness in her voice and eyes. "Why is doing the right thing never easy?"

"I don't know, but I'm sorry too. This isn't how I wanted to spend what might be our last hours together."

"Don't say that," she exhumed, rubbing her trimester belly.

Standing, we embraced each other. Holding on tight, we became misty. Looking into her beautiful, teary, almond-colored eyes, it ripped at my heart.

"I'm scared for you, Marc. I'm scared for us, and if you go and something happens to you, I won't even know it. I won't even remember what we've shared or about this child we're going to have. It would be as though we never met–that you never existed. Promise me that if you go, you'll remember me. That you'll come back to me so that we can live again as we are living now and have the family we're meant to have. Promise me…please."

"I promise, I'll never forget you, Angela–or our lives spent together. Never. And no matter how long it takes, I'll be back. I swear."

We closed our eyes and held each other close, unaware that the decision to join their cause was made the day they first visited us. For those of good conscience, refusal was not an option, and all that remained now were my memories of a love galaxies apart and a desire to embrace my wife who I was a stranger to.

Suddenly, the ship's alarm sounded, snapping me out of my deep thoughts. E'nie's voice boomed over the intercom and made me jump as my eyes went wide. Issuing an Elphah Black Alert, which was the equivalent to a red alert on Earth, I relinquished all thoughts of Angela, and my lingering pain and soreness. Jumping up off the sofa, I grabbed my Kaja, and called for a Hexagyn to transport me to my Juardian post.

In Throne Pryme, on screen the Pack looked at what was left of the Comini Defender's ship floating between two planets –blasted apart–its remains were scattered.

"Avedia, Arjenadann, cease velocity. Hold our position here," commanded the Elphah.

"Acknowledged," the Pylot replied, following her orders.

Performing a life scan was unnecessary, but the Twins did it anyway. One look at the wreckage, was evident that no one had survived. "The crew of the Comini never knew—" Sclee started to say.

"–What hit them. According to psionics –" Tonna continued.

"–They never fired their weapons," Sclee said, finishing the sentence.

"What in the cryda happened here?"

Missiles suddenly broke orbit of one planet, striking some debris from the Comini ship, and ripping through it, they struck the neighboring planet.

"There's your answer, Z'yenn," Joryd said.

"An interplanetary war?" Antonio said, perplexed.

"The Defender's ship must have been in orbit when the planets began firing," Laisere surmised.

"This can't be. The people of Doxini and Melmorn have been at peace for the past five hundred meads." Z'yenn stated.

"Well, something obviously set them off," Joryd countered as he stood up.

"Do you think they have been Influenced?" Avedia asked.

"Possibly–but before we call an Arjai Pride to inoculate, we need to investigate and confirm that they are not just behaving stupidly."

Tonna informed the Ra-Tuth, another word for Elphah, that long-range psionics had detected orbital weapons that have been launched by the Melmorn at the Doxini home world in retaliation for the attack.

The Ruling Planetary Governments were all well aware of Council laws pertaining to such action, and they knew once a conflict had expanded into orbit of their planet, it became the Supremacy's responsibility to stop the conflict…Wehtiko or not.

Joryd stepped down from his Throne, "E'nie, intercom." He commanded. "Pride, prepare to engage."

In every section where holographic stations were active, they vanished, and in their place would be solid stations. The technology in this galaxy continued to amaze me.

"Open channels to both planetary installations.

"Channels opened, Ra-Tuth."

"To the Ruling Governments of the planets Doxini and Melmorn, this is Joryd Kenton, Elphah of the Zahnobein Qi-Tahh. You are in violation of Council Law 42-A. I order you to cease and disarm immediately."

"Joryd, both planets are targeting us and firing," Laisere reported.

"Are they mad?" the Omegah asked, looking to the Elphah. "Their weapons are no match for ours." Z'yenn ordered the Tova to raise armor and shields, and to employ countermeasures to destroy all of the planetary defenses for both planets. Laisere acknowledged her and at once stopped the missile attack. The explosions lit up the blackness of space. The Velfin then targeted their planetary armaments and neutralized them as well.

"All planetary defenses have been destroyed."

"Now maybe they're ready to talk." The Elphah said, turning to E'nie. "Re-establish communications with the Ruling Planetary Governments."

However, before E'nie could acquire contact, Sclee-Tonna reported their psionics were detecting warships leaving both planets and heading toward them.

"They must be Influenced by the Wehtiko to challenge us," Avedia conjectured.

"Sclee-Tonna, identify warships," Antonio commanded.

"Saudi and—" Sclee started to say.

"–Rudarn class," Tonna finished.

"E'nie, warn them off," ordered the Elphah. "Influenced or not, I will not permit them to harm my Pride."

Though E'nie tried to establish communications, the warring planets refused to acknowledge his hails, and the enemy fighters continued their approach. Joryd's voice boomed over the intercom, ordering all Juardian Pylots to report to their fighters, and informed them that the attacking force were Influenced. They were to try to disable the fighters, but they were authorized to defend themselves at all cost.

"Arjai Packs, Mystiks, Wisards, and Boarding Juardians, meet me in the Hexagyn Bay." The Ra-Tuth commanded.

In standing, the Omegah's seat vanished. It was only active during use. "Avedia, Laisere, you're with us," Z'yenn ordered.

"Antonio, you have the Throne," Joryd said, turning and joining the waiting Pack inside the Portal.

"Yes, Ra-Tuth," he replied.

The doors closed, and the Hexagyn vanished.

Touching the Command chair, the Throne morphed into a seat styled for Battista, as he ordered the Twins to take the vacant Tova and Dicorp stations. They separated their bodies and split into two complete individuals. Sclee took weapons, and Tonna assumed navigation. Touching their seats, they, too, changed to chairs suited for their species.

"E'nie, contact the Sarten Arjai Pride and inform them that planets Doxini and Melmorn in the Grawnsom star system has been Influenced and to jamonaka provide arrival time for inoculation."

"Yes Deggzytepol," E'nie replied.

"Antonio, the Sarten Arjai Pride will rendezvous with us in one savner and fifty-one hotress."

"Acknowledged."

At the Gayr, the launch bay for the Xentous and fighters, the Juardians boarded their ships already attached to the space creatures and lifted off, Hexagyns appeared beneath them and they dropped inside. While in a nearby section, groups of Life Protectors entered Portals, and teleported once filled with a certain number were inside.

Ordered by U'kristu to remain onboard Arjenadann with a Juardian skeleton Pack in case of boarding, she made it clear that I was not trained in fighter maneuvers and was instructed to report to Throne Pryme…I had a front row seat of the battle.

Z'yenn was right. The opposing forces were no match for our Pride, and other than the suicide fighters who tried to kill us by making kamikaze runs, both planetary enemies were handled with no other lives lost. On their planets, the defense facilities were taken just as easily, and all attempts by the Doxinis and Melmorns to continue their senseless bloodshed were squashed.

The power the Supremacy possessed both frightened me and left me in awe. The Qi-Tahh did much more than simply police this galaxy. They were entrusted with the power to stop warring planets. If the governments wanted these battles, then they were allowed to have their senseless war, providing their citizens also wanted war. If their citizens decided otherwise or if their war spilled into their planet's orbit, then a Pride would be sent to stop it—peacefully if possible or by force if necessary. But one way or the other, the innocent were going to be protected. Wow, what a concept. I wonder if the people of Earth would accept such laws.

One thing was clear, the Wehtiko was a monstrous affliction. There was no limit in what acts those Influenced would do. The horrors they could create scared me. No wonder the Supremacy fought so hard to keep them under control. Slowly I came to understand the depth of the danger this contaminant possessed and why so many humans before me had given their lives to this alien cause. That was something I too, might one day have to do despite my promise to Angela, and especially if it meant preventing and ensuring this insidious strain never reached Earth. If it did, the evil and the atrocities that men have committed throughout history would pale in comparison to the new level of barbarism and cruelty this contagion would unleash within them. The thought of it made me shudder.

The Sarten medical ship arrived and inoculated the inhabitants of both worlds. Although there was no known cure for this diabolical disease, the Influenced could be treated. It was managed with inoculations, this affliction did not allow for preventive measures.

Questioned about the Wehtiko, neither race could tell us what sparked the war. Nor did they know how they became Influenced. Outside of the Comini Defenders, whose loss they mourned...and our presence...no other outsiders had entered their star system in months.

We thought this incident was routine. We thought wrong. How I wished my Pride and I arrived before what was to be, happened, but that simply was being not realistic.

"In truth…"

The door bell rung and my voice trailed off.

"Momja jamonaka suspend record."

"Acknowledged, recording suspended, Marc."

"Fasbi,"

The doorbell rang again. Though I was confined and could not leave my Habitat, did not hold the same restrictions for those who wished to visit me.

"Open, "I shouted and the door slid apart diagonally. Antonio, Torr and Syn-nar walked in and each hugged me warmly.

"How are you doing, brother?" Antonio was the first to ask.

"As well as can be expected I guess."

"We just wanted you to know that the Pride are behind you all the way." Torr confessed.

"Fasbi Tee."

"Can we get you anything?" Syn-nar inquired.

"Fasbi but no. Any word, yet?"

"About your case, no, and that's a good thing." Antonio said reassuring me.

"We can't stay, we're on our way to the Gayr." Syn-nar said.

"The Ghannies are at it again. I'll tell you all about it later," Torr said walking toward the door.

They each gave me a hug and a kiss and exited. The door slid closed and I thought how funny it was that I was actually missing the action–and fighting alongside my Pride.

I chuckled and shook my head. "I've gotta get my head examined." Suddenly I felt a renewal of energy. "Momja, jamonaka continue recording."

"Acknowledged…Jamonaka proceed."

"Fasbi. Thada Argen would turn out to be the epicenter of the problem we were having with the Influenced, and what we would later discover, happened before we were even sent there."

Days before the Grawnson incident, two star systems away on

the idyllic world called Thada Argen, this beautiful and lush green planet was shared by two sentient species. It was midday.

Flying overhead high in the sky, four pygmy-like creatures no taller than a half meter and resembling the colors of the forest they resided in, rode the backs of giant bats called Priorts. These winged rodents were three times the size of hawks, moved about during the day as well as night, and they were in service to the small people. Passing a huge nest, the four riders watched as a large mother bird resembling an alien vulture fed her younglings while her mate perched on the ledge of the nest watched protectively.

Continuing along their flight, one of the Pygmies spotted something down below and began making clicking sounds, pitches, and birdcalls. Their language was made up of a series of sounds with none of the normally recognizable patterns or vocabulary. Pointing, the lead creature jabbered excitedly and steered his Priort downward and forced the others to follow. Once on the ground, the small furry creature ran to the giant purple strawberries that caught his eye. They all commenced to feasting happily as the others complimented him on such a good find, patting him on the back and nodding their heads pleasingly, they enjoyed the delicious fruit.

Later, after they have had their fill, they returned to their mounts, but before they could climb aboard, they started feeling strange. They stopped and shook their heads. The affliction passed quickly, and they soon felt better. Clicking and jabbering briefly to one another, they believed the cause was from consuming too many berries too quickly. Mounting their bats, they took to the air and continued their journey.

A short while later, in the distance the Pygmies could see Acrea, the first of the Eanoi Settlements. Established fifty years ago after they escaped a Linksys Cleansing, the ragtag refugees found Thada Argen and settled here to colonize. Since then their colony had grown into thriving communities that represented a variety of different ethnicities who were agriculturists, builders, carpenters, and educators. Dispersed into several settlements, they felt each community would have a better chance of survival. If disease struck one settlement, it would not infect them all. The men and women worked hard, while the children were schooled and allowed to play. A five-year-old boy playing with other kids his age suddenly stopped and ran with his friends to a big, strong-looking man throwing large, heavy bustles of blue vegetation onto the back of a wagon.

"Daddy, the Dir-nays are coming," he said excitedly.

The man, shielding his eyes, looked up into the sky and saw the four riders approach. He instructed the youngster to go and tell the boy's two older brothers in the field. Acknowledging his dad, he took off while his father called out to the other men helping him load the wagon.

As the little riders descended, more of the Colonists gathered. Some had pitchforks, but a few carried axes and sledgehammers. As the Pygmies landed, the big man led the small group to meet them.

The Dir-nays dismounted, and pulling bags from their saddles, they greeted the Eanois warmly. The Pygmies were traders, peaceful and socialable and known to all of the Eanoi settlements. The Sukais returned their friendly greetings and welcomed them warmly as well. The big man and others who spoke the creatures' language, though difficult to master, had in return taught them to speak laimeguage, their idiom.

The bond between the two species began five decades ago when the Eanois first settled on Thada Argen. Many died from eating plants that were poisonous to them, and many more were sick and dying. But thankfully, the Dir-nays were kind and friendly, and they treated the Eanois with herbs that countered the poison and educated them about the plants and herbs that were safe for them to eat. The Colonists later learned the Pygmies were called Dir-nays.

The big man replied with clicks and clacks, "Edat," he said, using both Dir-nay and Laimeguage.

"Darr, it is good to see you, my friend," the lead Pygmy replied. "How is your mate, Karoline?"

"She is well, and we are expecting another child by this spring solstice."

"This is good."

The five-year-old returned with his older brothers, and ran up to the Dir-nay and threw his arms around his neck, giving him a hug. "Hi, Edat," the child said, smiling.

His father cleared his voice and looked to the boy with a raised brow. A bit of a smirk formed one corner of his chiseled jaw. "Justin," the big man said, drawing out his youngest son's name.

Breaking the embrace, the boy turned about and saw the familiar look of his dad, and facing the Pygmy he said, "Excuse me. I mean Hi Kadel Edat." Then ran to his father and hid behind him.

Justin heard another child call for him, and he replied by screaming back to his friend where he was and what he was doing, while the adults tried to have their conversation. Darr turned about, bowed, and ushered Justin to go and play with his friends.

Happily the little boy agreed, "Okay. Justin ran to meet his friends, turning back and waving, "Bye Edat," and began screaming and shouting for his friends like most five-year-old children did.

"Not Edat, Kadel Edat." Darr said, in a normal tone. Sticking a finger in his ear, he shook it, "Oh my God, I can hear again," and removed his finger from his ear. "Has your hearing returned?"

"That was nothing–you should hear the Dir-nay children Justin's age. Now their screams are deafening," Edat commented using both languages.

Darr and Edat communicated fairly well, and corrected one another with language skills when needed. Darr apologized and confessed he still needed practice with Dir-nay language, while Edat admitted the same for him with Darr's idiom. They suddenly bursted out laughing and hanging on one another, they were like two peas in a pod.

A five-foot-seven pregnant woman with sandy blonde hair and dark-colored eyes joined Darr and Edat. "What are you two laughing so hard about?" she asked in Dir-nay. She bowed to his level. "Greetings, Edat," she said, speaking fluent Dir-nay.

"Greetings, Karoline," he replied perfectly in Laimeguage.

They rubbed their noses together and hummed. Then they broke their connection.

"How is Magam?" Karoline inquired using the alien idiom.

"She is well. When are you due, my Oakra?"

"Next month."

Darr suddenly found himself out of the conversation as Karoline and Edat talked on his level. The women grasped the Dir-nay language with greater ease than the men, and so it was for the Pygmy females when it came to speaking the Eanoi language.

"I will tell her of your expectancy date. She will want to be there."

"She is always welcome, and I would love to see her as well, it's been awhile." she said. Karoline stepped closer to Edat. "Take care I have chores to get back to, but it's always a pleasure to see you." Again she bowed to his level and Karoline and Edat rubbed noses once more. "See you soon, Edat."

"Soon, my Oakra," he replied.

Karoline looked to Darr, "As for you, husband, you still have chores to finish, get to it, they're not going to do themselves." She said, walking away.

Edat clicked, hummed and spoke laimeguage. "I see why Magam and Karoline get along so well."

Darr and Edat bursted out in laughter, enjoying their private joke. They continued their conversation, as the Pygmy inquired about how Darr's harvest for this solstice was going. According to Darr, it was going very well, and he informed Edat they could expect delivery of the remainder of the gin-gyn in two days. Until then, he and his people had some moss ready to be taken now. Edat refused, and told Darr that they could wait. They still had a little left from the last trade.

"King Gutai would insist we wait and take the shipment in full." He patted Darr and smiled.

The blue vegetation grew only in select areas of the planet. It was difficult for the Dir-nays to harvest, but it was a great delicacy of theirs. In turn, they traded seeds for the Eanois to grow food, spices, and herbs, all of which they taught them how to plant safely.

"I appreciate that. Please have some, I picked these myself, just today." Darr said, prideful.

The Pygmies handed bags of seeds over to the Colonists, and Darr gave Edat and his friends the go-ahead to have some gin-gyn. They indulged, happily. Afterward, Darr walked Edat and the others back to their rides. He bid the Dir-nays farewell, and wished them a safe journey home.

"Please give our best wishes to King Gutai and the other Dir-nays, and we will see you soon my friends."

"Thank you Darr, we will see you soon." Edat replied, and smiled.

Both species raved about how they looked forward to seeing each other again. The Pygmies mounted their bats, and flew off. The Eanois returned to their duties.

Halfway back to the Coyoust Valley, where the Dir-nays dwelled, something in Edat and the other riders changed, and for no apparent reason, they began quarreling among themselves. Passing the same nest they passed earlier, Edat pulled out a spear from his saddle holster.

"Kill the Virggyte," ordered the Pygmy and attacked.

The others followed and joined the unprovoked attack on the bird creatures. The parents raced to intercept them, but they were slaughtered shortly after the engagement, killed for no reason other than a whim of Edat. He and another pygmy approached the nest and killed the defenseless young Virggytes inside. They rejoined the others and laughed at what they have done. Edat and his crew continued homeward.

Reaching their forest, the four dismounted and headed toward the dwelling of their chieftain. Edat angrily told their leader, Gutai, how the Eanois had betrayed them and that they were not the friends they thought, and demanded the Dir-nay King did something about it. Confused, the Chief sought clarity, so Edat began weaving him a web of lies about how the Colonists approached them hostilely with weapons, and refused to honor the trade agreement. They took the seeds, and did not give them the gin-gyn as promised. Edat told Gutai that when they protested, the Eanois gave them a little bit of the blue vegetation, but it was spoiled and made them sick. The Dir-nay King could not believe what he was being told, for the Eanois had been their friends for many years. Edat showed him the wounds he received in his fight with the Virggytes, but said it was the Settlers who had inflicted them. Gutai looked to the others, and they showed him their wounds as well.

Back at the Settlement, it was dusk. The people had finished a hard day's work, and now they were heading home. Justin, who first alerted his father, Darr, to the Dir-nays' approach, helped his dad, brothers, and uncles with the equipment. Looking up, the five-year-boy saw three of the creatures returning.

"Daddy, look," he said, pointing to the sky. "The Dir-nays are coming back."

"So soon," Darr said as he, too, looked up.

"Maybe they forgot something," Darr's eldest son, Sam stated.

Looking at the young man was like seeing a younger version of Darr, smaller, not yet as big.

"Maybe," Darr replied.

As the creatures neared, they soon saw what looked like the entire tribe trailing behind the three who led. The Colonists did not know what to think and wondered why the Dir-nays were returning so soon. Coming in as though they were landing, King Gutai hurled a spear at Darr. The lance plowed through his chest and caught the big man off guard. No one knew what had happened until Darr dropped what he carried, gasped, and fell to his knees. Justin screamed as another spear punctured his dad's eye and he collapsed sideways; blood trickling out of his mouth.

"Daddy," Justin screamed and ran to his father. "Mommy," the little boy shouted. Reaching him, he started shaking his father. "Daddy, get up. Sam, daddy's hurt."

Justin's two brothers were struck down before Sam and Caleb could act, both impaled through the heart.

"Mommy, daddy's hurt." Justin screamed.

Tears rolled down his face. Carrying a large basket full of clothes, the pregnant woman screamed and threw the basket. Karoline ran to her family. Wailing and confused, on hands and knees, she looked up and saw Magam, Edat's mate, riding a Priort. Karoline stood and Magam hurled a spear and struck her in the belly, killing her unborn child. In shock, the pain took a while before she fully felt it, and then Karoline began screaming. Magam swung around, withdrew her club, and smashed the back of Karoline's skull. She, too, fell sideways, dead.

Chaos erupted as everyone started fleeing in horror. The skies blackened with Priorts, the Dir-nays attacked the Settlers, and some of the Colonists tried fighting back, but they were outnumbered, outmatched, and unprepared for the unprovoked merciless assault by those they had called friends for many years. The Eanois at the Acrea Settlement were slaughtered.

Justin helplessly watched as his young friends and neighbors were savagely killed. In the air and on the ground, the once peaceful creatures and their bats viciously murdered every man, woman, and child–but one. Edat was about to kill Justin, when King Gutai told him to leave the boy alive and ordered him to help collect all the gin-gyn they could find.

Edat replied with a double click, "Why?"

"So he can tell them what we have done."

They both smiled, and bursted out in laughter as if what they had done were a joke. Before long, the Pygmies took their prize and left the sole survivor of the massacre kneeling next to his dead parents' bodies, silently weeping. Traumatized, Justin lay down between his parents, put his thumb in his mouth and curled up in a fetal position and did not move.

The next day neighbors from the nearby Settlement Vausch came to check on their friends when they did not show up the night before, and found the Colony destroyed. Shocked at the horror, the Eanois did not know what to think. They had no enemies, and the only remaining survivor could offer no answers. Justin did not speak, and he was taken back to their settlement for treatment. The others remained and searched for possible survivors and clues about what had happened. Later, more Colonists from Vausch arrived to assist with the dead and help to try to piece together what had happened.

Back at the Vausch compound, it was late morning when a horde of beetle-like insects swarmed the Settlement and commenced attacking everyone. Moving like a wave of black death, the Skarbs, insects in service to the Dir-nays, had begun eating the Eanois. A mother desperately trying to reach to her infant daughter was quickly overtaken by the voracious beetles, covered, and devoured. Many moved toward the crib of the crying infant and poured inside as the baby's screams escalated for a few moments, and then there was silence as they fed on her as well.

Entering the clearing with many of his people, King Gutai, Edat, and their mates Magam and Gulla led the group, and watched as the last of the Eanois were killed. Grinning at the bloodshed and devastation they had unleashed, the King issued a series of clicks and birdcalls signaling to the others that it was time to load the gin-gyn and return to their Valley home. In no time the blue moss was loaded, and the Skarbs and Dir-nays had all gone, leaving behind yet another senseless massacre.

Hours later the others returned to the Vausch Settlement with more questions than answers, and found everyone either butchered or partially eaten and again the gin-gyn was gone. Coming into the Settlement they suddenly stopped. Stunned at the last thing they would ever expect to see, a black woman muttered softly "Marie," and then screamed and broke the spell of shock everyone was in. "Marie," she screamed, dropped what she was carrying, and raced inside Vausch.

The woman found her seven-year-old daughter, she recognized the dress she made for her most recent birthday, and the only means of identification that could be made–the child Marie had most of her face eaten down to the bone. This time King Gutai left no one alive to question. Justin lay on the ground, dead, horribly disfigured, he was clubbed to death. Panic, tears, and horror plagued the Colonists as they looked and checked for family and friends. Although, this time they found hundreds of dead Skarbs, the same insects the Dir-nays used to aide them in cultivating the Eanois land and assisting in pest control. The Eanois discovered the gin-gyn was again missing.

Without warning, some of the Pygmies, who were ordered to wait for the others to return from the Acrea Settlement, attacked the Eanois, and mercilessly mutilated them. While their mounts tore some of the Colonists apart, the Dir-nays beat or stabbed the others to death. Mounting their bloodied bats, the bloody Pygmies left the slaughtered settlement and returned to their home in the Coyoust Valley.

The next day Settlers from the Glona community had become concerned when people they were expecting last night from Vausch had not arrived. Traveling to the Settlement to learn why, they arrived and were sickened by the sight of their neighbors' bodies. Animals tried to make off with a dead baby and leg of a small child, but the Colonists scared them into dropping their meal, and chased them away. Some of the Eanois went back to Glona to tell what was found. Some stayed and searched for survivors, while others proceeded to Acrea, the next closest colony, to inform them of their findings as well.

The Committee, the government for all the Eanoi Settlements on Thada Argen, called an emergency meeting to decide how to proceed before informing their people of the incidents at the Communities, but it was too late. Word of what had happened had already spread throughout the Settlements like wildfire, and it threw everyone into a state of panic. The reports the Committee received were unbelievable and terrifying—Colonists savagely slayed, ripped apart, or otherwise eaten down to the bone, with evidence of the monstrous acts among the bodies of those they knew. In addition, at every settlement the gin-gyn was taken. Unwilling to accept the possibility that the Dir-nays, their good friends and neighbors, had turned on them for the blue moss made no sense. The Committee instead convinced themselves and the other Settlement leaders that a renegade faction of Pygmies had gone mad and were responsible for killing their people. They believed King Gutai would help them, and decided to send volunteers, one from each remaining settlement, to journey to the Coyoust Valley to inform them of what had happened. However, as a precaution, the Committee would also send a message to the Council and ask the Ohdens for assistance as well. In the meantime, the Settlement leaders were to keep their community calm.

At the Glona Settlement, Clara, a large Latina woman, a member of the Committee and head of her community, gathered her people. Usually a breath of fresh air with her humor and sound advice, she was also a force to be reckoned with when necessary.

"Why would the Skarbs attack us?" an older man asked.

"We do not know," Clara replied.

"Do the Dir-nays know their bats and insects have killed our people?" an old woman inquired.

"They might. We found dead Pygmies among our people as well as Priorts and Skarbs, but we believe the assailants are renegades and do not believe their King is aware of what has happened," the female leader professed.

"I heard they're taking the gin-gyn, is that true," a teenage boy asked.

"Is that true? A woman holding her ten-year-old son, asked.

"Yes." Clara replied.

The commotion flared, and the people suggested they just give them the moss.

"I'm not finished," Clara bellowed over the raising noise. "Therefore, the Committee has asked for a volunteer from each colony to venture to the Coyoust Valley and request the King's help. I will also need volunteers to help maintain contact with the other Settlements as well.

"But what if you're wrong and the Dir-nays have turned against us?" a teen girl asked.

"Don't be afraid. The Committee has also sent a message for assistance to the Ohdens, who we are certain will dispatch the Qi-Tahh to investigate."

"No, she should be afraid," a booming male voice stated.

"Stop it. You're scaring the children," Clara said firmly.

"They need to be scared," the burly man said, pushing through the crowd until he was in the front row.

"And you need to be quiet now, Darwin. Yes, I am a member of the Committee, den mother to some of you, midwife to others, and above all I am a lady. But none of this means a damn thing because if you're gonna insist on scaring the children, that's when the gloves come off. Now, do I need to come over there and beat your ass. Stop talking foolishly, or I will take off my earrings and necklace and come over there?"

Darwin said nothing further on the subject. Soon another question was directed at Clara, and a man angrily asked what she was going to do about the Pygmies in the meantime. She told him that in the meantime she and the Committee had devised a plan in readying themselves in case of another attack.

"But we're no fighters. We're farmers, builders, and teachers," a middle-aged woman shouted.

"And what if they do return tonight? What are we supposed to do?" a young father asked, clutching his two small children.

The crowd began to shout—some out of fear, others out of anger. Some believed they should leave, and others thought they should stay and kill the Pygmies. Soon all were quarreling amongst themselves and forced Clara to shout over their ruckus.

"Listen to me! Listen," she shouted and managed to settle them down. "Somah, c'mon up here."

A Caucasian woman as large as Clara made her way to the platform and joined the Community leader.

"Somah is my second, you do what she tells you. Somah, take people and gather all the burning oil we have. We're going to pour a huge circle that's big enough to surround Glona, and should the insects attack here, we'll light it and burn 'em up."

"What good will that do?" Another middle-aged woman shouted.

"If the Dir-nays are involved, the fire won't stop them," a husband shouted, standing next to his pregnant wife.

"But we do not even know if their tribe is involved," another man professed.

"I'm-not-finished," Clara shouted. Morgan, if you're so concerned about the fires not stopping the renegades, then you'll be in charge of fortifying this Settlement." Clara faced her people, "If they try flying in then we'll find a way to knock them out of the sky," the Latina leader stated strongly.

"Knock them out of the sky? With what?"

"What do you suggest we do? Wait and end up like Everett's Community or Carson's?" she asked. "Volunteers, see me. All strong men see Morgan, and everyone else see Somah." Clara clapped her hands, "Come on people, move, we've got a lot of work and little time to do it."

"We should leave," a brown-haired teen shouted.

"And go where?" Somah replied. "Running is not the answer, baby. Besides, the Committee has instructed its representatives to do likewise at the remaining Settlements. This discussion is over. We have much work to do. Let's get to it," Somah commanded.

The crowd dispersed and followed their instructions. The Settlers worked hard and by night fall the Eanois were ready. They posted sentries in case of an attack, but aside from a couple of false alarms, nothing took place that night.

The next day the representatives traveling to the encampment of the Dir-nays set forth while the Settlements remained on high alert, and still, there were no attacks, leaving some Eanois to believe that maybe the Dir-nays were not involved. However, others were still jumpy and on edge.

Later that day, the Emissaries led by Tami, a Korean woman with a medium build, arrived at the entrance to the Coyoust Valley with the others. Forced to continue on foot, their mode of transportation was too big to enter the forest. Not long after entering, several Pygmies appeared from all around, putting the representatives on guard. They stopped, almost confused by the Eanois defensive posture. Tami started to chatter and mimic animal sounds.

Warmly, the furry creature approached and greeted her, "I am sorry we frightened you, Tami."

Surprised, she said, "That's all right, Bashaun. You probably weren't expecting us. But something serious has happened, and we must speak with King Gutai," she said, speaking fluent Dir-nay.

"I do not understand," he clicked and chattered. "Come, my friends. We will take you to him."

The Eanois exhaled, relaxing their posture and letting the creatures know it was all right to embrace them. They were taken to the encampment and shown to their King's tent. One of the creatures entered and began clicking, clacking, and bird calling. He came back and escorted them inside. Giving Gutai his due respect, Tami explained the reason for their visit.

The long-haired, dark eye woman told Gutai of the massacres committed by some of his people. The terrorists had used Priorts and Skarbs to aid them, and after each attack, the marauders stole the gin-gyn. Though they did not believe the King or most of his people were involved, evidence supported that the Dir-nays were responsible.

"We ask you for your help in stopping these renegades."

King Gutai was shocked and could not believe all that he was told about the horde of senseless violence as well as the women and children who had been butchered and eaten. Grief-stricken, he offered the weary travelers a tent where they could rest and eat. The King promised to return with them to their Settlements and guaranteed the Eanois their safety.

Back at the Glona Settlement, the Eanois continued their high alert vigilance while waiting for the renegade Dir-nays to return, but they never did.

The following day at the Coyoust Valley, Gutai reassured Tami and the others that the problem would be handled, and he and his people took the Emissaries back to their homes. Thanking him and his tribe for everything, Tami and the others mounted the bats and held tightly to their riders as they took to the skies.

Tami and Bashaun reached the Glona Settlement first, and upon their approach, Clara and many of their people clustered to meet to them. Landing, the Korean woman quickly dismounted and talked fast to calm those who were upset by the Dir-nay's presence. As big as they were, Clara and Somah drifted through the crowd unobstructed by the gathering, and were soon front and centered.

"Clara, great news," Tami said excitedly. "We told King Gutai of what has happened at our Settlements, and he knew nothing about it. He sends us all his condolences, and will do all within his power to find who has done this and help us protect our Communities."

"Thank God," Clara said, facing the rider and clacking to him. "Thank you so much, Bashaun."

"You're welcome, and I am sorry this happened," Bashaun replied in Laimeguage.

Somah and Tami hugged and the Settlers relaxed and started hugging and kissing each other.

"Look… In the sky," a young girl shouted pointing.

"Don't be afraid," Tami shouted. "They are here to protect us. King Gutai is leading them," she said, smiling, and suggested others do likewise.

The Priort riders approached no differently than the other times they visited before, and though they had brandished weapons, in light of everything that had happened, the Dir-nays were welcomed as though all was normal. Coming in for a landing, Clara was especially pleased to see Gutai himself leading them. Dismounting, the King, Edat and their mates Magam and Gulla approached, and greeted them each warmly.

Several Dir-nays stood behind the King and his party. They suddenly hurled spears into the crowd, striking two preteens. The boy and girl were among the first to die. Hit in the heart, the boy's death was quick, he hit the ground with a loud thud. The girl suffered before dying. Struck on her left side, the spear perforated her lung. She fell to her knees and fell forward. The spear pushed through her body, her hands dangled, and with her last gasp, she died. Blood trickled from her mouth.

A spear punctured a man's throat. He gasped gurgling blood. His eyes rolled up, and he fell onto the ground. Before the Colonists could act, a flock of Priorts swooped down and attacked.

Chasing a family of five, the husband handed the baby to his wife and told her to take the children and run. He picked up a torch from off the ground and tried hitting them, but he was plowed down instead. Once on the ground the bats covered him and began biting and clawing him until he was dead.

Fleeing, his wife led the family into the path of Skarbs that overtook them and attacked. Eaten alive, the mother and children screamed horribly until they too were dead.

A man wielding a torch was struck by Priorts. They knocked him down, the torch flew out of his hand and set a house on fire.

The Dir-nays charged the unsuspecting Eanois, impaling men, women, and children with their spears, or beating them to death with clubs, as their bats and beetles fed on the wounded, the living, and the dying. One woman on fire, was clubbed by two Pygmies. Desperate to get away, she accidentally set a shop on fire, and ran out the gate. A Dir-nay struck her, and she fell on the circle of oil. Igniting it, the Village was encircled in flames.

Darwin, the big burly man challenged Gulla, Magam and one other. The three Dir-nay females laughed as they took turns beating him. Magam shattered his kneecaps and crippled Darwin. From there on, he was at their mercy, for which they had none. Gulla poked the big man, and then smashed him across the face. The other Dir-nay clicked and clacked, and then struck him twice and he gasped coughing blood.

Magam spoke to Darwin in perfect laimeguage, "Careful, big man, it sounds like you may have a collapsed lung." She looked to the other Dir-nay. "If he doesn't already have one, see to it that you give him one."

The Pygmies smiled, approached Darwin, and without a word the three began beating him and together they smashed his skull and broke his body. The Dir-nays left to join their mates. Blood dripped from their clubs, and they laughed loudly, amused by their heinous acts.

A child on fire running out of a burning house screamed until two spears found his body and silenced him. He fell forward to his knees, and onto the ground. Unmoving, his eyes stayed opened as his body continued to burn. Two Pygmies approached to admire their work.

Many of the Eanois frantically scattered, trying to escape, while others tried to fight back. In the end, except for Clara, Somah, Tami and the two who managed to escape the siege, all others were either dead, dying, or would soon be dead. The King laughed as Gulla and Magam approached and enjoyed the horror and confusion he saw on the Eanois' faces. The Settlement around them burned.

"I know all about the attacks on the other settlements, Clara. It was I who ordered it." Gutai said, speaking Dir-nay.

Gulla stabbed Somah with her spear, and she cried out. Grabbing a hold of it she pulled the spear out and punched the Pygmy, knocking her to the ground. Somah raised the spear screaming and readied to attack. Before she could act, Magam charged and stabbed her in the side, and knocked Somah off her feet. She was approached by an angry Gulla.

"You dare strike me…I am a Queen."

Suddenly hundreds of beetles formed a protective circle around Gulla.

"Tear her apart," the Dir-nay Queen shouted.

The Skarbs attacked Somah. The heavy set Eanoi woman cried out horribly as the insect tore her to pieces. A short while later, Somah's screams had ceased, and neither Clara nor Tami could bring themselves to look at her mutilated body. Powerless to help Somah, the King and some of his subjects had prevented the women from interfering.

Shocked by what she had just seen and surprised by the news she had heard, Clara asked, "Why? We are your friends."

"You are our enemy. How could we be friends with anyone as ugly and repulsive as an Eanoi. The very sight of you sickens me," Gutai bellowed in Dir-nay.

Clara and Tami's eyes widened as Bashaun suddenly smashed Tami's knee with his club. Crying out, she fell to the ground in agony. Gutai and Gulla held up their spears and positioned themselves and again prevented the large Latina woman from aiding another of her friends.

Looking up fearfully, tears poured from Tami's eyes, as Bashaun, a Dir-nay she had known for years, struck her across the jaw and knocked her flat onto her back. Clara stood by helpless to act, and watched as Bashaun and Edat beat her friend until she was bloodied, broken, and dead. Blood spayed them as they continued with their merciless attack. Speechless and scared, Clara looked down at Gutai, who shoved his spear into her stomach and twisted it. He yanked it out and she dropped to her knees, blood spilling from her mouth. Clara covered her wound with her hands.

Still confused, Clara asked, "What have we done to deserve this?"

"You were born," Gutai replied coldly in laimeguage, and thrust his spear into her heart, pushing until she fell back flatly. Looking down at her, Gutai watched as she gasped deeply, loudly, and then gasp no more. Clara was dead. Bracing a foot against her face, the King withdrew his spear and spat on her corpse.

At the Argenta Settlement, a community not far from Clara's compound, the thick smoke could be seen in the distance. Committee member Matsu, a Japanese man and the leader of this community, had his people scramble to travel there and help. However, before they could, the two survivors who had escaped, along with others from this settlement who were aiding them, arrived and warned them of the massacre the survivors witnessed. The refugees told them of the Dir-nays' involvement.

Stunned, the Eanois could not fathom why their former friends had betrayed them and murdered their kind, but nor were they going to just stand by and let the Pygmies do the same to them. Not like the Linksys had done fifty years ago. They prepared to fight, not realizing how futile such an engagement would be.

Matsu took charge and informed the Colonists that he had informed the Council, and despite waiting like Clara chose to do, he vowed not to make the same mistake or allow such violence to go unpunished. Though he hoped help would arrive before the Dir-nay's next attack, he was not going to place their survival solely on that prayer or his second, more frantic call to the Ohdens.

It was now days later, and back in present time in another part of the Jhanctum galaxy at one of their Defense Directories, the disturbing news of what was happening on Thada Argen had reached the Ohdens.

"In the past few niyas, we have received more than normal reports of Wehtiko outbreaks throughout the galaxy, and it is not known why.

"I believe the outbreak and Wehtiko on Thada Argen are connected," Rhetnig-Sux said. *"If we trace the path of Influenced, we would discover it originated from the Thada star system."*

"The Eanois on planet Argen have reported being savagely attacked by the Dir-nays, Priorts and Skarbs, and have twice requested assistance; the last more desperate than the first." A pewter colored brain said telepathically aloud. *Evidence points to the Dir-nays."*

"First the Linksys annihilated their world, and now this," Kerebrol's twin voices of male and female remarked sympathetically.

Wahn-Jemm interjected, *"Unleashing the Priorts and the Skarbs against the Eanois without provocation would seem to point to one conclusion–the Dir-nays have become Influenced, and have turned the two life-forms they control into terrifying weapons."*

"How many Eanois have been killed since the outbreak?" Heshe asked in twin voices.

Rhetnig-Sux answered, *"Four hundred and three deaths have been reported thus far."*

Kaivessh added in her thoughts, *"Kerebrol, you know as well as I that the sukais of that world are powerless to defend themselves against the Pygmies, and at this rate the Dir-nays will wipe out the entire population of Settlers within a verstix."*

Told to dispatch the Symborach Life Protectors to help protect the inhabitants until the Arjai ship Doryes could arrive and treat the Influenced, Gy-ew reported that he was in telepathic contact with his Qi-Tahh Elphah as they spoke, but unfortunately they were already contending with a confirmed Wehtiko incident. Kerebrol ordered Wahn-Jemm to send her Qi-Tahh to assist. They would provide reinforcement for the Symborach, and help contain the Influenced before going to Thada Argen and doing the same until the Healing vessel could arrive and commence treatment.

Again Heshe's plans fell through. They were at the other rim of our galaxy and were too far away to be of any assistance." The sea foam green hue cerebellum replied.

"There is only one Pride close enough to Thada Argen to be of service, and I understand your reluctances in sending them, but if the Eanois are to survive they must have help now." Wahn-Jemm stated.

The Council understood Kerebrol's reluctances, and sympathized with Heshe. They knew Kerebrol was still coping with loss after the Linksys incursion two meads ago, had killed many of Joryd's Pride, but there were no other Life Protectors available that they could send.

"I will inform my Qi-Tahh, but presently they are busy trying to corral the Zonnyan Assembly who have been Influenced," the Elphah Ohden replied telepathically.

"Before you do, Kerebrol–know that if the Dir-nays succeed in killing all the Eanois, it may be the catalyst that ignites this epidemic. If that happens, the Wehtiko will erupt exponentially, not just in the Thada star system but will flood out over all the star systems," Wahn-Jemm offered.

"If it does, neither we nor our Supremacy will be able to contain the madness that will follow. In that event, our galaxy will be

consumed and the Wehtiko Influence will spread throughout the universe unchecked. To insure this does not happen, I recommend Containment Protocol III." Kaivessh added.

"But what if you are wrong, Sister?" Rhetnig-Sux asked

"What if she is right, Brother?" Another cerebellum creature asked.

"Are you willing to take that chance?" Gy-ew added, *"It has been thousands of meads since the need to implement Containment Protocol III. Are you certain this is our only other option?"*

"Yes, but only if Joryd and his Pride fail. I do not expect them to fail. However, I will make it clear that if they cannot stop the Dir-nays before the situation reaches critical mass, they are ordered to destroy Thada Argen and kill every living thing on the planet, including all Pridesmen on the planet." Kerebrol replied.

Ancient Evil

V

Elsewhere on a planet in another galaxy and far beyond Jhanctum, a different kind of insanity was being fought. An army of Amazons on flying Platforms stealthily approached a heavily guarded fortress and landed unseen on the rooftop. Gaining entry, they quietly approached the four sentries standing guard and slit their throats. They hid the bodies, split up into cells and checked the Palace for their objective.

One group led by a tall African female with long thin braids stopped suddenly and silently ordered the others to do likewise. Without saying a word, she informed them as to the six soldiers positioned outside the Throne room. A brunette Amazonian, shorter than the others peered around the corner, waved her hand and caused the sentries to vanish. No trace of them remained. Racing for the door, the taller Black warrior with braided hair aimed her staff at the doors and blew them open. At once she and the other Amazons commenced firing their staff weapon at the creature sitting in the royal chair. Moving his arms about, he created a barrier protecting him from their attack. The sounds of laser fire soon brought enemy soldiers running to them.

The shorter Caucasian woman with piercing blue eyes, faced her Amazon Captain. "Talah, go help our sisters. I've got this."

"Mheria, are you sure?"

"Yes, now go." She commanded.

"Yes, Imperial Empress."

The African warrior and her sisters turned and raced to engage the soldiers, while the young Amazon faced their nemesis.

"I find these raids of yours tiresome, Thakien."

"Get used to it, monster. I will not stop until you are dead."

He laughed as he stood. "Or until you and your pathetic Amazons are. And just what is it, child, you think you can do to me?"

Speaking her native language, her hands glowed, and she conjured up a ghostly form to break through his protection spell. Grinning, the Sorcerer found the endeavor amusing–her magic could not disrupt his spell. Raising his hands and forming the Earth's devil sign for the jackal, his eyes glowed, and he destroyed the apparition. Again, he laughed. "A futile attempt, child. You have none of your mother's strength."

"Oh, yeah?"

Casting her spell, the young Empress animated the Throne chair behind the unsuspecting creature. It rose up displaying humanoid features and attacked the Sorcerer. The chair slammed him against his own barrier, pinned him, and held him there.

The Mandrake creature cried out as his protection spell was used against him. The energy field was cooking him alive. Though he tried to push away from it, the young Sorceress maintained the chair's force and kept him pressed against it. Suddenly the barrier vanished, and the Sorcerer stumbled forward, but quickly caught himself. Turning about, the creature grabbed the chair by its arm, and threw it at her. The Sorceress caused the chair to vanish, and reappear moments later above him. It came crashing down on top of the Sorcerer.

Unprepared for that particular retaliation, the large seat pinned the malevolent being to the floor. Before he could act, the Sorceress directed the chair to pick him up and begin slamming him into the floor. With each tremendous blow, the Sorcerer's body reverberated and broke. Again and again, she made the animated chair punish and pulverize him, and it did not stop until there seemed nothing left of the creature. Thakien levitated him off the floor and slammed him once more with anger. There he lay, apparently dead. The young Sorceress changed the chair back to its original form, held it over the Sorcerer, and bashed him with it until he lay in a pool of black blood.

In the hall the Amazons finished off the last of the soldiers and rejoined the Imperial Empress, who was breathing heavily after expending such energy, and she continued to breathe like that until her heart and pulse rate steadied. Facing her Amazon sister of African descent, Mheria said nothing while Talah placed a gentle hand on her shoulder.

"Are you all right?"

"I will be, Talah, once Telus' death has been confirmed."

Suddenly, the pile of rumble began to slowly move as the creature underneath stirred and started to unearth himself. Surprised, they stood and watched as he slowly stood, bleeding and hurting but very much alive and very angry. His eyes glowed red and he fired a high-intensity optic blast at the one who had hurt him so badly. Quickly, Talah pulled Mheria out of harm's way, and the female warrior standing behind them was hit. Crying out in agony, the eye beams paralyzed her and began incinerating her. The young Sorceress cried out. Raising her hands, she was about to help, but it was too late, and with her final agonizing scream, the Amazon dematerialized.

"Missed," Telus said malevolently.

He began firing his optic blasts at all the female warriors. Moving quickly, the Amazons dodged and evaded his assaults. Looking to the Sorceress, his gaze again blazed, but just as he discharged, the Amazon Captain threw her staff at him. Telus' beams exploded the staff directly in front of him, blinding him. He cried out in pain and covered his face with one hand, while unseeingly firing energy bolts with his other hand.

"Mheria, we've gotta get out of here…now while he's blinded." Talah said, looking to the Sorcerer.

"No, Talah, we need to finish Telus while we can."

Talah glanced to the Tyrant. "Sister, Telus' blindness is only temporary. Get us out of here."

"No, not while the monster lives."

Talah grasped Mheria's head and forced eye contact with her. "Listen to me, sister. More soldiers are on the way, and our sisters are injured. Look at him," she said, releasing her.

Mheria did as Talah instructed and saw the truth of their situation.

"Telus is already starting to regenerate. If we don't leave now, our mother's sacrifice would have been for nothing." The young Sorceress again looked to the Warlord. Again, Talah forced Mheria to look her in the eye. "We die. He wins–period."

Reluctantly, Thakien nodded, closed her eyes, and displaced herself and all her warriors at the enemy fortress, to her Palace ship where it remained hidden from the Sorcerer and his invading force.

At her Throne ship, Mheria picked herself up off the floor, looked to her sisters briefly, and left the room. Talah followed. In her private chambers, the Imperial Empress paced angrily and was soon joined by her Amazonian Captain.

"I should've continued fighting. I should've killed that monster when I had the chance."

"No, sister, killing him would've been too time-consuming, and time was something we were out of. If we didn't leave when we did, he would've killed us all."

Mheria exhaled hard. "You're right," she admitted solemnly as the fury of her pacing subsided. "Talah, we're losing this fight. It's now painfully apparent that we can't stop Telus and his soldiers by ourselves."

"No, Mheria, you can't. You haven't the right."

"The decision has been made."

"Sister, no. It's not their fight, this is not their problem."

"I said the decision has been made, Captain," the Imperial Empress retorted, angrily.

Talah stepped back, knelt down, and bowed her head. Crossing her arms in front of her, she replied, "Yes, Imperial Empress."

"Now go. I need to rest. I'll need my full strength to accomplish the task ahead."

Without further discussion, the Captain bowed once more, rose, exited, and closed the doors behind her.

Back in the Jhanctum galaxy, my Pride and I were busy in the Divergia star system trying to stop the Zonnyan Assembly. They had launched ships to slow our incursion, and give their scientists—their bakoryms as they were referred to in this galaxy, time to fire their terrible weapon…a Sonic Wave Emitter.

Inside the Zonnyan moon, Zendox, the facility housed the controls for the weapon, and the three creatures who created the device were making their final adjustments.

The Sonic Wave Emitter was similar in concept to what we humans referred to as a Rail Gun, or its colloquial aperture, a Mass Driver. Imagine if you would, a weapon that used huge, long magnetic coils capable of attracting large fragments of mineral-enriched asteroids or large chunks of meteors. Now imagine these chunks could be fired with accuracy at any targeted area of choice. The Sonic Wave Emitter worked on the same principle—except instead of collecting rocks, this weapon attracted and stored the gravimetric energy fields that all planetary bodies produced, with the capacity of firing and with far greater accuracy.

Aboard Ship-Arjenadann, the Elphah and his Ra-Tuths were in the Strategym, a place where conferences and strategies took place.

"The potential of such a weapon is unimaginable," Joryd said, looking at the Wave Emitter on the holographic display screen.

"I do not have to imagine. When I was still a Vardyn, I saw the Hykard use it to push a moon out of orbit and send it crashing into the planet Ehindo, annihilating both the planet and its populists," U'kristu interjected. "That weapon must be destroyed at all cost."

In Throne Pryme, the naked Twins had separated. Sclee wore a tan scarf and silver belt, and she had the Throne, while Tonna who was posted at their science station wore a blue scarf and gold belt. All holographic consoles were replaced with solid stations.

In the gay'r, we launched Xentou-Fighters to combat the Zonnyans, once the ships were occupied and Ported them into space. Ja-Challah, positioned to leave first was delayed by her brother, Renn.

"Sister, how are your tendrils?"

"They're fine, Renn."

"Have they healed completely?"

"Yes–stop babying me, I got a clean bill of health from Kahnu in Arjai."

"I'm not babying you, Ja-Challah. I'm concerned."

"Don't be–Syn'nar's here, we gotta go."

Once the Pylot was ready, the Xentou rose up, and a large Hexagyn appeared beneath Ja-Challah and Syn'nar, and they dropped inside the Portal.

Outside Ship-Arjenadann, the Portal opened and they exited and awaited their back up. Within moments, Renn, Nyrit, Saffron and their Pylots joined them. They were the first line of defense and raced to meet the approaching enemy ships.

The Juardian-Omegah led a Juardian Pack of five, including me, to the moon to stop the Bakoryms and destroy the Emitter. Hexagyning through their defense screens, the doorway opened in the weapon's control room. Armed with Gauntlets, we stepped out with Syn'nar at Talon's side. He led the way. The Scorpilyn and Zigong shot all the guards in the room before any of us could get off a shot. Damn, Talon and Syn'nar were fast.

"Stop," shouted Talon in Zonnyan. He raised his gloved hand and aimed at them.

The lead scientist faced us. "You are too late, Qi-Tahh," he replied in Zonnyan and fired the weapon.

They looked grotesque—soft and shapeless like large mollusks without their shells. Pus oozed out from their bodily orifices.

"In less than three—"

In a wink of an eye, Syn'nar threw her Gauntlet arm out to the side, and transformed it into a Dysk. She struck the lead scientist across his face in midsentence, and dropped him. The Juardian-Deltah caught her returning Dysk and morphed it back into a Gauntlet as the Zonnyan hit the floor.

Though I did not understand their idiom, I did comprehend their body language. They were angry at us, and we fired. We hit them with a heavily charged of plasma energy. The discharge shook their bodies and they cried out in pain before dropping to the floor, unconscious. The plasma shock setting on our Gauntlets had the same yield control as weapons with a stun capacity, and if what Talon had said earlier about this setting was true, the Zonnyans were going to be out for hours.

I ran to the weapon's system, stopped and stared at the control panel. I searched for some familiarity with the controls, but found none. I did not recognize these symbols or system's configuration, and I was going to need time to figure it out.

Joining me, Talon told me we did not have the time for me to learn the system or Zonnyan. I heard the reptilian's Holo-Com beep. He tapped the micro dot and opened communications.

"Talon, this is Sclee. The weapon has been fired."

"We know. We were too late to stop them."

"The Sonic Wave will hit the planet Signius in precisely two hotress and forty-three et'nims," Tonna replied.

"The controls are in Zonnyan and unknown to me." I said cutting in on the conversation. "I need time to comprehend the device." I said as my eyes scanned the alien controls.

Again I was told that was time we did not have.

"But I must learn the language before I can even begin to try to hack the system, and then I will need to decipher the technology before even attempting to disarm the weapon, especially one with a virtually unlimited energy capacity."

The space battle against the Zonnyans was fierce. Two war class fighters were on Ja-Challah, and soon she and Syn'nar found themselves cornered. The Xentou's only remaining defense involved her using her tentacles.

"Ja-Challah, use your tendrils, they are our only hope." Syn'nar ordered.

"I cannot, they hurt too much."

"What?" The Pylot said, surprised.

"I lied to Renn, I never kept my Arjai appointments, I was afraid Torr or Nahni would ground me if they found out."

Renn arrived and saw what was happening. *"Sister, use your tendrils, they are your only hope.*

"I can't." Ja-Challah reluctantly admitted.

In Throne Pryme, Sclee-Tonna replied that I had two minutes and thirty-two seconds before the Wave impacted with Signius.

"E'nie, you and Laisere join Tonna and me in pseudo form to assist Marc," Sclee commanded as she activated her Throne controls. Activating their holographic forms from their stations, they also operated the controls, and allowed the figures to move independently of their true selves.

They joined the Scorpilyn and me on the moon Zendox, at the weapon controls.

"Talon, have your Juardians transport the Zonnyan bakoryms and their guards to the Juardian Maximum Enclosure wing, and be certain to scan and search them thoroughly. They are to be kept separated and sedated."

Talon bowed. "Yes, Ra-tuth," and then he faced the other Juardians and shouted, "You heard Sclee." His eyes narrowed. "Juardian Protocol Five, execute!" he said, roaring the order.

Syn'nar called out, "Port."

A Hexagyn appeared, and the Echelon and the other Juardians gathered the scientists and guards, and placed the ugly unconscious creatures inside. I was glad I did not have to assist. Aside from their grotesqueness, the smell of Zonnyans alone could make a spy talk. Although, what most amazed me was how many people the Portal held. There were nine bodies placed inside the Hexagyn, and there was still plenty of room for the Pack. I should not have been surprised though. The Supremacy held the secret to fourth-dimension technology where the inside was always larger than the outside.

The Scorpilyn's tongue slid between his parted lips as he looked over my shoulder at the controls.

"Sclee-Tonna, problem. The weapon is rigged to fire if the trajectory is changed without the proper encryption code," Talon reported.

"Can you deactivate the trigger relay?" the Elphah-in-charge inquired.

"Maybe—" Laisere answered uncertain, as his Holo-Form looked over the controls.

In space, Renn raced to his sisters, who could not help themselves. The older Xentou managed to destroy the Zonnyan fighters and saved Ja-Challah and Syn'nar, but Renn was seriously injured in the process. They raced him back to the ship to receive emergency medical attention.

On board the Mothership, the Tova's voiced trailed off as he returned fire on two class-five Zonnyan cruisers.

"Sorry, Zonnyans." Laisere said, looking at the controls.

"We must try. Time of Wave impact with planet Signius is one hotress and fifty-two et-nims," Tonna added.

Deactivating the trigger relay was only one part of the problem. We still needed to break the code if we were to change the Wave's trajectory. E'nie asked if I could do it if they talked me through the technical parts. I did not know and continued to stare at the controls with uncertainty.

"We are running out of time," Talon bellowed.

"He's right," Sclee said. "Work it out," she commanded.

Aboard Arjenadann, the Elphah-in-charge took the Tova's post so that Laisere could concentrate on the task before them, and Tonna took over on communications to free up E'nie.

On the moon, the Twins' pseudo images vanished. Now unburdened by the battle, E'nie and Laisere assisted me, as we only had a minute and forty-one seconds before the Wave struck and obliterated the planet and killed the millions of people of living there.

"Tell me what to do."

With me acting as their hands, we raced to save Signius from destruction. Talking me through the procedure, Laisere helped me through the technical portion and watched me closely as E'nie translated the language.

"No, Marc," the weapons specialyst suddenly said, halting my action. "First remove the paradyne isotope rectory and then the inverted initiators. All right, now cross-connect the regulators and insert them into circuits A-17 and C-5." Laisere said motioning his hands. "Now…very carefully disable the rely switch and remove the sonic trigger. Do not touch the sides. If you do, we are dead."

I successfully removed the trigger rely and deactivated it, and then proceeded with the encryption code and discovered the Zonnyans, like the ancient Egyptians of Earth, used hieroglyphics to represent their alphabet and numbers, but the Zonnyans use was created with greater complexity. The Zonnyan language was written from down to up diagonally. Fortunately, the Ginsung, E'nie, could read it, and I was able to place the weapon in diagnostic mode. But we still needed to access the controls to shut it down, and time was not on our side.

"Marc, hurry." The communications specialyst shouted.

Feeling the pressure, I asked about our time. They told me the Wave would impact with Signius in forty-three seconds.

"Marc," E'nie's holographic form again shouted.

"You know, you shouting my name every five et-nims isn't helping, E'nie. I've almost got it."

"Time of impact thirty-one et-nims," Tonna called out.

"Almost," I said.

"Thirty, twenty-nine, twenty-eight, twenty-seven—"

"I'm in. Accessing trajectory controls and firing into space." I said typing away. "Damn!"

"What is it?" Laisere asked.

"The system requires an actual target, or it won't alter target lock."

Listening to our conversation, Tonna commenced scanning for a new target and soon found one. "Target the Zonnyan asteroid, Screel. Psionics show the asteroid to be devoid of life."

E'nie inquired, "Are you certain?"

"Yes," she replied, and though Tonna believed she was, the acting Elphah had her Twin run another psionic sweep.

"Affirmative," Tonna reported back. "Transmitting coordinates."

"Receiving coordinates," I said, typing the numbers in.

"Eight et-nims, Marc," E'nie said, panicked. "Seven, six, five, four—"

The Sonic Wave suddenly changed course and veered away from the planet Signius, and headed toward Asteroid Screel. All congratulated me and cheered except for Talon, who simply crossed his arms in front of him, cracked a half of grin, and nodded once sharply. Forgetting he was a pseudo image, I went to slap Laisere's clawed hand and passed through it. The Ra-Tuth-in-charge reported the Wave would collide with Asteroid Screel in a little more than two minutes.

"Well done. Now destroy the facility," commanded Sclee.

"And we will see you both aboard Arjenadann when finished," Tonna added.

Tapping the micro dots behind their ears, Talon and I closed communications and the images of Laisere and E'nie vanished. We drew our Kaja-Gauntlets, and following Talon's instructions, I mentally raised the weapon's yield to force five and prepared to fire when Arjenadann's voice boomed in our heads.

"Talon, Marc, do not fire. I have just detected life-forms on Asteroid Screel."

"Ow… Not so loud," I shouted verbally.

"Apologies."

"What?" Talon said, roaring.

"Why the hell did psionics not detect them sooner?" I asked.

"The asteroid is composed of Urinnite, a mineral the Zonnyans used in conjunction with screens to give off false readings. It deceived ship's instruments and temporarily fooled my senses."

"Numbers," I asked, shouting.

"Five thousand."

Holstering my Kaja, I raced back to the controls to try to change the Wave's trajectory.

On board Arjenadann, Joryd and Z'yenn exited a Hexagyn in Throne Pryme, and the Elphah demanded a report from Sclee, who relinquished the Command chair back to him, and remerged with her Twin. Quickly she explained the situation. Weighing his options, the Ra-Tuth asked if they used all Hexagyns, could they evac all of the inhabitants in time?

"No, there isn't time," the Omegah replied. "Where are the Packs?"

"All Pridesmen are already back–," Sclee replied.

"–On board except for –," Tonna added.

"Talon and Marc, they—" Sclee was in the midst of saying.

"Where are they," Z'yenn demanded.

"Still at the Zendox facility," Sclee-Tonna said simultaneously.

Joryd at once contacted Talon for a status report, to which I interrupted and told him that I was attempting to again alter the Wave's trajectory. Laisere told Joryd the Sonic Wave would strike Asteroid Screel in fifty-two et-nims. The Elphah ordered Talon and I back to the ship, and I refused and continued to work the Zonnyan controls.

"Marc, you are endangering the Pride unnecessarily, return, now. Talon, evacuate the complex…now!"

"No, Joryd, I can save them. I just need a little time," I said, desperately trying to complete the task.

"You're out of time," Joryd shouted. Hexagyn back, now." he commanded.

"No, I'm almost there."

Aboard the Mothership…

With twenty-three seconds remaining, the Elphah ordered me to return to the ship at once. Instead I argued that I could not, and was close to reconfiguring the system. I nearly had it.

The Velfin updated the Pantherus, "Joryd, seventeen et-nims."

"Laisere," Z'yenn said, approaching his station. "On my mark, extend armor and shields over both Arjenadanns."

"Yes Tas'r."

"Avedia, Arjenadann, set course for the nearest Cosmic Corridor and prepare for Emergency Maximum Light Speed jump."

"Yes Ra-Tuth.

"Joryd, even with armor and shields, the shockwave from that explosion—"

"Will rip us apart. I know, Z'yenn."

"Shockwave will hit Asteroid Screel in eleven et-nims," reported Laisere.

"E'nie notify the Pride that we'll be jumping to maximum light speed. "Joryd said, facing him. "Talon, I want that weapon destroyed, and you and Marc back here immediately. That's an order, Juardian-Omegah."

At the facility...

"I am sorry, Brother."

Talon picked me up and carried me away from the station, as if I were a piece of luggage. He called for a Portal and then pulled something from his belt. Stepping inside the Hexagyn, I protested, but was powerless to do anything about it. The Scorpilyn tossed what he was holding, and destroyed the weapon's controls as the door closed, and we vanished.

"Noooo," I cried out.

In Throne Pryme, the Portal appeared.

"Laisere, now," Z'yenn ordered.

The Xentouwish and Arjenadann were encased in armor and force fields.

"Avedia, go," Joryd commanded.

Talon and Marc exited the Hexagyn.

"Five, four, three..."

Laisere continued to count as we traveled twenty-seven times faster than the speed of light. The Sonic Wave struck Asteroid Screel, obliterating it almost instantly. Not configured to be used on something as small as an asteroid, the awesome power of the sonic vibrations violently tore the space rock apart. We raced to escape the explosive chain reaction that followed.

"All sections, standby for shockwaves." E'nie shouted over the intercom.

The Sonic Wave caught Arjenadann, and she and the ship were rocked and tossed, as were I and the Pride, but we managed to enter a Cosmic Corridor and escaped before the full effect of the Sonic Wave destroyed us.

Z'yenn looked to Joryd. "That was too close."

"Agreed," he said, looking back to her.

The reality of what I had done, pissed me off, and I ran to Joryd, the source of my anger. "You mother fucker," I screamed.

Joryd turned causally, and I struck him across the jaw. His head darted to the side.

"I could've saved those people, you son of a bitch," I shouted.

"Va-lim," U'kristu called out, surprised by the attack.

"Hawkins," Z'yenn shouted in anger.

Turning, the Elphah roared angrily as he faced me. His orange and green eyes narrowed, the bridge of his nose wrinkled, and Joryd bared his teeth, and raised his huge paw.

U'kristu cried out, "Joryd, no!"

But the big cat's retaliation was swift and powerful. Striking me across the chest, I sailed to the other end of the Throne Pryme, and felt the burning of my bleeding wounds. Slowly, I got up. Now angrier than ever, I was ready to fight.

"Because of you, five thousand innocent people are dead. You used me! Why?

"Arrest him," the Omegah ordered.

"Delay that," the Elphah countered. "But get him out of my sight," he commanded through gritting teeth.

"I'm not finished."

Joryd roared loudly, "Yes, you are," he shouted back, and glared at me.

"Va-lim." U'kristu said, slowly moving her head side to side as a warning not to proceed any further.

My Ket-sho offered Torr's Habitat as my confinement space,

which the Tas'r hissed at, until U'kristu reminded Joryd and Z'yenn that was where I currently resided.

"As long as he does not leave, it will suffice."

"Fasbi Joryd, I will see to it," U'kristu replied. "Port," she shouted.

Angrily, I joined U'kristu who stood in the Hexagyn's threshold, waiting for me. I cursed Joryd to hell along with the rest of the Throne Pryme Pack, and stepped inside. The Portal closed, and we vanished.

Z'yenn faced Joryd and said with anger, "Hawkins should be going to a Juardian Enclosure, not Sivgins' Habitat."

"The decision has been made."

"Elphah? According to regulations—"

The Pantherus growled lowly, "I've had enough belligerences for one niya, Z'yenn."

The Zahnobein stepped back and bowed deeply. "Jamonaka forgive me, Ra-Tuth. I meant no disrespect."

The Omegah took her Acquil-Throne and said nothing more on the subject. Instead she pressed a button, and addressing the Damage Repair Pack, she commanded they report all damages to the Deggzytepol.

"Avedia, you and Arjenadann, exit the Corridor and hold our position. Laisere, suspend defenses once we've cleared the Corridor." The Elphah commanded.

The Pylot turned her head 180 degrees, "Acknowledged, Ra-Tuth." Avedia replied and turned to face the screen.

"Yes Ra-Tuth."

"What's wrong?" Z'yenn asked facing Joryd.

"I want to check our status before returning to the Divergia star system, that was a rough ride."

The Acquil-Omegah approached and gave his report. The ship suffered minimal damage, and all Damage Repair Packs have been dispatched. Antonio also reported that eight were injured in our battle with the Zonnyans, and Renn was in surgery being healed by Torr and Nahni.

Exiting the Cosmic Corridor, Avedia and Laisere followed Joryd's commands. The ship was stationary and defenses deactivated. The ship suddenly wobbled as if it stumbled. Then it happened again. The Omegah inquired what was happening, and Avedia told her it was not her, or her systems at fault, it was Arjenadann, and she was in need of healing. Hurt by the Sonic Wave, the Xentouwish again felt off balanced and wobbled again, she rocked the ship.

Z'yenn ordered separation. "Avedia, ease us off Mother as gently as possible."

Yes, Z'yenn.

Outside, the prods retracted, ports closed, and the ship raised off of Arjenadann, and hovered beside her.

Joryd glanced to Z'yenn, who in turn contacted Arjai Quoni. The Omegah explained Mother's condition, and though Torr and Nahni were in surgery with Renn, Kahnu, Healer second-in-command, replied that he and Cougg, another arjai technician would check her out and report when finished.

Outside of Torr's Habitat, the Hexagyn opened, and U'kristu and I stepped out.

"You were wrong to strike Joryd. We do not hit our Elphahs… ever," she said, sternly.

I stood at Torr's Habitat, still seething about what had happened. I told my Ket-sho, Joryd was lucky I did not hit him again, although he did have a good hit and he was stronger than I thought. I had to remember that, including how well he controlled his claw extensions. "The next time—"

U'kristu grabbed me by the arm. For such a petite humanoid, she had a strong grip. She turned me to face her. She was angry. I had never seen her angry before, and truth be told, I never thought it was possible to make her so–until now. U'kristu always seemed so calm except during training, but that was because she took our sessions very serious. Now I was seeing a whole other side of her.

"Marcus Anthony Hawkins, listen and listen well. We do not

strike our Elphahs," she said emphatically and released me. "There will be no next time, and if there is, I will be the one that hurts you, not Joryd. Are we clear?"

I paused for a moment and studied her body language. U'kristu was not bluffing, so I stepped back and bowed. "Yes, Ket-sho."

We entered the Habitat, and U'kristu saw my anger, and she told me to be angry if I must, but remember what she said about striking our Elphah. As for the incident on Asteroid Screel, U'kristu was sorry for my pain.

"You see, that's just what I mean." I said explosively. "This is my pain, my hurt. Don't you feel anything anymore, or have you been killing so long you've grown numb to it?"

"Would you rather the Zonnyans won?" She asked with an even tone.

"Of course not."

Regardless, and appearances aside, they were still a sentient species. People who could think and feel, love and hate like any human, and now five thousand of them were dead. Rixx attempted to convince me that I could not have saved those people in the time we had. Her reply did not even begin to answer my question, and I told her so.

"Now, if you don't mind, it's had been a long fucked-up day, and I want to be left alone."

"As you wish." U'kristu walked toward the door. "I will need to secure you inside, and you are to remain here until Joryd says otherwise. But we are not finished discussing your actions, or your use of profanity, and we will speak more of it, koroxsu.

"Ask me if I care."

"Jamonaka, do not try to leave. We will know if you do, and it will only make matters worse."

"And what makes you think I want to be around a bunch of fucking murderers?"

"Again, Va-lim, I am truly sorry."

U'kristu exited, and in the corridor I heard her order Momja, our living computer, to secure the Habitat and not allow me to leave.

Using her Juardian-Elphah authorization code, Momja followed her orders.

Outside the ship, the Octopi healer and his Arjai Pack finished their preliminary examination of Arjenadann.

"Kahnu to Throne Pryme, acknowledge."

"Yes Kahnu, how is Mother?

"Mother's injuries are more severe than she believed, Joryd, and Arjenadann requires surgery as well.

A section of the ship opened up, and the Arjai Pack, helped Arjenadann move inside the vessel.

In Throne Pryme…

"Avedia, once Kahnu and his Pack have secured Mother in the Surgical Bay, close section and set course for the Divergia star system–light speed six."

"Yes, Tas'r."

"Laisere, raise armor and shields, and ready weapons." Joryd commanded. "We don't know what kind of reception we're going to receive."

"Acknowledged, Ra-Tuth."

In Arjai Surgical Bay One, Torr, Nahni and their Pack of healers, raced to save Renn's life, while Kahnu, Cougg, a Cat life-form, light brown fur, short rounded ears, and orange colored eyes, and their Arjai Pack moved Arjenadann into Surgical Bay Two.

The specially designed state-of-the-art medical facilities were made especially for the Xentouwish and her children. It was their Healing Center, filled with whatever was needed to arjai one of their kind. Arjai Quoni-X was absolutely incredible. Although, if not for the advancements these creatures possessed in fourth dimension technology, none of this would be possible.

Scared for her brother–and herself, Ja-Challah entered the minds of the Arjais working on Renn. She saw through their eyes, and the truth of her brother's condition. The young Xentou wished she had not done so. She was sickened by what she saw, saddened, by what she felt, and utterly guilty for what she had caused. Then Ja-Challah felt despair when she saw Kahnu and his Pack bring their mother into surgery.

We returned to Zonnyan space and encountered no problems. With most of the Assembly's forces destroyed along with their weapon, the Zonnyans were taken easily, and held until treated. We had notified the Council as to our progress, and were instructed to head directly to the Thada star system–planet Argen once we were finished. Further instructions would follow.

Later, in Arjai recovery, both Arjenadann and Renn had been healed, and though Mother would return to active duty in a few hours, her son would require a much longer period to arjai. Ja-Challah visited her mother and brother.

"My daughter," Arjenadann said weakly, addressing the Xentou telepathically with a loving tone. *"I sense you are unduly upset."*

"This was all my fault. What happened to Renn was because of me."

"Do not think like that, your tendrils are still healing–your brother knew that. That is why he stay close to you."

Ja-Challah then told Arjenadann the whole story. How this started two years ago during the Linksys incursion of Seregaia. It was when her tendrils were severely damaged battling a Linksys Attack Drone.

Arjenadann confessed to recalling the incident. Torr and Nahni repaired Ja-Challah's tendrils, and Sivgins gave her a prescription to see Kahnu for physical therapy.

"I stopped my rehabilitation."

"What? Why?"

"After going for awhile, I felt better and thought continuing was a waste of time. I bedazzed Kahnu into thinking I was still receiving therapy, so no one would know."

"What changed?" Arjenadann asked, in a neutral tone.

The battle with the Doxini and Melmorn. The young Xentou

admitted to discovering her tendrils' sensitivity to pressure, but kept it quiet. She confessed, Renn had tried to check with her about her tendrils before the engagement with the Zonnyans, but she had blown him off.

"And now he may die because of me."

"Your brother is not going to die, but you will have to tell him the truth."

"He will hate me."

"Renn loves you–very much. He always has-and he always will." Arejenadann assured Ja-Challah. *"Then, you, your father Joryd and I are going to have a long talk about lying to family, and the misuse of your Bedazz abilities on a fellow Pridesmen."*

"I understand."

"No you do not–you do not have any idea what you have done. Or the seriousness in what you have done–but you will. I am angry–and very disappointed in you. Now, if you would excuse me, I need to rest"

A conversation between two telepaths exchanging information, was far quicker than any verbal form of communication, and in a very short time, the talk between mother and daughter was over.

Later that day, my anger had still not lessened when the doorbell sounded, and I shouted for whoever it was to come in. The Elphah entered, and I bowed. Joryd told me it was time we talked, he said approaching me. He asked me to please sit, but I was not in the mood, and told him so. The Elphah stepped in close to me.

"That wasn't a request. Sit…down."

Reluctantly, I complied. Joryd confessed he understood that I was upset, but added, that still did not give me the right to behave the way I did. The Pride did not deserve my disrespect. He knew my issue was with him. Joryd told me to leave the Pride out of it and keep it between us.

Standing back up, I was enraged and shouted to Joryd that he understood nothing. Before I joined this killing squad, I had never killed anything larger than an insect, and in one fleeting moment, I was turned into a mass murderer. And for what?

"You told me we were Life Protectors. That was a lie. You're not Life Protectors. You're glorified warmongering murderers, and because of you, I'm responsible for the deaths of five thousand Zonnyans, you son of a bitch."

The Elphah roared loudly, "That's enough. You will show me the proper respect, or I will beat it out of you." His orange-green eyes narrowed, and again he roared. "Do not try me, Cub."

I stepped back and bowed deeply.

Again Joryd ordered me to sit down, but this time he added for me to shut up and listen to what he had to say. Yes, five thousand Zonnyans lost their lives, koniya, but the millions who were in danger were saved. It was always tragic when the innocent got caught in the crossfire, and Joryd was not just talking about those on the receiving end of the Wehtiko, but those Influenced as well. I did not believe him, and asked why did he not give me the chance to save them if he cared so much.

"I did. I am sorry you can't see that, but time was not on our side. We safeguard the ones who were on the receiving end of the threat first and then those who were the aggressors second–if possible."

"You turned me into a monster," I screamed.

"No, we're teaching you how to fight monsters and to defend those who cannot protect themselves," Joryd countered angrily and began to pace. You stopped the Influenced from eradicating a planet with millions of inhabitants. What of them? Would you rather the Zonnyans had succeeded? We are Qi-Tahh. We kill when we must, not when we wish. I am sorry if we don't fit your idea of nobility, but this is our way."

I was now solemn, all my rage had suddenly died out. "That may be, but this is not my way. My joining the Supremacy was a mistake."

"No, it wasn't."

I stood and started to pace as well. "So is this what I'm supposed to be for the next six years? A killer?"

"No, not a killer, not a murderer, but a Life Protector, a Qi-Tahh."

No one knew for certain why I of all people was chosen by Kerebrol to join the Supremacy. However, Joryd and I did know that the Ohdens were very selective when it came to choosing and recruiting humans–which they have been doing for thousands of years. They were well aware of the dangers should they ever enhance a human who was incompatible or turned evil.

"Why me? I'm no warrior or soldier."

"You're wrong. I see the same thing Kerebrol sees in you—great potential."

"You say that with such certainty."

"I am."

Joryd asked me to trust him, and trust in our Pride. They needed me, or so he said, and whether I believed it or not, I think I needed them too. Maybe he was right. Joryd told me to think about it and suggested I get some rest. I would need it.

"We are still in the middle of a crisis, and I need your help in stopping this ancient evil." Joryd turned and walked toward the door to exit.

"You could've killed me in Throne Pryme.

The Elphah turned and walked back over to me. "Yes, that's right," he said, as a matter-of-factly.

"Why didn't you?"

"What, kill you over something you do not yet even understand? And if I had, how would you have learned from your mistake?"

He was right, there was still much I needed to learn. For starters, how the hierarchies within the Prides worked. When I struck my Elphah, and in front of my fellow Pridesmen, unbeknownst to me, I was actually challenging Joryd for leadership of the family. This was usually a death match. No wonder U'kristu was so pissed with me. As for the rest of the Pride, they took these matters very seriously.

"And I suggest you do likewise."

"I apologize for hitting you, Joryd. You didn't deserve that."

"No, I did not, and you are forgiven, but be warned. It had better not happen again outside of training, or else next time I will not be so forgiving. Am I clear?"

"Yes, Ra-Tuth, I understand," I said, and bowed deeply.

"Good. We cannot expect you to know everything, Marc, at least not yet, but we can correct your way of thinking when wrong. See U'kristu regarding disciplinary actions and good daiot, pleasant slumbers." Joryd walked back to the door. "Momja, jamonaka discontinue confinement status for Marc Hawkins, Betah.

"Acknowledged Joryd, confinements have been nullified."

"Fasbi," he replied, and exited.

Thada Argen

VI

In my room at Torr's Habitat, I laid on the bed staring at the ceiling lost in a swirl of thoughts. Restless, I sat up and started to pace.

"Private Journal 2022. My Xentou brother had pulled through, the Arjai Packs had managed to save Renn's life, thank God, and they healed Mother though her life was not in jeopardy, I was still glad to hear Arjenadann was released back to active duty. However, my brother's recovery would take longer as his injuries were more severe.

I, on the other hand, could not forget the lives my actions had taken. I had never killed anyone, and in the blink of an eye, I had murdered five thousand people. Though I saved another planet's population, I could not justify the means regardless of the circumstances. And the worst part was my Elphah and Pride, though saddened by the loss of life, were also fine with what I had done. I wish I could let my mind drift off to a less traumatic time right now, but I did not have that luxury. It was time for my shift, and I was still expected to perform my duties regardless of how I felt emotionally. I would have to indulge my desire for a mental retreat later." I ended the journal and left to make my Juardian rounds.

We were enroute to the Thada star system and still had not heard from Kerebrol.

Arriving in Throne Pryme, I tried to leave behind all thoughts of the Zonnyan incident. Torr, who seemed to enjoy accompanying me when he could, made it easier. His humor and high spirits were welcomed, and gave me comfort. We stepped out of the Portal together, and onto the floor of Throne Pryme.

"Oh, my God, there's a blind woman flying the ship," the Fonchuai said jokingly.

"Good niya, Torr," Avedia said, smiling.

Torr and I approached Joryd and Z'yenn and bowed to them both, something that was customary and expected. We gave them our greetings and then started to walk the Command Center as Torr guided us toward the Twins.

"Grumbah, Cinnamon," Torr said and kissed Tonna on the lips.

Making his way to their other side, he continued. "And Grumbah, Spice," he said and kissed Sclee on her mouth.

"Grumbah, Torr." Sclee-Tonna said in unison, and smiled.

Interrupting my stroll of Throne Pryme, Torr dragged me with him over to the Ginsung, our communications specialyst, who was busy working underneath his Holo-Station.

"Whoa! Whose four-toe sasquatches are those?" I asked, stepping over them, and continued walking.

"E'nie, just the person I wanted to see." Torr stopped and stooped next to the dark blue grasshopper, who seemed more interested with what he was working on than with what Torr had to say.

"Hey, my blue brother buddy, I've got a new pahfa for you. What would happen if you replaced the word koroc for the word kill?"

I turned around, thinking there was no way he was going to tell that joke… Not here…at least not now.

Continuing to work, the Ginsung asked, "Torr, is this one of your vact goxs?"

"No, it's not a sex joke. At least I don't think it's a sex joke. Okay, may be it could be a sex joke, but that doesn't matter. Just listen."

The Icsiedoa crawled out from underneath his construct station. "All right, I'm listening."

"What if you replaced the word kill for the word koroc?" Torr then changed his voice. "Okay, Sentinel, we're going to koroc you now…but we're going to koroc you slow."

I was shocked at what came out of his mouth, and I was about to say something when the Pack began laughing out loud. Except for the couple who missed the joke–myself and of course, Z'yenn, who hissed like an angry cat because that was what she did, everyone else including Joryd was cracking up.

"Neither of you have anything better to do?"

"Excuse me, Z'yenn, but I am making my Juardian sweep. Throne Pryme is part of those rounds.

The Omegah looked around and saw a few Pridesmen, including the Elphah, still enjoying Torr's joke. "You two are sick," she remarked hissing at us.

"You're absolutely right, Z'yenn. This is all Marc's fault." Torr said, pointing to me.

"My fault? I asked, looking to him surprised.

"I'm glad you admitted it."

"I admit to nothing. How the hell do you figure this is my fault?"

"It was you who told me the joke, was it not?"

"Yeah, but—"

"Well then," he cut me off. "All I did was change it so that most got the punch line, but it was you—" Torr shouted as he again pointed at me. "Who, had it not been for, none of this would've happened. Besides, it has to be your fault…otherwise it would be mine, and that can't be right…I'm a professional."

Z'yenn looked to Joryd. "Furlonus, give me strength. I am going to kill them both."

The Elphah tried to hold back his continued chuckling from Sivgins' joke, but failed, and the Omegah growled at him.

About to reply to Torr's remark, the pseudo image of the Council Elphah, suddenly appeared next to me, and scared the fuck out of me.

"Greetings my Pride." Kerebrol said.

I jumped, and morphed my Kaja to Gauntlet, before disarming after I saw who it was, and handled my fright badly, to say the least.

"Whoa. What the fuck, Chuck? What the hell is the matter with your mind? You can't be suddenly appearing next to people like that. What are you trying to do give me a heart attack? Ring a bell, knock on a door–give a brotha some advanced notice before your ass pops in beside him."

Suddenly realizing what I was saying, I stopped and began looking around as everyone in Throne Pryme stared at me in disbelief. Even E'nie had crawled from underneath his holographic station to see who I was addressing so disrespectfully.

"I'm sorry, did I say that out loud?" I asked, already knowing the answer.

Nodding his head and sporting a big grin, Torr replied, "Oh Yes, you did my brother, oh man did you ever."

"Oops, my bad," I said, addressing the Pack. "Apologies," I said, facing the holographic Elphah Ohden and bowed.

Joryd dropped his head and shook it. He then faced Heshe, "Jamonaka tell me that you did not pop in as a spot check on Marc's progress." He looked to me. "As you can see, there are still some areas that we need to work on, such as how to address the Elphah of the Ohdens."

I cracked a nervous smile, and Joryd faced Kerebrol once more.

"I wish it were that simple, my opo, but there is civil unrest on Thada Argen. The Dir-nays have been Influenced, and as a result, they have turned on their Eanoi neighbors. The Council believe this is the source of the increased infection activity occurring throughout our galaxy. For fifty meads the Dir-nays and Eanois have lived peacefully, ever since the Eanois settled on Thada Argen after the Linksys Cleansing nearly wiped out their species. Now they are being slaughtered by the Dir-nays, who control the Priorts and Skarbs, making each attack far more bloodier than the last."

"Defenses," asked Z'yenn.

Kerebrol replied with twin voices. *"None to speak of. Thada Argen is an agricultural planet. If the Dir-nays succeed in wiping out the Eanois, we believe this will cause the Wehtiko to become cataclysmic and sweep across the galaxy with such virulence we would not be able to stop it or contain it. Once that happens, it will spread throughout the universe unchecked,"*

"When are we to rendezvous with the Arjai Pride?

"You won't. Because of the urgency of the situation and the unavoidable lateness of the Arjai vessels, the Vitalyst and the Mirren, they will meet you at Thada Argen, and your Pride will assist in inoculating the Dir-nays. However, if you are unable to stop them before the situation reaches critical mass, which is when the Dir-nays have eradicated all the Eanois, you are hereby ordered to carry out Containment Protocol III."

"I understand," Joryd replied with a grim look. "However, that won't be necessary–we'll handle it."

"I know you will...good luck."

The Ohden vanished as instantly and quietly as Heshe appeared, and the Omegah ordered the Dicorp to inform Arjenadann to set course for the planet Argen light speed twelve. The amphibian contortionist corkscrewed her body around and informed Z'yenn that she had anticipated the order, and was already in the process of doing so. Avedia turned back around, and faced her holographic console.

"Course and speed laid in, Omegah."

"Arrival time?" the Zahnobein asked, twitching her whiskers.

"Two savners, twenty-two hotress and eight et-nims."

"Execute." Z'yenn ordered her Pylot.

"E'nie, have all Ra-tuths report to the Strategym at once." Joryd commanded.

The Icsiedoa followed his instructions, and opened the channel with his three-fingered hands while his two clawed hands performed other tasks, and rested his two praying mantis arms on his console.

Torr called for a Hexagyn, grabbed me and raced us inside.

"I can't believe you threw me under the bus like that with Z'yenn. That was koroced up, almost as much as your addressment to Kerebrol, bro."

We stepped inside the Portal.

"What'd you want from my life, Heshe scared the hell out of me. I mean, who does that to people? Suddenly appearing next to someone like that. What the fuck? And I'm supposed to be okay with that shit? I'm tellin' you, Kerebrol was lucky I didn't blast Heshe's holographic ass."

"Kerebrol scared you, really? Because I thought you were smooth and played it off very well. I doubt anyone even noticed." Torr smiled broadly.

I looked to him for a moment, faced forward, and saw Joryd talking to Avedia and Sclee-Tonna. "Fuck you, Torr." The Hexagyn closed and we vanished.

The Elphah turned the Throne over to Avedia, and he invited Sclee to attend the meeting, while Tonna took over navigation. Uncoiling herself out of the Pylot's chair, Avedia divided her serpent body into four parts and walked over to the command seat. She touched the chair with her webbed hand, and it morphed into the same configuration as her Dicorp seat. She then coiled herself into the Throne and sat comfortably.

"Z'yenn, Antonio, and Sclee, let's go." That was all Joryd said.

At the Strategym, a meeting place for the department Elphahs to come together and strategize, Torr laughed as we stepped out of the Hexagyn.

"You think I'm joking. You don't know how close Heshe came to being shot. Construct or not, Kerebrol should know better than to do that to someone armed–this is how accidents happen," I said, taking my seat across from Torr. "And when did I ever throw you under the bus with Z'yenn? And who taught you that Earth phrase, anyways?"

"Anishaa, don't try to change the subject. You told Z'yenn you were in Throne Pryme as part of your Juardian duties."

"But I was," I replied, confused.

"I know, but once you said that, I no longer had any legitimate reason to be in Throne Pryme."

"And this is my fault, how? You rarely have reason to be in Throne Pryme–that's never stopped you before. So then tell me… why were you in Throne Pryme?"

"To see the Twins, of course."

"Of course," I said, shaking my head.

A Hexagyn opened, and the Elphah and four Ra-tuths exited, just as more section Elphahs arrived. Looking at me, they took their seats, and their chairs morphed into whatever seating was comfortable for them. Except for Sclee, who remained standing. It seemed I was in her chair, so I motioned to get up.

"Marc, these proceedings are normally for Ra-tuths and invited Omegahs. You are here now, so you may stay, but do not make it a habit."

I nodded once to Joryd, retook my seat and remained silent.

"Momja, we need another chair, and jamonaka adjust for table size to accommodate it."

"Acknowledged. Jamonaka standby."

A chair for Sclee appeared, and the table increased its size to accommodate the extra seat comfortably. The Priccaryan, though always naked, never seemed to get cold, and sat crossed leg and rested an arm on the table.

"Most of you are aware of what has happened on Thada Argen. For those of you do not, Z'yenn will explicate," Joryd said, glancing to her briefly.

"The Dir-nays are Influenced with Wehtiko, and as a result, they have begun attacking the Eanoi Settlements. They are using life-forms they control to aide them. Before they were infected, the Dir-nays and Eanois shared the planet peacefully and lived as friends and tradesmen for more than fifty meads. Now the ground is stained with their blood."

Joryd dropped his head before raising it up high. "If we cannot restore the status quo before the situation reaches critical mass, which is when the Pygmies finish massacring all the Eanois, we are ordered by the Council to implement Containment Protocol III to keep the affliction from spreading."

"Oh no," Sercrom said.

"What is Containment Protocol III? That's the second time I've heard it said."

"It is the total destruction of a planet and its inhabitants, Va-lim." U'kristu looked from me to Joryd. "How much time do we have?"

Talon cut in, "We should have not released the Zonnyans. They lied.

"Of course they lied. They were Influenced,' Torr interjected.

"Joryd, you should have let me question them after the inoculation."

"Why? Killing five thousand of their people wasn't enough? Now you want to interrogate them?" I asked.

"Influenced or not, the Zonnyan Assembly present a clear and present danger to Supremacy security, and their lying could place us and the galaxy in great danger."

"Or…they may not have an agenda toward us, and all they want to do is just pick up the pieces of their shattered lives and find the strength to go on." I argued.

The Elphah tapped his claws on the table. "That's enough. Talon, make your report. Include your reasons of suspicions and present all evidence, and I'll view it after this assignment. For now, we have a planet full of people who need our help."

"Eanois or Dir-nays," I asked.

"Both," the Elphah replied.

We did not know how much time we had. For all we knew, the deadline had already occurred, and the infection was spreading even as we spoke. However, Joryd did not believe that was the case, and he surmised if that were true, Kerebrol would not have given us a time frame at all.

I was curious about why the Eanois chose Thada Argen for their new home, it was a great distance from their home planet and star system, so Sclee explained. I learned the two planets shared the same type of atmospheres. There were few planets in the Jhanctum galaxy that had a carbon dioxide environment.

The Acquil-Omegah interjected, and added "Unlike most sukais, the Eanois on Thada Argen, although they look human, their internal system were completely different. The Eanois breathed carbon dioxide and exhaled oxygen as their by-product."

Torr took the opportunity to also warn Antonio to be careful. While on Thada Argen. His strength, speed, and mental powers would be compromised, and reduced by 68 percent.

"And that is with your Life Support Device, active."

Battista acknowledged his warning. "I will be careful."

The Arjai-Elphah also shared Renn's condition. The Xentous would be out of commission for the next few vertixs–the injuries he suffered were severe. Torr also reminded Joryd that he had removed Renn from active duty until further notice.

The rest of the meeting was spent brainstorming, profiling, and working as a Pack, sharing our thoughts on the best way to subdue the Dir-nays without killing them. We felt that killing the Pygmies, would produce the same catastrophic results if the Dir-nays were to kill the Eanois.

The first on the agenda was finding a way to break their

connection to the Priorts and the Skarbs, thus taking away their advantage. Sercrom suggested that we might be able to construct a hypersonic frequency disruptor that could be channeled through our communications array, but Z'yenn countered, that the frequency needed to block their connection could quite possibly kill the population in the process.

"Why not have Arjenadann use her telepathic powers and turn the creatures against the Dir-nays or at the very least break their control? From what I've been told, a Xentouwish's mental powers are formidable."

"Stay out of this Hawkins. You are here as a privilege, not to—"

"Hold on a et-nim, Z'yenn, Marc may be onto something." Joryd interjected. "Arjenadann join us jamonaka."

"Acknowledged, Joryd. I am present." the Xentouwish replied telepathically.

"Mother, how are you feeling?"

"I am well, Kahnu and his Pack had healed me completely."

Glad to it… Arjenadann, given what we know about the Dir-nays and their abilities to communicate and control the Priorts and the Skarbs, would it be possible for you to turn the creatures against them or at least stop them from being used by the Pygmies?"

"An interesting concept– Perhaps."

"Think about it, Mother, and get back with me," the Elphah replied, and then he faced me. "Fasbi, Marc."

Though it was not said, the threat we were about to face was great, so much in fact that the Council were sending two Arjai ships– where one was usually enough. Torr told us he had never met Keelan Sopa, but had only heard of him. He was Zahnobein, and Elphah of the Mirren. The Fonchuai went on to say that he however, was familiar with the Vitalyst's Elphah, Rheeza, and thought she was one of the best in her field.

"Is that what you call it here, when you sleep with someone?" I did not mean to say that, at least not aloud. It just slipped out. Ever since I was augmented, I noticed my sarcasm was becoming second nature like Torr's. "Sorry," I said, looking to everyone.

"Do not be," Sclee said, looking to Torr with her head cocked to one side, her arms crossed in front of her chest and one brow raised.

Laughter from the group took the nervous edge off, and now Torr seemed to be in the hot seat with Sclee. Sivgins smirked, smiled, and shirked his shoulders, but said nothing. The laughter quickly died, and Joryd continued.

"The two Arjai Prides, though en route, will not reach Thada Argen for nearly three niyas, and there are no other Prides close enough with the skills to handle this size of an outbreak. We can. Our mission is to keep the situation under control until they arrive."

"The Kerevene Arjai Pride is closer and could help in handling the Influenced, but they're busy battling an outbreak of Nyphomadaxel in the Zeffron star system. It's a parasitical infection that absorbs all fluids in a body. Regardless the species, it reduces the host to a few pounds of crystallized remains," the Arjai-Elphah said.

"Torr, why not send the Vitalyst to the Zeffron star system and have the Kerevene rendezvous with us?" I asked.

"Arjai protocol prevents it. From the moment the Kerevene entered the star system, it became bah-rodft."

"You guys can quarantine an entire star system," I asked in disbelief.

Annoyed, the Omegah hissed. "Getting back to our present situation—"

"No," the Elphah said. "We'll stop here for now, but we will reconvene in one savner. I want options other than committing genocide. I will not have that as my only choice. I want those other options...dismissed," Joryd said, nearly roaring the words.

Everyone but he and Z'yenn exited the Strategym.

"As much as I hate to admit it, the Council may be right this time. Planetary eradication may be our only option."

"I won't accept that, Z'yenn. There are always more than one solution to a problem." Joryd pushed himself away from the table. "You know, my grandfather So'blom had a saying, 'There are many paths to the same place.'"

"That sounds like Granddad Blom," Z'yenn remarked, pushing herself away from the table. She walked over to Joryd.

"You know, you're the only one he ever let call him Blom. He loves you very much, Z'yenn."

"I love him too, and I miss him very much."

"Defona, on our next leave, let's visit him. It'll be a wonderful surprise for him and a nice change for us."

She smiled broadly, "I'd like that, Suncol."

Joryd's smile suddenly faded, and he frustratingly slammed a huge paw onto the table. "No, I will not visit my grandfather and tell him I destroyed a world. There's got to be another option."

"Were that true in most cases. With the Influenced, the solution is not always a peaceful one." Z'yenn purred near his ear, and gave Joryd a loving lick and exited, leaving the Elphah to make the hard decisions.

We were approximately an hour and a half from the Thada Argen. The Cosmic Corridor, which enabled ships to travel far greater distances throughout the galaxy in a much shorter time, without it our journey would have taken weeks even at traveling twenty-seven times the speed of light.

In Arjai, Renn was still recovering. At his side, Ja-Challah kept her Xentou brother company. Though part of her punishment was to help Renn with healing, she was there for other reasons. Ja-Challah was ordered to complete her physical therapy, and she was not to Bedazz anyone until further notice. Furthermore, Ja-Challah was to see U'kristu regarding the remainder of her disciplinary action.

An hour later we all had reconvened in the Strategym, and after going over everything that we knew about the Wehtiko, and compared that information to our profiles of the Dir-nays, we figured out which direction their madness would drive them.

The Elphah and Omegah listened to what we devised. Sitting between Torr and U'kristu, I remained silent as the Scorpilyn told us that he and his Juardian Pack had psionic the planet and compared the data they already had with the new information. Consequently, they were able to extrapolate the Pygmies' plans. Meva profiled the Dir-nays' behavior and found a pattern to their attacks. Their assaults were not random but strategically coordinated. The gin-gyn seemed to be what was driving them.

Standing, the Sk'tier walked to the head of the table and activated a 4-D holographic image of Thada Argen.

"The Dir-nays are systematically wiping out the Eanois. They first destroyed the Acrea Settlement," U'kristu said, pointing to it. "Then the Vausch, and last was the Glona Settlement."

"Joryd, that leaves only eight settlements remaining." U'kristu reminded him. "If we are correct in our evaluation, the next settlement attacked will either be Argenta or Dumaus. Both are potential targets."

Surprised to hear about two possible objectives, the Elphah studied the holographic world, and the colored dots displayed were referenced to a particular species. The blue, for instance, represented the Eanois. The red were the Dir-nays. The brown were the Priorts, and the black were the Skarbs. The red and brown dots covered the sky in large clusters, while the black moved like a plague destroying everything in their path. I asked Z'yenn, who replaced U'kristu at the table's head, why we could not simply stun the Dir-nays and keep them sedated until they could be inoculated. But the reply I received from her was heated impatience. My Ket-sho, however, had a much higher tolerance and explained that our weapons had no stun setting.

That did not make sense to me. Having weapons with a stun capacity would solve a lot of problems; beginning with this one. What I did not know until U'kristu explained was that most species in Jhanctum galaxy were resistant to such settings.

Again, I had demonstrated my inexperience, but I still nonetheless had a few burning questions. "How are we supposed to protect the Eanois and stop the Dir-nays without killing them?"

Z'yenn's shortness with me exploded. "Hawkins," she bellowed.

"This is not a teaching group, and unlike you, we know exactly what we are doing."

Mother-Arjenadann rejoined the meeting and telepathically informed us that she had empathically scanned all of the inhabitants of Thada Argen. From the Dir-nays she picked up feelings of rage, hatred, and sadistic tendencies, confirming they have been Influenced, but the Eanois projected fear, confusion, some anger, but mostly terrified. It was exactly what she knew she would find. Arjenadann telepathically observed the relationship between the Dir-nays and the Priorts and Skarbs.

"Breaking the bond between the Priorts and the Skarbs may not be possible. The frequency the Dir-nays use is very precise, and each life-form responded to a different frequency."

"Arjenadann, you must keep trying. It may be the only way to keep us from having to annihilate the Priorts and Skarbs–two species that are vital to Thada Argen's ecosystem," Antonio replied.

"Acknowledged," was all she said.

"Fasbi, Mother-Arjenadann." The Elphah countered.

"We need to turn their attention away from the Colonists and toward us," Talon commented, flicking his forked tongue between his lips.

"He's right," Joryd concurred.

Studying the world map, the Elphah agreed and reminded us that the Dir-nays were as much a victim as the Eanois were, and made it clear that we were only to kill as a last resort. Joryd looked to Z'yenn, and informed her she had the Throne and was to remain aboard ship.

"I am not joining the ground forces?"

"Not this time."

"Why?"

"This will be an extremely deadly encounter. One of us is expendable, not both. Besides, you will be needed to oversee our last option should it become necessary. I'm counting on you, Tas'r."

"Yes Ra-Tuth, I understand," she said. Though disappointed, she did indeed understand. She faced the Juardian-Elphah. "U'kristu, you are personally responsible for the Elphah's safety," she said in front of everyone.

"Understood," she replied, bowing her head.

"Marc, you're to remain aboard Arjenadann as well. As a Betah, you're not yet trained enough to handle this kind of situation, and you do not yet speak Dir-nay. Besides, after Divergia, I believe you will best serve the Pride working with your brother Kileo in Ashanti. I hear you have an aptitude in this field."

"And I suppose everyone who is going, speaks Dir-nay?"

Answering me in the Pygmies' native language, I looked to him, confused. So he replied in Zahnobein, "Yes, and quite fluently, but this is not the issue. You are to assist your brother Kileo in readying the Star Prysm, and should it become necessary, you will help to fire the weapon. Am I clear?"

"Yes, Ra-Tuth," I said and bowed slightly.

Z'yenn hissed, "Are you sure this is wise?"

Joryd looked to Z'yenn, "He will be fine," and he turned to me. "As long as no one suddenly startles him. After all, we wouldn't want you firing out of fright–now would we?"

Joryd had seen me form the Gauntlet back in Throne Pryme when Kerebrol's Holo-Form scared the hell out of me. Torr looked to me, surprised, and I shrugged my shoulders.

"What part of Heshe scared the fa…," I let the word die before finishing it and darted a look to U'kristu, who was looking at me with a raised brow. "The blank out of me didn't you believe?"

U'kristu simply smirked.

"Meanwhile, the rest of us will tah the remaining settlements. Half the Pride will go to Argenta, while the others defend Dumaus. A skeleton Pack will remain aboard ship." The Elphah stated.

"I don't like this Joryd. What if he—"

That was all the Omegah said before the Elphah cut her a glare that silenced her quickly. Z'yenn had stepped over the line of tolerance, and knew once an Elphah had made their decision, all discussions on the subject were over. Joryd instructed the Ra-Tuths to ready their Packs and dismissed us.

Outside the Strategym, I waited for the Pantherus–I did not have long to wait. “Excuse me, Joryd. May I speak with you for a moment?”

He sent Z’yenn ahead and waited for me to approach, “This isn’t a good time, Marc. Can it wait?”

“I don’t believe so,” I said, stopping before him. “I don’t believe working with Kileo is such a good idea.”

“I understand your reluctances, my son, but what you did on Screel was the right move. And in doing so, you saved an entire civilization.”

“And killed thousands to make it happen.”

“I cannot get into this with you right now, but know I would not have posted you in Ashanti if I had any doubt you could do it. Now please report to Ashanti. Your brother is waiting.” Joryd turned to leave.

“Excuse me, Joryd.”

The Elphah turned about and roared loudly. “That was not a suggestion… Go!”

“Okay, okay, you don’t have to roar about it. Sheesh.”

Turning back around, he continued to walk away, while I headed to Engineering.

I arrived at Ashanti and found Starone staring at the giant Prysm, patiently waiting for me. I apologized for my tardiness and inquired about Kileo. He was not here, but I was told he would join us shortly. The Elemental showed me everything from the enormous crystal that drew and held energy in its applicator to working of the controls. He taught me everything that is except what it felt like to kill an entire world. This weapon was a planet killer, and I was assigned to help fire it should it become necessary.

The Marten life-form came hopping into Ashanti at that moment, and on his third leap, he landed beside Starone and me. Kileo told Starone that Sercrom was waiting.

“Take over. Our brother knows everything about CP-III up to the inversed phasing and the pulsar array. "Good luck to you both," the Elemental said, turned to vapor and exited through an air vent.

Picking up where Starone left off, Kileo continued with my education and taught me things Starone had not. "In the event the weapon is fired and we need to dissipate the discharge, the abort code must be entered by an authorized user either verbally or manually within fifteen et-nims, or else there will be no stopping the discharge. I doubt even Avedia or Meva's majik would be able to stop the beam."

We reached Thada Argen, and tensions were high. The Pride broke up into Packs led by their most experienced Ra-Tuths, and they all Hexagyned to the planet's surface. Joryd's Pack however, went to investigate a trio of Dir-nays they detected that were separated from their tribe and far away from the conflict.

Exiting the Portal, U'kristu made a brief survey and then called to the others. Antonio spotted a lone Pygmy child trying to evade a giant vulture-like creature. The young Dir-nay dove as the bird swooped down and missed. The Pygmy was now on his feet and running. The winged predator missed again, when the child tripped and fell. Circling back around, the creature was intent on catching its prey. The Deggzytepol touched his Kaja and hurled a shield between the Dir-nay and the giant vulture, and protected him.

"That Virggyte isn't finished yet," Battista said after the shield returned to him.

The red and brown alien vulture circled back around as Antonio knew it would. Starone raised an arm and prepared to fire, but Antonio stopped him.

"No, don't kill it," he said, lowering the Elemental's arm. He looked to the Elphah. "The Virggyte is not Influenced."

"Be careful, the Virggytes may not be Influenced, but the Dir-nay may."

He nodded to Joryd, and raced to help the Pygmy child.

Tackling the youngling, Antonio used his shield and deflected another attempt by the Virggyte. Battista rolled onto his back and morphed his Kaja into a Gauntlet. He fired shots around the Virggyte to discourage it, but he did not wish to harm it. Eventually it fled back to its nest.

Checking on the child's safety, the Deggzytepol introduced himself. Then he introduce the Elphah and the rest of his Pack as they joined them. The boy was named Wagg. He told them how two Virggytes had taken his parents to their nest, and he pointed to the high mountaintop. Joryd calmed him and promised to help.

"E'Dol, you and Antonio rescue the parents." The Ra-Tuth ordered.

The Netureal, the same species as Meva, was not much taller than she, and his fur was dark brown, not sandy blond like hers. He transformed himself into a giant winged creature, a scaly reptile with a rainbow of colorful feathered wings. The Human-Augment mounted him. Sitting on E'Dol's upper back, Antonio gripped the long neck spines tightly, and they took off with the Animorph flapping his beautiful colored wings. They approached the nest.

At the nest the captured Dir-nays struggled to keep the baby Virggytes from feeding on them while the parents watched. Before they could help their babies, the adult Virggytes caught the approach of E'Dol and Antonio and left to challenge them.

"E'Dol, can you handle the parents without killing them?"

He nodded his dragon-like head.

"Try to take it easy. They are only trying to feed their young. I'll get the Dir-nays."

Again, the Animorph nodded, and once the parents were in range, E'Dol exhaled a long, thick stream of plasma fire and forced the Virggytes to evade, cutting a path through and allowing them to pass. The parents circled around and raced after them.

"E'Dol, get near the nest, and I'll take it from here. I'll call for you when I'm ready."

He again nodded his head, and the Human-Augment stood up on his back and leapt off, dropping a 132 feet. Quickly morphing his Kaja into a metal winged suit, Antonio glided to the nest, but found he could not maintain it for long. The device went null, and he plummeted. Creating a grapple, Antonio fired a line into a stone outcropping and swung to the nest–he landed sure-footed and safe. Watching briefly as the Dir-nays fought to keep the young birds at bay, the Deggzytepol formed his Gauntlet and mentally reduced its setting to its lowest yield. Firing near and around the baby creatures, Battista deliberately missed in case the setting was still strong enough to harm them irreparably. Antonio strained to control his Kaja–he managed with difficulty.

Frightened, the young Virggytes retreated into their dwelling, and the Life Protector cautiously approached the Dir-nays. He still did not know if they were Influenced or not. However, once he was certain they were not infected with Wehtiko, Antonio relaxed. The parents at once began jabbering excitedly at him.

"Calm yourselves," he replied, speaking Dir-nay as he squatted to their level. "My name is Antonio Franco Battista, I am Qi-Tahh, and I'm here to help." He said with his thick Italian accent. "What are your names?"

Again, they chattered excitedly.

"Yes, your son, Wagg, is safe. He is with my Elphah and Juardian-Elphah."

"I am Nextus, and she is my mate, Pisana."

"Let's get you out of here."

Pointing to the sky and jabbering, the Deggzytepol turned and observed the Netureal battling the protective parents.

"Don't worry. E'Dol can handle them. Watch."

The Animorph, controlling the intensity of his plasma-breathing held the adult Virggytes back with a constant exhale, but when they began to move against his fire, he increased its strength and pushed them back.

In the nest, the young Virggytes' fear had started to subside, so Battista fired near the younglings and sent them ducking back into the security of their outcrop. Nextus climbed on Antonio's back, and Battista picked Pisana up in his arms and then called to E'Dol.

Ceasing his attack, the Animorph turned and flew to the nest. The stunned creatures shook off the effect of his assault and pursued him. Raising his arm, the Human-Augment awaited the Animorph's approach. Looking back, E'Dol blew a thick, smoky cloud out of his nose between him and the Virggytes. Facing forward, E'Dol swooped down and grabbed Antonio's forearm at the same time he grabbed his scaly ankle, and pulled the three of them from the nest.

Temporarily blinded by his diversionary tactic, the adult Virggytes struck the side of the nest, and though stunned, they were not seriously injured, however, nor were they able to continue their pursuit.

The Qi-Tahh and the Dir-nays returned to where the rest of their Pack and the boy waited. Dropping low to the ground, Antonio and the Pygmies landed safely, and both parents immediately raced to their child, expressing joy that they were all unharmed. Landing, E'Dol returned to his natural form, and joined them.

Nextus told Joryd and the Pack how things were before the Dir-nays changed and why he and his family were not infected with the others. Nextus, Pisana, and Wagg were travelling to the Glona Settlement to visit their friend Clara and her family, but Wagg's Priort became ill and forced them to rest until he was well enough to continue. It was late by time the Priort was able to travel, so they returned home and heard King Gutai's gloating over how he killed Clara.

"We saw what they did to the few that had not changed," Pisana said, dropping her head. She held her small hands over her mouth.

"I had no idea my people were capable of such heinous acts, so I took Pisana and Wagg, and we fled."

"Your people are not responsible for their actions. They've been Influenced with Wehtiko, a disease that brings forth one's darkest nature," Joryd explained.

"We were on our way to the Argenta Settlement to warn them, but we ran into those Virggytes," Pisana added. "They forced us down, and our Priorts took off."

At the Argenta Settlement, Avedia and her Pack arrived to a community under siege. A family of four running from a group of Priorts soon found themselves cornered. As the bats attacked, the man, woman, and two small children turned translucent, and the Priorts passed through them and smashed against the structure behind them. The frightened family looked around, confused as they reverted back to their solid forms.

The Mystik joined them, speaking Laimeguage, "Do not be frightened. My name is Avedia, and I am Qi-Tahh."

Though not every species knew of the Wehtiko, there were few who had not heard of the Supremacy. They exhaled, relieved, they managed to relax a little. Suddenly, one of the children screamed and pointed behind the Mystik. She quickly turned and saw a flock of Priorts heading for them. Facing them, Avedia muttered something the family did not understand, and the bats turned to hard clay and crashed into the ground, shattering on impact.

Avedia faced her Charges and said, "Stay close. I will not allow them to harm you."

Elsewhere inside the Argenta Settlement, the Skarbs cornered several Eanois and closed in to feed when the ground suddenly split open directly in front of them and swallowed most of the horde. The land then closed up again and looked as though it had never been disturbed. This did not deter the insects, and the remaining beetles continued to advance toward them. Meva levitated the Eanois up out of harm's way, and then she formed a ring of fire around the insects, uttered a couple of strange words, and closed the fiery circle, burning the Skarbs to death.

At the Dumaus Settlement, the Colonists were overrun by dozens of Dir-nays armed with clubs and spears, and though they tried fending them off, the enemy's numbers were too great. The alien Pygmies knew this and moved in for the kill. They raised their weapons to attack, and while some of the creatures prepared to hurl their spears, others decided to simply lunge.

Before they could act, Kaja-Dysks severed the heads of all the spears and turned them into sticks. Surprised, the Dir-nays turned and saw Syn'nar Sivgons standing there, now armed with her Gauntlet.

They attacked, but the Scorpilyn interceded, spun around and swatted them with his powerful tail. He knocked several to the floor. Reaching down, Talon grabbed two Pygmies by their throats, flicked his wrists, and broke their necks. He dropped their lifeless bodies and picked up another two by the back of their necks, and prepared to smash their heads together.

"Talon, kasauj!" Syn-nar shouted. "Brother, remember kill only when necessary. You are Qi-Tahh. Control your Scorpilyn nature."

Taking control of his cold-blooded nature was not easy for Talon, he was born of a savage race where killing and death was second nature. Though he still bumped the Dir-nays' heads together, he only knocked them out as opposed to shattering their skulls as he had intended. Tossing the Pygmies to either side of him, another group attacked, and the Juardian-Omegah spun around with his tail, and knocked one set of Pygmies into the others.

Picking themselves up off the floor, the uncontrollable rages forced the small-sized creatures to charge the Scorpilyn, who again spun about and dispersed them all with his powerful tail. He sent them back to the floor. Sivgons fired her Kaja-Gauntlet and plasma shocked them into retreating.

The Qi-Tahh had the Dir-nays on the retreat.

Outside, a commotion brought Syn'nar running. Watching her cousin, Torr nerve blocked one Dir-nay's shoulder, and paralyzed the hip and leg of another Pygmy. While one of them held his unmovable arm, the other dragged his leg.

Syn'nar faced her Mirrepo. "Torr, stop nerve blocking the Dir-nays, they're trying to retreat."

Two of the small creatures suddenly jumped Torr and knocked him to the ground, where he wrestled with them.

Again Syn'nar shouted, "Torr, stop playing with those Dir-nays– they had enough and we got work to do. Let them go." She said, and shot the creatures off him with a respectable level of plasma energy.

Back at the Argenta Settlement, overpowered, outmatched, and unprepared to battle the Pride, the Dir-nays retreated, and took their Priorts and Skarbs with them. Joryd and his Pack arrived with the Dir-nay family just as the last of the Influenced were leaving. The Pack were all stunned by the carnage the Pygmies left behind. Screaming and shouting as they flew off, the Dir-nays left the Settlement.

Avedia slithered over to the Elphah and his Pack. "We managed to turn the invaders away, and according to the Packs at the Dumaus Settlement, they were able to fend off the Dir-nays' attacks as well."

"That may be, but as a precaution, I want the Pride to remain on guard until further notice," U'kristu said, adding herself to the conversation. "I will inform Talon and Syn'nar as well. They are at the Dumaus Settlement."

"And what of the Colonists here?" Joryd inquired.

"Unfortunately, we were unable to save them all, and most of those still alive are in need of medical treatment."

Joryd looked to Nahni, the Arjai-Omegah, who had already assembled her medical Packs and were busy helping the Eanois. The Elphah, Mystik, and Juardian-Elphah surveyed the area, while others searched for survivors. Joryd had Saffron and Nyrit, two Xentous, go to the Coyoust Valley to keep tabs on the Pygmies.

Although they managed to save most of the Eanois at both settlements, the Elphah was still not happy, even though the Eanois considered this a victory.

"Thank you," a bald black man offered. He had his son at his side, a young black boy with short curly hair. They approached Joryd and his Pack. "Thank you."

"You are welcome, I am sorry we could not have arrived sooner to prevent this," Joryd said, offering them his condolences.

"We are grateful for those of us you were able to save. My name is Lucan. This is my son, Sorn. Welcome to what is left of Argenta."

"I am Joryd Kenton, Elphah of the Zahnobein Qi-Tahh. Where is Matsu? I thought he was—"

"Matsu was one the first killed," Lucan said, dropping his head. "He died protecting some children from the Skarbs." Sniffing, he wiped his eyes of tears.

Antonio and the Dir-nay family stepped forward, initiating a wave of hostility from the Eanois. Lucan shouted and drew others to him. The Colonists picked up stones, clubs, and whatever else they could use as weapons and approached the Pygmies.

"Kill the traitors. Kill them all," Lucan shouted.

"No, stop," the Elphah shouted, but the mob kept coming.

E'Dol and Antonio stood in front, guarding the innocent creatures, as the Pantherus roared loudly. U'kristu stood before Joryd protectively. She formed her Gauntlet and aimed her hand at the crowd. The Elphah roared again even louder, and halted the rest of the approaching mob.

"I said stop!"

"Come no closer," U'kristu warned.

"They're Dir-nays," the bald black man shouted.

"They murdered my father," a woman screamed. She picked up a rock and threw it.

With telekinesis, Antonio stopped the projectile just inches from striking Pisana. Then he moved it off to the side and exploded it. Normally, this was an easy feat, but now he felt the strain from his action, it left him feeling weak, and he nearly failed to stop the stone altogether. Another Eanoi threw a rock, and one threw a Dir-nay's spear. Avedia waved her hand, and they vanished in mid-air.

"They're Dir-nays. Why are you protecting them?" a heavyset man asked.

"They're responsible for killing our people. Kill them," another woman shouted.

"No, they are not. They haven't been Influenced by the Wehtiko and are not as the others are," Battista shouted back.

"Please. I will explain everything later, but first, we need to treat the injured and secure your Settlement," Joryd said, trying to defuse the situation.

The angry Colonists ceased and listened. The Ra-Tuth looked to the Dir-nay family, and speaking their language, he told them that neither he nor his Pride would allow them to be harmed. Joining them, Nahni gave her report, and it was not good, but reminded the Elphah it could have been worse–much worse. Noticing the Dir-nays' injuries, the Arjai-Omegah offered to treat them and escorted them to her makeshift hospital. Antonio followed to protect them while the dispersing crowed glared at them with hate and fear.

"That was close. For a hotress, I thought we would have to fight the Eanois to tah the Dir-nays."

"The Eanois are scared, U'kristu."

"C'an you bl-ame 'em?" E'Dol asked.

"No, no, I can't," Joryd replied.

"At le'ast for th' mom'ent it is o'ver," E'Dol commented.

"Over?" Joryd said, surprised. "This is just beginning."

Blindsided

VII

By evening all of the Eanois were transported to the Denizen Settlement, the new Elphah Site which the Ra-Tuth believed would most likely be the Dir-nays' next target. Accommodations were cramped, tensions were high, and patience were thin, but the compound was secured and protected by the Pride. Joryd gathered the Colonists together, many of which were scared to death about what would happen next, and with good reasons. The Argentas and the Dumaus heard that this community would undoubtedly be attacked next, and that did not sit well with most. Nor did they understand why the Qi-Tahh had brought them to Denizen. Fear and apprehension spread quickly, and though some were ready to retaliate against the Dir-nays, most still were confused about their former Pygmy friends, and why after fifty years had they turned on them.

"Why are they killing us? And why were our so-called saviors now protecting the very people killing us?

"Firstly, the Dir-nay family you've been eyeing with hatred, resentment, fear, and discontent were never Influenced. There is no blood on their hands." Joryd looked to the Eanois. "Secondly, there is strength in numbers. Prides are strong because we fight as one, and we will be able to protect you more efficiently if you are together."

The Elphah went on to explain that the Dir-nays were infected with a disease and were not responsible for their actions. They themselves were victims of this affliction.

"Disease?" a healthy woman said. "I have two children, should I be worried?"

"What kind of disease? Are we all going to go mad like the Dir-nay?" a boy asked.

Joryd attempted to make them understand that the Wehtiko was unlike any pathogen they ever heard of, and the likelihood of them contracting it was slim to none since it had not already happened. This explanation settled their minds, and they believed what they had been told. With their fears addressed, their anger quickly rose to the surface. The Colonists demanded the Qi-Tahh ousted the Dir-nay family and send them back to their people.

"No," Antonio said, stepping forward and standing beside Joryd.

"They will either become Influenced, or the others will kill them as outsiders."

"So what? That would be three less of them to deal with," an old man shouted.

"Have you always been such a closed-minded fool, or is it your senility acting up?" Battista asked, upset. Our Elphah just told you that the Dir-nays were victims, did he not?"

"We will do all that is within our power to keep you all safe, but you must follow our instructions without question. We have dealt with the Wehtiko before. There are two medical Prides on their way. They will arrive in less than three days to inoculate the Dir-nays. Until then our assignment is to protect all of you and keep the Pygmies at bay." Joryd stared at the crowds of Eanois. "Now…let me be equally clear. So long as they Dir-nay family remain uninfected, they are under my personal protection. Anyone—" he said and scanned the Colonists. "And I mean anyone who tries to harm them will regret it. Am I clear?"

Mumbles and slight head bobbing followed, but no one in the crowd gave any real verbal affirmations, so the Pantherus roared loudly, startling some. Then he let out another fearsome roar and scared others. "I repeat–am I clear?" And again he looked out over the crowd, awaiting an answer.

At once, they all verbalized their acknowledgment.

"Good. Make certain you do." Then he waited for them to settle down.

Joryd sympathized with the Eanois. He understood their fears and apologized for their circumstance, and even offered them his condolences on their loss. A middle-aged man shouted out that the Dir-nay had killed his kid brother, who was no more than twenty years old, and questioned the Life Protectors' allegiance.

Antonio explained that the Wehtiko was an insidious strain and that for whatever reason, it did not affect all who were exposed. It was neither viral nor organism-based; however, once Influenced, the victims would be forced into unleashing their darkest nature.

"Yes, the Dir-nays in their present state are monsters." Antonio's voice softened as he continued, “But they are also your friends and tradesmen, and they need your help. They may be monsters now, but they do not want to be monsters.”

A short, heavyset woman shouted, “So why not kill those Wehtiko people?”

Joryd looked to Antonio, who dropped his head and exhaled with frustration.

“Are you sure these Eanois aren’t descendants from my home planet?” Battista asked.

“I’m hoping it’s just something in the water,” Torr said, stepping forward and joining the conversation. “I’ll run tests on it later and check back with you.”

Looking out to the crowds, the Ra-Tuth was losing patience with their closed-mindedness, and he replied through gritted teeth, “The Influenced are victims. Do not make me repeat myself on this issue again.”

“How long does the treatment take to reverse the infection?” a young man asked.

“The reversal is almost immediate,” Torr replied. When the Pride healers arrive, they will inoculate the Dir-nays as well as all of you.”

The Eanois were mystified as to why they had to be inoculated too. They were not infected. Why could they not receive a preventative injection. The Arjai Ra-tuth explained that because of the nature of this particular strain, only the worlds that were Influenced could be inoculated. The Eanois questioned why they could not be transported to the Qi-Tahh ship until the Dir-nays could be treated.

“It is against medical protocol, and we cannot risk possible infection. Though it is highly unlikely that you Colonists are carriers. But as a precaution–”

“Torr, stop talking,” Antonio suggested, looking at the growing confusion on the Eanois’ faces.

An elderly woman spoke, “But aren’t you and your Pride already inoculated?”

“Yes,” the Fonchuai concurred.

Joryd interjected, “I see where this is about to go, and I will say this only once. We are not going to transport any of you to our ship, and that is final." The Elphah gazed at the crowd, and though many showed that they were upset about his decision, no one challenged his ruling. "Now I suggest all of you ready yourselves for meal and sleep. You are safe. My Pride will see that no uninvited guests enter the Settlement."

A middle-aged woman asked, "How will you ensure it?"

"We have it covered," U'kristu added.

With that said, the gathering slowly dispersed.

Later that evening at the lodgings where Antonio and others slept, the female Dir-nay, Pisana, entered and approached the Acquil-Omegah. Startled, Battista awoke in a defensive posture–armed with a Gauntlet, and disarmed once he saw it was Wagg's mother.

"I am sorry to disturb you," she said, bowing her head. "But Nexus and I are having trouble getting Wagg to sleep. Would you help?

"Why me?"

"I noticed how taken Wagg was with you earlier," she softly chattered.

"Saving someone's life will have that effect."

Battista agreed, quickly dressed, and they left the guarded house together.

Antonio and Pisana entered the lodgings, and watched as the father, Nextus, tried to coax the child to sleep, but he was not getting anywhere. Antonio and Pisana approached. Smiling, the Deggzytepol greeted the father and sat beside Wagg. The parents stepped back while he spoke with the child in their native tongue.

"Hey, my little opo, what's going on? It's late. How come you're not asleep?"

"I am afraid and cannot sleep."

"Afraid…of what?"

"Everyone hate us. The Eanois…they want to hurt us because we are not like them. Our people want to hurt us because we are not like them. And those creatures want to hurt us."

"Wow. That is a lot for one so young to think about. What are you–six?"

"I'm seven," he blurted out, correcting him.

"Seven, huh? Well Wagg, you're still too young to have so much on your mind. But do not be afraid, I will not let anyone harm you or your parents."

"Promise?" he asked, wide-eyed.

"Promise," Antonio replied, grinning. "Now…in you go." Battista pulled back the covers.

Wagg slipped down, resting his small furry body on the mattress as the Augment pulled the blankets up and covered all but his head. He wished him a good night's sleep, and started to get up to leave when the child sprung back up and begged for him not to go. Wagg's parents step forward, and Nextus told the child that it was late and Antonio had to leave. Wagg protested. Pisana tried to explain that Battista needed his rest, but the Pygmy child was not hearing it. He did not care and was beginning to get more and more upset.

"Hold on. I have an idea," Antonio interjected as he activated his Holo-Com.

A moment later the image of a tired Pantherus appeared as a holographic image to Antonio and inquired about the reason for the call. Battista briefly explained the small situation he had at the Dirnays' lodging. Assuming the worst, Joryd asked if more Juardians were needed, and Antonio informed him that it was not that kind of problem. He needed to stay with the family tonight, but there was no need to panic. The pseudo image of the huge cat granted him permission and then sleepily signed off.

"I can stay the night, but only if it is all right with your parents."

Excited, the child asked, "You will?" and then he looked to Nextus and Pisana. "Oh, please can he stay?"

His father glanced to the boy's mother. "All right, but you have to go to sleep."

"I will. I promise," Wagg said, plopping into the mattress. "Antonio, you sleep next to my bed," he said gleefully.

"I will get you some covers," Pisana offered. "Thank you."

Antonio helped Nextus move a twin-size divan over to where Wagg had his bed, and the Dir-nay father thanked him for his help. Returning with the blankets, both parents again thanked him as he readied his bed. Smiling, he let them know that he was happy to help. Wagg hopped out of bed and assisted them. When finished, the tired Augment tucked the child in again, and Nextus and Pisana wish them both a restful sleep before they retreated to their bedroom. Before long Wagg and Antonio were slumbering deeply.

The next morning Wagg sat beside Antonio, enjoying their meal, as the two laughed and joked. Afterward, the Ra-Tuth gathered the Pride and Eanois together and informed them of his plans. The Qi-Tahh were to install pseudo imagers, holographic projectors that would show the Eanois as they were during a normal night and day, while we transported the Colonists to another community where they would be safe. The Dir-nay family would remain close to the Life Protectors since some Eanois still meant them harm. Nextus and Pisana agreed.

Though everyone was busy, Antonio took time out to teach Wagg some basic martial arts techniques. Educating him in how to stand, balance, move, and fall, the two had quickly grown close in the short time they have been together.

Watching them, Joryd understood Battista's connection to the youngster. Antonio had a little brother he left back in Sicily, one he loved very much. Now it seemed he had adopted another little brother. The big cat grinned before he continued overseeing the project.

Later, Antonio and Wagg approached Joryd. The child had told the Deggzytepol about some of their plants that had powerful medicinal properties that could be beneficial to the Pride against the Pygmies. Battista requested permission to investigate.

"Are his parents aware of the excursion both of you wish to take?"

"Yes, Elphah," the child replied. "And they will say yes if you do. Please?" Wagg asked, drawing out the word, 'please.'

Chuckling, Joryd replied, "All right, you have my permission, but be careful and stay vigilant. The planet might harbor dangers other than the Dir-nays and their controlled life-forms. Know your limits."

Joryd and Antonio exchanged looks, and with a sharp nod from Battista, he agreed.

"Don't worry, Elphah. Antonio's with me," Wagg said proudly, and looked up at them. "I'll keep him safe. I promise."

They smiled, amused by Wagg's enthusiasm. Antonio rested a hand on the small creature's shoulder, and they left. U'kristu arrived and inquired if it was wise for them to leave the Settlement. Joryd assured her that Antonio could handle himself. As for the child, he was safe with him. With that said, the two continued overseeing the operation.

Later a good distance away, Antonio and Wagg arrived at the forest the child spoke of, and the Deggzytepol examined the floral and thanked the little Pygmy.

"Those plants are poisonous to the Eanois, but these plants here." The seven-year-old showed him and said, "Taste peppery, try some." Wagg handed Antonio a small piece.

Battista sampled a bit. "You're right, it is peppery," and coughed. "Maybe a little too much." He coughed again.

"Why do you call everyone in your Pride your brother or sister?"

"Because they are. This is part of what a Pride is. We're family."

"Do you like everyone in your family?" asked Wagg.

"No, but that doesn't mean I would not lay down my life to save theirs. They are family, and like blood relatives, we do not get to choose who's in our family."

"Wow, we do not have families such as your Pride. We only have the family we are born to."

Antonio stopped walking. "And did you have a say in who your family was to be?"

The adorable expression on the young Pygmy's face as he thought about what to say, and about what they have been discussing made Antonio smiled and fought his urge to laugh.

"No," Wagg finally replied, shaking his head, and looked up at him. "You are so lucky."

Wrapping his small arms around Antonio's legs, the Deggzytepol broke his grasp and picked him up. Tickling him, he threw Wagg up in the air and caught him as he came down. Again, he threw him up higher and higher with each throw and caught his laughing body. Throwing Wagg up in the air again, the Human-Augment suddenly felt dizzy and weak, and he nearly dropped the Dir-nay when he caught him on the last toss. Not noticing, the child joyously laughed, but Antonio told him that was enough for now and that they needed to get back. Battista turned to walk when Wagg grabbed his arm.

"Stop," he said, still pulling on his arm.

"Why? What is it?"

"That large patch of earth is not solid. It is a sinking hole."

"A sinking hole? A sinkhole?" Antonio asked surprised.

Wagg nodded and led them around it.

Suddenly ambushed, a group of Pygmies attacked, and while two wrestled with Wagg, trying to secure him, the others jump Antonio. Knocking two of them unconscious, the Deggzytepol flipped a third into the sinkhole and nearly fell in himself. However, when four of them rushed him as a group, they pushed Battista in. Trying not to struggle for fear of sinking faster, the Qi-Tahh spotted his Kaja lying on solid ground just out of his current mental reach, and he could not bring the device to him.

Wagg, who also saw his weapon, was powerless to help, as he was held by adult Dir-nays and could only watch as Antonio sunk deeper. The Pygmies laughed as Battista slipped into the earthy abyss, while Wagg continued struggling against their hold. Remembering what Antonio had taught him, the boy elbowed one adult in the stomach, back fisted him in the face, and broke his nose. He used his palm to strike the other Dir-nay in the face before he could react, and then Wagg grabbed him, stepped back, and flipped him into a third assailant. The fourth Dir-nay raced to apprehend him, but the boy slid between his legs, grabbed the Kaja, and threw it to Antonio just as he went completely under. Recapturing him, the Pygmies secured Wagg more firmly and watched for signs of life from Battista.

The Dir-nay child screamed for Antonio, and watched–as did the others, but there was no sign of the Augment. Another moment passed and then another–and then one after that. Convinced he was dead, Wagg began crying while the others started laughing.

Suddenly, a grapple shot from the sinkhole, penetrated one of the tall trees and pulled the Deggzytepol out of the deadly pit. Steadying himself on one of the thick branches, he shook sand from his hair, and morphing his Kaja into a Gauntlet, he fired four energy pulses, and plasma shocked the Dir-nays into unconsciousness. He again willed the device to become a grapple and swung down, landing next to Wagg, who wrapped his small arms around Antonio's leg.

"Thank you, Wagg. Your quick thinking saved my life."

"I thought I lost you."

"Never."

"I love you, Antonio."

Uncoiling his grip, the boy stood in front of Battista, who knelt down, wiped away Wagg's tears, and hugged him. "I love too you, Wagg." He broke their embrace. "Let's head back, and let's keep this little incident to ourselves. Deal?"

Wagg looked to him and smiled. "Deal."

The day had come and gone, and night was in full bloom, but there was no signs of trouble. With early morning approaching fast, the Xentous still had not reported any Dir-nays leaving the Valley. Avedia checked in with Nyrit and Saffron, and no sooner than Nyrit finished his mind-link with Avedia, he discovered the Pygmies were gone. What they thought were the Dir-nays at their encampment was only their psychic residue.

Aboard Arjenadann in their Habitat, Z'yenn spoke privately with Joryd in Holo-Form. She argued with him to transport the Pride back to the ship, along with the Eanois, whom they could place in stasis until we remedied the situation. The Elphah refused and would not surrender the planet. He reminded the Omegah that placing the Eanois in stasis might not defuse the situation, and the threat of critical mass could still exist. Joryd ordered Z'yenn to make the final preparations to implement Containment Protocol III, which might now be necessary.

"When the deadline hits, regardless of any personal feelings, you must follow through–our galaxy, possibly the entire universe depends on it.

"You can count on me–Suncol."

"Do not look so grim, I will see you again–my Defona.

Z'yenn closed communications and left her and Joryd's Habitat.

Back on Thada Argen, Joryd received an urgent message from the Rydia Settlement, who were given a communications device, were under attack. The Elphah ordered Avedia, Meva, and E'Dol to transport as many Pridesmen as possible to the Rydia Settlement. He would gather the others and Hexagyn over ASAP.

Within moments, the Mystik, Wisard, and her apprentice arrived at the Rydia Settlement with twenty-three Pridesmen–their transport limit. The compound was in chaos. Houses and buildings burned brightly, engulfed in flames set by the Dir-nays, while Eanoi bodies littered the ground. Several dead Pygmies were discovered among them, but their numbers were insignificant compared to the lives the Influenced had stolen and the misery they had caused.

"Spread out, and stay in teams of two. Meva, you, Torr, Syn'nar, and E'Dol search for survivors, but be careful," warned Avedia who looked at their surroundings.

The Wisard and her apprentice suddenly vanished, leaving those they brought with them, as they all scrambled to find any Eanois still alive.

"Starone, the scent of the Wehtiko in these Dir-nays smell different than other Influenced species I have detected. I cannot explain it. She looked to the Elemental. "Stay here with me and assist in putting out those fires."

The Elemental moved closer to the houses "Cyrivedian V should do the trick. The foam works fast and will smother those flames in no time." He transformed his body into foam and prepared to extinguish the fires.

The Mystik heard what sounded like a child's cough, and slithered toward the burning community barn. She stopped and swiftly turned and looked to the houses.

"Avedia, not too close. This chemical foam is lethal." Warned Starone.

The Mystik closed her eyes, and her pendant turned green. It glowed as she opened her eyeless lids and saw a group of small children trapped in one of the houses with unconscious adults in another house, and there were animals in barns, some injured others dead, killed by the Dir-nay out of spite.

"Starone, no. There are people inside."

About to discharge, the Elemental ceased and spun around. "What?" he said, surprised. "Where?" he demanded to know.

Avedia's eyes and pendant returned to normal, and she pointed out where the Eanois were. "There are three adults overcome by smoke in that house, and the children are in that one. I will get the children. Whoever finishes first will save the animals in the barn."

Starone turned to stone and raced through the fire, as his body absorbed the heat all around him. Running inside, the Elemental found the adults, soaked them with water, and encased them in carbon dioxide while he extinguished the flames and led them out.

Inside another house, Avedia used her mystikism to locate the children and wrapped them in a protection spell. Levitating them through the fire, unharmed, she deposited them safely away from the flames. Speaking words of her mystik order, she extinguished the fires.

The fires were out, and the people safe, but they were too late to save the animals. Avedia told the people to go to the house with the least damage where they would be safe. The young children held onto the adults' legs, shaking their heads, frightfully refusing. She tried to convince them that her spell would protect them, and still they refused.

A Hexagyn opened and out stepped U'kristu palming her Kaja. She briefly surveyed the area, and then signaled for the others to follow. Joryd lead the Pack as they exited the Portal, and Avedia slithered to him quickly, and explained their progress. The Elphah dispatched most of the Pack on a search-and-rescue mission, while he managed to convince the Eanois to retreat to an undamaged house.

Before Avedia could cast her spell of protection, an energy sphere appeared suddenly, enveloped her and vanished. Another ball appeared, and U'kristu morphed her Kaja into a Gauntlet and stood in front of Joryd and fired. The energy ball continued toward them and she fired twice more before raising the yield and changing to rapid fire. U'kristu blasted the sphere. Unaffected by the energy beams, the ball enveloped both her and Joryd and they too vanished.

High above Rydia, Laisere, pursued by a flock of Priorts, tried as he may, could not evade them. He flew up and looped, spiraled down and swayed back up, but they stayed with him. The Velfin drew his Kaja and flung his Dysk, but the bats separated their forces and avoided the weapon. Boomeranging back around, the Dysk sheared off a wing of two bats and sent them crashing into the ground. The Dysk returned to Laisere, who morphed the device into a Gauntlet and fired. Most of the Priorts avoided the blasts and still they continued their pursuit.

Down below, Laisere spotted Talon barely staying ahead of a horde of Skarbs that were beginning to close in on him fast. He was unable to help. The Scorpilyn took a wrong turn and was now cornered. The reptilian drew his Kaja-Gauntlet and commenced rapidly firing. Unfortunately, this did not make any significant difference, and the beetles continued their march toward him.

Spotting a nearby water tower, Laisere raced toward it and fired two shots. He destroyed the front support legs, and toppled the tower. As the drum hit the ground, it split wide open and unleashed thousands of gallons of water with the force of a river that overtook the Skarbs and washed them pass Talon, who had hopped up onto a small rock formation just moments before the insects were swept away.

Still chased by the Priorts, the bats were now starting to close in on the Velfin when they suddenly stopped. Looking back, he noticed the winged rodents were no longer gaining on him, in fact, they turned around and fled. Laisere faced forward, and ran into an energy ball that appeared directly in his path. Unable to evade the sphere, he flew inside and vanished.

At the heart of the Rydia Settlement, several Eanois fled to a store, slammed the door shut, and tried to barricade themselves inside, while outside a group of Pygmies armed with spears and torches battered the door to gain entry. Unable to do so, they decided to burn the Eanois out and began setting the building on fire. However, before the flames could blaze, a solvent put them out along with the creatures' torches. Turning about, the Dir-nays saw the Elemental's arm returning to normal. They hurled their spears at him, and his hand turned to fire, and Starone reduced them to ash. He raised his other hand and hosed the attacking bats with liquid oxygen and froze them solid. Their icy figures broke and shattered, and the Pygmies retreated. Starone spotted some Skarbs racing toward the same store, and sprayed them with a chemical mist designed to discourage them. When it failed, he changed his composition, but was enveloped by an energy ball and disappeared.

On Ship-Arjenadann, in Ashanti, the engineer section, the Star Prysm pulsated with power. The yellow substance contained within the red crystal was pure power. Kileo finished my education on the intricate workings of the deadly device, and I now knew all there was to know about the Star Prysm.

"This is wrong, Kileo. It is our duty to find another way. We are Life Protectors. Our responsibility is about saving lives, not taking them."

He argued, "True, and because we are Qi-Tahh, we kill only when we must. None of our Pride want to do this. It comes down to simple hardcore logic. The planet's survival or the galaxy's."

Kileo was dedicated to following orders, and nothing I said was going to deter him from his duty, so I changed the subject and ended up doing something that set off an alarm. My brother quickly corrected my minor error and taught me what I had done wrong. I apologized. Handing me a checklist, we followed procedures and ensured all was done correctly. Calling out each step in the order they were listed, I checked them off after he confirmed them. The Prysm was ready for firing.

The Omegah arrived in Ashanti still sporting a grim look. We bowed as she approached and gave her the proper respect.

"Kileo, you and Marc jamonaka make the final preparations to fire the weapon. Charge it to full power and stand by."

"Yes, Z'yenn," Kileo replied.

"Are we really going to kill a planet full of people?" I asked.

"If we have to."

"Damn Z'yenn, that's cold. Are you really that callous about taking lives? I can't believe you're fine with killing our Pride along with every other living creature on Thada Argen."

Z'yenn fired back, "Listen. I don't like this. I don't like this any more than you do, but we have our orders."

"Then let's find another way."

"I don't have the time or the desire to debate or entertain a fabricated split-second decision scenario with you, Hawkins. So I will say this just once. Listen and listen well. If the Dir-nays succeed in this insurrection, the Wehtiko within them will reach critical mass and the Influence will spread beyond this planet, becoming a full-blown contagion that will one niya envelop the Universe. To stop that from happening, I will destroy everyone on the planet."

"Our Pride included, even though the possibility of them contracting the disease is negligible?"

"Those are Council orders, and every one of our Pridesmen know it. If we do not follow through, billions of people will be Influenced, and hundreds of billions could die. Neither is acceptable, and this discussion is over. Assist your brother in readying the weapon, or I will reassign you and post someone else."

"That will not be necessary. This is my post, Tas'r... and my responsibility."

She looked to Kileo. "Notify me when ready."

Bowing to her authority, she glared at me and turned to leave when a ball of energy appeared and moved toward her.

"Z'yenn, behind you," I shouted, moving as quickly as possible.

Reaching her just barely ahead of the sphere, it overtook us before I could push the Omegah out of harm's way, and we and the ball vanished.

On Thada Argen in other parts of the Rydia Settlement, many of the Pride were unaware of what was happening to their family members as they fought to save the Eanois. Trailing behind a horde of Skarbs, Dir-nays chased after the Colonists.

Displacing themselves, Meva and E'Dol appeared between the Eanois and the threat pursuing them. Transforming herself into a giant alien wasp, the Animorph, about to act was suddenly enveloped by an energy sphere and whisked, leaving E'Dol alone to cope with the Skarbs and Pygmies.

In another part of the compound, Antonio used the little majik he knew to dismount the furry riders and slam their Priorts into trees and structures. Physically trying to remove one of the community center's porch support beams, Battista tugged on it, and by the third yank, it finally gave way. He strained to hurl the beam at another wave of Dir-nay Priort riders. Taking out three of them, he had to evade their bats. Antonio felt his reduction in strength, and felt winded and fatigued–he was slow to get up. The Priorts turned about and charged him. Syn'nar arrived, killing the charging bats, she drove the other Priorts and Dir-nays off.

King Gutai, who had been observing the battle, signaled for his forces to withdraw, and just as suddenly as they appeared, the threat vanished. But the aftermath of the engagement remained.

"Antonio," Syn'nar said, helping him up. "Brother, are you all right?"

"I'm fine, this planet is really messing with my augmentations," Antonio replied raising the protection yield on his L.S.D. "This is the second time I've had to increase my forcefield. Torr was wrong… the decrease of my augmentations are much greater. At least 84%, another 16% and I'll be a normal human." Antonio turned about and suddenly saw a look of puzzlement and worry on his sister's face. "What is it, sister?"

"My mirrepo," she remarked, confused.

"Your cousin—what about Torr?"

"He's gone. Some sort of energy sphere enveloped him, and he disappeared."

"What?" Antonio retorted, surprised.

As the Qi-Tahh regrouped, they discovered that many of the Colonists were badly hurt. Some required surgery, and then there were those who were dead. The suffering seemed to never end for these people. Nahni and her Arjai Packs scrambled to help those they could.

The Deggzytepol was flooded with a mix of anger and sorrow, as he stared at what was left of the Rydia Settlement. We had underestimated the Dir-nay King, and it cost the Eanois dearly. Talon and E'Dol joined Antonio and Syn'nar to report Laisere and Meva's abduction. Battista called to notify Z'yenn of the situation, but Sclee told him that both she and I not long ago were taken as well.

The Acquil-Omegah took charge. "None of the Eanois are to know about this," he said softly.

"What about the ones present when Joryd and U'kristu were taken?"

"There were Eanois around us all. How could we possibly conceal what I count to be nine missing Pridesmen, including our Elphah?" The Juardian-Omegah added.

Antonio looked to the others and then closed his eyes, *"Arjenadann, we've been blindsided. Request mind-link. We need your help,"* he said telepathically.

"I am sorry, Antonio. Blindsided? I do not understand."

"It's a human expression. I'll explain later. For now I need you to mind-sweep our area. Joryd and eight of our brothers and sisters have been abducted. We do not know why or by whom."

"At once," she replied telepathically.

"But first, I need you to Bedazz the Eanois. They must not know about what has happened to the others. Not until we do."

"I understand. I will take care of it and inform you once done."

"Fasbi, Mother."

"Wurz kuyo, son."

Antonio opened his eyes and felt dizzy. The effort required to mind-link left him greatly drained. He stumbled and Talon caught him. "Fasbi brother, I'm all right."

"Are you sure? Maybe you should return to Arjenadann?"

"You know as well as I do, Talon, that is not an option. I'm fine." Battista said ending the conversation.

"What about the Dir-nays? Some of them had to witness our family's abduction."

"Syn'nar is right," Talon said, validating his Echelon Juardian.

"Then we'll deal with it. For now, get the survivors to the Denizen Settlement and contact the other compounds–I want a progress report." Antonio looked to Talon. "It's doubtful the Dir-nays will return again tonight, but I want everyone at our Elphah site to maintain an Elphah Black Alert status. And until Joryd and Z'yenn are found, I am Elphah. Talon, I'm making you Juardian-Elphah. You are now in charge of security. Select your new Juardian-Omegah.

"I choose Syn'nar… Now, what of our family?"

"Easy, brother. I am just as worried about them as you are. Unfortunately, this inoculation assignment takes precedence," Antonio said and touched Talon's back. "As soon as we're finished here, we'll find out what happened to Joryd and the others… I promise."

"Transport all supplies to our Elphah site, and I want a casualty report and an explanation as to how this happened…and I want it now," Antonio said, shouting his orders.

The Rydia Colonists were relocated back to the Denizen Settlement, where Syn'nar had doubled the Juardians posted for the Dir-nay family after this latest attack.

"We will see to it, Ra-Tuth," Talon replied, glancing to Syn'nar, his forked tongue darting out between his parted lips. "Until further notice, you are my Juardian-Omegah, and the Elphah is your Charge."

Both Juardians faced Antonio and bowed. Talon left and Syn'nar remained.

"In the meantime, let me arjai you," Nahni suggested. "C'mon, Antonio," she said coaxing him.

Sadden by recent events, Battista asked his Juardian bodyguard, "What have we done?"

"The best we could of course." Sivgons stated proudly.

"It does not feel that way."

"If you want answers–you're the Elphah–get them." Nahni said adding herself to the conversation.

Antonio looked to her and smiled. He instructed E'Dol and V'Hil, two Animorph to infiltrate the Dir-nays' encampment and discover how they eluded them. Feeling weak, Battista sat down. Nyrit and Saffron were still at the Coyoust Valley, and would expect them.

He told them all to exercise extreme caution and report back when they have the answers he seeked. The two apprentice Wisards teleported themselves to where the two Xentous waited.

After they left, Arjenadann mind-linked with Antonio and reported there was no information on the abducted Pridesmen, but that she had completed Bedazzing the Eanois, and just prior to a mob of angry Colonists approaching. Syn'nar stepped forward, her hand poised to touch her Kaja.

"You're supposed to be helping us," a man shouted.

"Please stop and come no closer," the Juardian-Omegah warned touching her Kaja and morphing it into a Gauntlet. Syn-nar aimed at the crowd.

The Colonists stopped for a moment and then continued.

"They're killing us, and you're doing nothing to stop them," a woman screamed.

"We are doing the best that we can," Battista replied.

"The best that you can?" she said, repeating the words as though it were a joke.

"Tell that to my dead baby girl, Life Protector," another woman shouted, clutching her remaining child.

The Eanois were soon clustering around them, and Sivgons activated her com.

"Talon, out front–we've got a situation."

"On my way."

"How did they know which Settlement to attack?" An elderly man asked.

"We don't know, we're investigating what happened," the acting Elphah replied.

"Where's your Elphah? Why isn't he talking with us?" a Latin-looking man asked.

"And where's that fish woman?" a heavyset Indian-looking man inquired.

"And that stone man?" a young girl asked.

"They are working elsewhere. My name is Antonio Franco Battista, and I am the Elphah of this Pride… Talk to me."

"Why not ask the Dir-nays that you've been protecting?"

"The family had nothing to do with this," Antonio shouted back.

"That's what you say, but ever since your arrival, many of us have died."

The crowd started to close in around them, and though Syn'nar warned them, they continued their approach. Suddenly, the loud angry roar from the Scorpilyn scared the Eanois into stopping.

"Keep away from my family," he yelled, and walked toward them fast aiming his Gauntlet.

"Please. We will stop the Dir-nays. They will be treated, and peace between you and them will return."

Lucan ignored Antonio and spoke to his people. "I don't know about the rest of you, but I don't feel safe with them here, do you?"

The crowd was starting to become rowdy and unruly again, and despite what any of his Pridesmen attempted to say, the Eanois just frustratingly walked away from them. Deep down, the Life Protectors could not blame them, for they too, felt as though they had failed them.

Before long the Juardians protecting the Dir-nay family soon found themselves facing the same an angry mob. The Eanois wanted the Pygmies, and were hell-bent on killing them regardless of what the Qi-Tahh said. Carrying torches, clubs, pitchforks, and whatever else they could find, Lucan and the Colonists approached, forcing the Life Protectors into taking a defensive posture. The Juardians aimed their Gauntlets at the Eanois.

Syn'nar ordered Lucan and the other Eanois to stand down, informing them that if they did not comply, they would be shot. Screaming and shouting, the Colonists continued their approach, but suddenly, stopped when they heard the loud thundering angry roar of the Scorpilyn walking toward them hostilely.

The Elphah, though he was still feeling weak, ran ahead of Talon and the mob and stood between the Eanois and Dir-nays' house. Lucan, holding a club demanded Battista and his Pride turn the family over to them and they moved toward the house. Joining his family, the Scorpilyn fought hard against the impulse to injure the Eanois as he moved through the crowd unobstructed. At Antonio's side, Talon crossed his massive arms in front of him.

The Elphah argued that the Pygmies in their care were innocent and not traitors, but despite this, the ugliness of the mob continued to grow.

A teenage boy with a pitchfork threw it at Antonio, and in a blink of an eye, Syn'nar raised her Gauntlet and vaporized it. Lowering her weapon but maintaining its activation, she addressed the crowd.

"I understand your anger and sympathize with your plight, but I cannot and will not allow you to harm my Elphah, my Pride, or the

Dir-nay family, and I will hurt the next one who tries. Please do not force me to do so."

An older man pushed his way to the front of the crowd brandishing a hatchet, he raised it and Sivgons shot him in the chest with a plasma pulse. He sailed back, hit the ground, and whimpered in pain.

"You shot Irwin Copple," an elderly woman shouted.

"You didn't have to do that," another man yelled.

"Be thankful I only plasma shocked him. Had it been Talon, he would have killed him. Scorpilyns are not known for their patience. This is not a game, and I am not going to tell you again," Syn'nar said, angry over what they had forced her to do. "That was your last warning." Then she increased the Gauntlet's yield. "The next one of you who raises a weapon gets seriously hurt."

"You would rather hurt us instead of them?" a heavyset woman asked.

"She's bluffing. They won't hurt us," a middle-aged man said, holding an axe.

"They're Qi-Tahh. They don't harm those they are to protect."

The Juardian-Omegah aimed her Gauntlet at him, "Please do not force me to hurt you."

He spat to the side. "C'mon, she won't shoot."

He raised his axe, and his wife raised a pitchfork. And together they approached. Syn'nar lowered her arm and head, and exhaled frustrated. She raised her head and threw her Gauntlet arm out to the side, and morphed it into a Dysk that boomeranged around, and sheared off the heads of the axe and pitchfork. Returning to her, the Dysk morphed back to Gauntlet, and she shot the couple with strong plasma shock pulses. Lying on the ground, screaming in pain, the two shook. After they stopped shaking, the others of the group helped them up.

Syn'nar looked to the crowd. "Now…anyone else think I'm bluffing?" The lavender skinned Juardian asked raising a brow.

Stunned, the crowd lowered their weapons and approached no closer.

In my Habitat, "Momja," I said, tiredly. "Suspend recording, jamonaka."

"Acknowledged, Marc, recording suspended."

"Fasbi. I'm tired. Jamonaka wake me in four savners, I'm going to lay down."

"Understood. Sleep well."

I returned to my bedroom and dropped onto the bed.

Three hours had passed, and after a restless slumber, I awoke. Went into the kitchen for something cold to drink, and after a couple of gulps of some alien nectar, I returned to the living room.

"Momja, jamonaka disregard wake-up call," I said, taking another gulp of the beverage. "Let's resume entry."

"Acknowledged Marc," the computer replied. "One moment, jamonaka. Ready."

"Back on Thada Argen, outside the Coyoust Valley, the two Xentous, Nyrit and Saffron, were cloaked. The space creatures used their chameleonic abilities and blended into the background of the large forest, making them seem nearly invisible, and had moved farther beyond the Valley after the Dir-nays nearly discovered them. They continued to keep the Pygmies under surveillance. Suddenly appearing, E'Dol and V'Hil arrived and began looking about for their brother and sister.

"Ny-rit, Saf'f'ron sh'ould be h'ere," V'Hil said, continuing to look around.

"Th'ey are. I see y'ou both. St'ay in ca'mel'leon'ic m'ode.

V'Hil and I're goi'ng in." E'Dol said, transforming himself into a Priort. V'Hil was next to morph into a giant bat, and together they flew to where the Dir-nays made their home.

Entering the Pygmies' encampment without arousing any suspicion, they joined the other Priorts hanging from a tree upside down and listened to what was being said.

A Pygmy approached King Gutai and reported, "Again, they

intervened and thwarted our slaughtering of the Eanois." He chattered and whistled while at times screaming like an angry chimp. "They kill your people. They have killed many of our Priorts and Skarbs and saved many more Offworlders."

Having finished his report, he looked to several others who now joined him. "Gutai, you are not a good choice for leadership of our people, our pets. I believe I will make a better leader than you." He looked to the tribe. "I will lead a force that will crush the Qi-Tahh." He said stepping forward. He turned and stepped in close and faced the King. "I will do what you cannot."

Gutai looked to his mate, Gulla, and faced the Pygmy. "No one will follow a dead Dir-nay," Gutai replied, and pushed him back.

Grabbing a spear from one of his guards, the King thrust it into the Pygmy's stomach and twisted it. He ripped the head out, and then shoved the spear into his heart.

"The Dir-nay who would be King—do not worry. You will not die alone for this treachery." Gutai pushed the spear deeper into the Pygmy's heart. He pushed until the Dir-nay was on his back then stabbed him wildly.

Ripping the spear out after the last impalement, Gutai looked to one of the traitors and hurled the spear through his eye. The spearhead partially penetrating the back of the Pygmy's skull.

"Seize them," the King shouted, pointing at the remaining four.

Complying, the Pygmies apprehended the traitors as their leader angrily approached. Gutai snatched a spear from another Dir-nay and thrust it through one Pygmy's throat, and pushed until the spearhead fully penetrated the back of his neck. He yanked it back out, and the guards released him and let the dead creature fall to the ground.

"I am King. No one else," he shouted, repeating his execution on two more who dared follow another, and sent a message to all.

Kicking and screaming, the last Dir-nay tried to break free, while he cried and begged for his life. But his plead mattered not, for his fate had already been decided, and this King was law. After Gutai killed each traitor personally, he threw the bloodied weapon back to a Dir-nay and ordered them to clean up the mess he had made.

Fuming, ranting, and raving, the King finally calmed down and faced his people, laughing. Stopping as suddenly as he started, his smile faded and his malevolence took its place once more.

"Qi-Tahh," he yelled wildly. His mate and their people joined in the incomprehensible chattering until he silenced them. "Their arrival changes nothing, and as far as I am concerned, the Life Protectors are just as much Offworlders and trespassers as the Eanois. And if they insist on interfering, they too, will share the same fate as those they choose to help."

Before continuing, the King had some of his females sniff the air, which the Animorphs found strange. They seemed to have a greater sense of smell than the males, and appeared to be checking for alien scents, possibly the Xentous, which they might have detected earlier. Gulla and Magam reported negative findings, and Gutai gloated. He was pleased with how well this last siege had gone. Though they had not succeeded in killing all of the Colonists at the Rydia Settlement, he was happy with the number of Eanois they had killed.

"The trust the Qi-Tahh had with the Eanois has been damaged. They had no idea we had discovered their spies, and though we could not see them, we were aware of their presence." The King continued to gloat, "Feeding them false information was easy, but to use it to cripple them—that was genius."

Yes, Gutai was pleased with how well the siege had gone. His people joined him in celebration for what they agreed was a victorious assault. They laughed and cheered.

"Soon, all Offworlders will either be dead or gone, and the planet will be ours alone once more," the King shouted and laughed again.

With their celebration commencing, some of the Priorts took off, so E'Dol and V'Hil did likewise.

Out of the Valley, the Animorphs transformed back to their true forms and mind-linked with Nyrit and Saffron. Sharing what they had learned, E'Dol ordered the Xentous to remain where they were and not to venture any closer, while they left to report their findings to Elphah Battista. The Animorphs became Priorts once more and left for Denizen.

Later, at the Settlement, the standoff between the Qi-Tahh and the Eanois continued to escalate, until several Colonists noticed the approach of two Priorts. Panicked, they readied the primitive weapons they carried as the big bats came in low, but Antonio and Syn'nar warned them not to harm them. Frighten of what the Juardians might do if they attacked, the Eanois allowed the creatures to land unharmed. Returning to their true forms, they approached Antonio.

"Th' Dir-nay fam'i'ly are inn'ocent of th' acc'u'sa'tions pl'aced on 'em," E'Dol shouted.

The crowd stepped closer as the commotion rose from mumbles to coherent words.

"Th' Dir-nay K'ing kn'ew we 'er s'pying on 'em, and fed us fal'se in'form'ation."

"It is t'ru. Th'y set us up," V'Hil added.

"Explain," the Elphah commanded.

"Th'y w're aw'are of Ny-rit and Saf'f'ron's pres'ence, and tho th'y co'uld not see 'em, th'y co'uld s'mell 'em. It seems th'fe'males have an un-can-ny sense of s'mell."

"If that is true, then they know you were there again," a skeptic woman voiced.

"No, th'y do n'ot," E'Dol said, shaking his head. He glanced at her and then faced Battista. "Not th'is t'ime. Th'y st'ayed outside the Va'lley and bey'ond th' Dir-nays abil'i'ty to det'ect 'em. V'Hil and I wit'nes'sed 'em ch'eck'ing for th' Xen'tous but co'uld not s'mell 'em.

"Why should we believe you?" the same woman asked.

Antonio stepped forward. "Because we have not given you any reason not to."

"Are Nyrit and Saffron still positioned at the outer rim of the Valley?" Antonio asked.

"Yes," V'Hil answered.

Looking to the Juardian-Elphah, who had not moved from his protective position, the Elphah suggested the Colonists return to their lodgings to sleep; however, their fear and anger still had not totally dissipated, and again, they became quarrelsome.

Syn'nar disarmed, "Please return to your Habitats. The Dir-nays have finished for now. Sleep. No harm will befall you. We will see to it."

"Like you have been doing?" a bitter woman asked.

"And if we refuse, what are you going to do? Shoot us into compliance like you did to Anton and Marya? They still feelin' the effects from your weapon," a man said, equally upset.

"I am sorry about that. But I did warn them, and they chose not to listen." Syn'nar explicated. "Regardless of what I had to do, please know that we really are here to help you, and we need your cooperation."

"Who are you to tell us what to do? You're not our Elphah, and you're not our community leader or the Committee. So why should we listen to you or do anything you say?" a middle-aged woman shouted.

The Scorpilyn stepped up and stood forward of Antonio and Syn'nar, his arms crossed in front of his massive chest as his tongue slithered between his lips. Sivgons saw a look she recognized in the reptilian.

"Oh, shit, this isn't good," she said, looking passed Talon's bulk to Antonio. "Talon is pissed."

"You should listen because our Elphah has asked you nicely to return to your lodgings," Talon said as his forked tongue again slipped through his parted lips. "Because my Juardian-Omegah had respectfully requested your cooperation." He uncrossed his arms, took another step forward, and roared like an angry dinosaur, glaring at the crowd with an arctic stare. "Because I am telling you to." The Scorpilyn shouted.

Someone started to speak.

"Shut up and do not say another word. I have heard enough. In fact, I strongly suggest you all quit while you are ahead and alive. I am tired of your stupid whining and arguing. You're making this assignment to save your ungrateful asses harder than it need be, and it stops now!" Again, Talon roared angrily. "From here on, you will do as we say when we say it. Show your ungratefulness again, and I will be very, very irritated." He said glaring over the mob–his tongue slipping through his lips as he crossed his arms in front of him. "Now… Go-to-bed." Talon then roared once more for good measure.

"Go to bed? Fuck, after that, my ass would be getting under the bed," Antonio commented.

The crowd began to disperse, but they were moving too slow for the Scorpilyn, so he roared loudly brought, uncrossing his arms he down his fist, he smashed the thick heavy wooden porch column. Everyone stopped and looked at the seven-foot reptilian. Momentarily frozen, the Eanois looked to one another, and then as though a starting pistol were fired they, without so much as a word or mumble quickly dispersed. They ran to their dwellings, entered their lodgings, closed and locked their doors. In no time the streets were cleared of all except the Life Protectors.

"Fasbi, Talon," Antonio said, looking up at his Juardian-Elphah.

Nodding sharply, his tongue slid out and back in.

Antonio, Syn'nar, Nahni and Talon were joined by E'Dol and E'nie.

"I think the Eanois are now more afraid of Talon than they are of the Dir-nays and their creatures," Nahni speculated.

"Can you blame them? I'm family, and there are times when he scares the lopsin out of me," Syn'nar admitted.

"Oh, Syn'nar," E'Dol said as if she were being silly.

"'Oh, Syn'nar' my caraf," she replied, looking at the huge reptilian.

"I have to agree with Syn. There are times when Talon scares me too." Battista again looked to the Scorpilyn. "No offense, my brother. I love you. You know that, but truth is truth. You're scary, especially when you're pissed off."

Talon simply smirked and walked away.

"I'm so glad he's on our side," Syn'nar interjected.

Antonio watched Talon leave and then informed the others that he doubted they would have any more trouble from the Eanois or the

Dir-nays tonight, but as a deterrent to those feeling stupid, he ordered the Juardians presence for the Pygmy family to remain.

"Yes, Ra-Tuth, I will see that it is done," Syn'nar replied.

"Fasbi, Syn." Then he glanced to all of them. "As for the rest of us, we should turn in as well. Koroxsu is going to be a long niya."

Feeling tired and weak, Antonio asked E'Dol to establish a mind-link with Nyrit for an updated report. The information exchange was quick yet detailed, and soon their nonverbal communication ended. The Xentous would remain where they were, and it seem that the Dir-nays were still celebrating, pleased with the number of lives they had destroyed with their subterfuge.

In light of the news, the Elphah-in-charge bid his brothers and sisters a good sleep and escorted by Syn'nar, Antonio joined the Dir-nays, who were already asleep. He needed a way to subdue the Pygmies using non-lethal measures, and also had the equally daunting task of figuring out a way of not killing all the Priorts and Skarbs. Doing so would change the planet's environmental balance. But Battista was exhausted. His battles with the Dir-nays and Eanois had left him drained, and he had no choice but to turn in as well. Quietly, he climbed into his bed, which was still positioned next to Wagg's. By morning, Antonio would have a plan, but for now he needed to sleep. He drifted off just as an idea occurred to him, and it made him smile. Tomorrow would indeed be a busy day.

Early the next morning, a welcome sight greeted the Life Protectors and Colonists when the two medical Prides finally arrived. Antonio no longer felt the need to implement his idea from last night now that the Mirren and the Vitalyst were here. Their presence made what he had thought of, useless.

Antonio and Syn'nar joined Talon and Nahni, as they met the Elphahs. Keelan Sopa introduced himself. A Zahnobein male, the Black Panther was tall and buffed and led the Arjai Pride, "Mirren." Next to him was Rheeza, a Syth whose coloring differed from the Syths they knew. Her brown, green, and white coloring gave her a most exotic look.

Rheeza coiled her vine-like arms around the Arjai-Omegah. *"Nahni," she said, hugging her warmly. "How long has it been?"* the Syth asked telepathically.

"It's been a long time, Rhee." She returned her hug and kissed her on her plant mouth.

"How is your family? How is Mama Chytyck?"

"They're well. If we survive this, I'd love to catch up, but we're rather pressed for time right now," Nahni said, directing her. "This is our Elphah, Antonio Franco Battista"

"Excuse me. I thought Joryd Kenton was the Zahnobein Qi-Tahh Elphah?"

"And where is your Omegah, Z'yenn Kaira?" inquired Keelan. His eyes narrowed. "What's going on here?"

"Not here. Aboard your shuttle," Battista said, waiting for them to lead the way. "Much has happened since our arrival. I'll bring you up to speed, but privately."

Keelan and Rheeza looked briefly to each other, and then without another word, they led the Pack to Rheeza's ship.

Aboard the Syth's medical ship, the two Arjai-Elphahs were informed of the situation, including the mysterious disappearance of Joryd and eight Pridesmen. Antonio told them of the memory block Arjenadann had employed on his orders, and their race to meet a deadline. Battista also informed them that they had to forego any investigation into the disappearance of their missing family until the medical mission was completed. They worked on a plan to inoculate the Dir-nays, and one that covered all possible contingencies.

With all of their lives in the balance, Antonio was not leaving anything to chance, especially after last night's attack. Their meeting was short, and the Qi-Tahh and Arjai-Prides were soon ready. Keelan and Rheeza had come prepared, and issued the assault Pack, dart rifles along with two extra clips. Each cartridge held twenty-nine darts.

Nahni and the Arjai-Elphahs took over the duties of treating the Eanois, and the Ra-Tuth decided he would lead the strike force.

But before departing, Antonio had E'Dol contact Nyrit and Saffron and check on the status of the Dir-nays. They reported back that the creatures were still slumbering after their late celebration, which had ended only a couple of hours ago. E'Dol relayed Antonio's orders to the Xentous, who were to remain at their post and to expect the Elphah and a large Pack. The Netureal ended their telepathic link,

"Excellent. This will be the best opportunity for us to inoculate the Dir-nays without any more bloody engagements." Syn-nar stated.

Assembling a large Pack, the rest of the Pride remained at the Settlement.

"Talon, you are Elphah until we return. Maintain the Elphah Black Alert just in case this siege goes south."

"You are going into battle and leaving me here to watch children?" he said, upset.

"We are not going into battle. We are simply going to inoculate the Pygmies. As for the latter, I need you here just in case, because I know you will do all within your power to protect these so-called children."

Talon's tongue slipped through his parted lips and slowly receded. "Yes, Elphah," he said, bowing.

"Listen up. As soon as we're finished here, we'll be able to search for our Pridesmen. We'll be back soon," Antonio said and walked away.

The Elphah had decided to shuttle over as opposed to Hexagyning. He could not risk exiting upwind and give away their advantage. Boarding a shuttle with no Xentou attachment, they left for the Valley.

On the outer rim of the Valley, the Pack arrived and quickly disembarked while the Ra-Tuth consulted with Nyrit and Saffron outside the Coyoust Valley and confirmed the Dir-nays were still asleep.

Straining their majikal powers, E'Dol and V'Hil transported twenty-six of them inside the encampment unheard by the sleeping creatures. Stealthily, they positioned themselves throughout the

Pygmy Village, and once everyone was ready, Antonio gave the order to fire.

Striking them, the sharp, pointy darts suddenly—and painfully—awakened the creatures. Jabbering while they pulled out the darts, the Dir-nays looked to the Qi-Tahh and suddenly stopped talking. Neither side spoke. The air was thick with anticipation as the Pack waited to see if the Dir-nays had been treated.

"Kill the Offworlders," ordered King Gutai chattering.

Battista's eyes widened. "Fire again," he shouted.

Again, the Pack shot them, and again, but the vaccine failed to inoculate the Dir-nays. How was this possible? For whatever reason, the inoculation was not working now.

The Qi-Tahh soon found themselves battling an entire village of angry Pygmies. Though they still were no match for the Pack, the Elphah ordered them to use non-lethal force, but all of that changed when Priorts and Skarbs arrived to help the Dir-nays. The Pack, forced to retreat, were not fast enough. As a result, four Pridesmen were killed, and over a dozen were seriously injured. The two Wisard apprentices transported the Pack out of the encampment.

The Dir-nay King screamed in his native tongue, "Run! We're coming for you. We're coming for you all. You are all dead!"

Later, at the Denizen Settlement, the Arjai-Prides finished healing all of the injured. The sight of the Xentous returning with the shuttle filled both Qi-Tahh and Eanois with smiles as they cheered and began hugging one another. Yelling and cheering, they all ran to greet the Pack, but when Antonio and the others exited, the cheering slowly died out as the battered Life Protectors helped the injured.

"Antonio, what happened?" Nahni asked reaching him first.

"We've a got a problem. We've got a big fucking problem. Vaccine W does not work on the Dir-nays."

"That is not possible. Vaccine W was engineered to be fast-acting and effective on all species, and it has never failed." Keelan offered.

"Not only is it possible, but they're coming with everything they've got to finish what they started. And if we can't stop them within the next eleven savners, the Council has ordered us to implement Containment Protocol III."

Rheeza gasped. "Total planet eradication," she said softly.

Far from Home

VIII

Displaced to some unknown planet, my Pack and I awoke confused and scattered throughout a small clearing. It took several moments for us to get our bearings, and I was surprised to find that Z'yenn and I were sporting standard equipment we did not previously have with us aboard ship. Our Life Support Devices were activated indicating the atmosphere was inhospitable to us. Finding each other was easy enough, those taken together remained so, and once reunited, and our initial bewilderment wore off, did we began with the questions.

"Is everyone all right?" The Elphah inquired.

We all acknowledged that we were.

"Is this everyone?" the Omegah asked.

"Wow," I said, looking up at the sky and our surroundings. "Is this Thada Argen?"

Joryd looked up, "No, it's not. By the look of things, I would say we're most likely in another galaxy."

"How do you?" I asked.

Z'yenn cut me off, "This planet's rising moons have double rings. No planet in our galaxy have such moons."

"How many of us were taken?" the Pantherus asked, looking about.

"I don't know. I'm here because I tried to save Z'yenn," I replied.

"Fasbi for trying," she said.

I nodded my reply.

We tried to use the Psionic configuration on our Kajas used to scan, but for whatever reason they did not work. Joryd turned to Avedia and asked her to find out.

The Mystik touched the centerpiece of the necklace she always wore and dropped her head. When she raised it, an eye had appeared on her forehead. The eye, the vacant canals of her eyes, and her medallion turned soft blue, as she entered into some sort of Trance. In her mind's eye, Avedia witnessed nearly everything about our abduction and saw all who had been taken, but she could not see our abductors. When she came out of it, she looked around before finally directing her attention to the Ra-Tuth.

"Except for Meva, we are all accounted for, but I cannot tell the whereabouts of our sister."

Z'yenn began inquiring if any of us had seen her, but the truth of the matter was that until now we did not even know Meva was missing, let alone that she had been abducted with us.

"Why take only Meva when they captured us all?" I asked.

"I do not know," Joryd commented.

"Neither do I, so find her…now," Z'yenn shouted.

Activating his gi-brey, Joryd tried contacting our Pridesmen by communications, but became frustrated by his inability to reach her and closed the channel. Deducing that the Netureal was either unable to respond, or that their signal was being blocked was of little help. The Elphah ordered us to begin searching our immediate surroundings for her. Later after a futile search, we regrouped, and Joryd decided on a different strategy.

"Laisere, give me an aerial assessment of the area and look for anything that might lead us to Meva."

"Yes, Ra-Tuth."

The Velfin untucked his two powerful wings, which lay hidden beneath his fur, and prepared for flight. We all stood back because of Laisere's giant wingspan and gave him the space he needed to ascend. Bending his knees slightly, the weapons specialyst pushed off, and he was soon high in the sky.

I was amazed. "You can fly?" I said, surprised. "You never told me you could fly. I've know you for two years."

"Oh, that's right. We never had combat training together," he replied, facing me briefly before flying higher.

Soaring upward, he flapped his great wings, and I could only watch in awe. Hovering over us, he surveyed the area and looked for the least ominous clue. Sniffing and tasting the air around him, the Velfin paused before finally rejoining us.

On landing, he recoiled his feathers and reported, "I've discovered a possible direction Meva might have been taken. I spotted where she landed upon arrival, and I was able to pick up her scent. It is faint–as is the scent of the other."

"The other?" Z'yenn asked, puzzled. "The other what? What has her? What's abducted our sister?"

"I do not know. The scent is new to me."

The lion commander asked, "Which direction?"

Laisere raised an arm and pointed, "That way."

"Then that way it is. Everyone, maintain Elphah Black Alertness until we know what we are dealing with," U'kristu commanded, and immediately stepped in front of her Elphah and Omegah. "I am sorry, Joryd, but under the circumstances I must take the lead in this hunt until the danger has been identified and its intentions are revealed." She stepped in even closer to Z'yenn. "This is not open to negotiations, and I will not tolerate a stunt like you pulled on Seregaia two meads back. Am I clear?"

"Yes, Juardian-Elphah," she said and bowed slightly.

The Zahnobein had no choice but to acquiesce with the Sk'tier, and even though the hunt belonged to the leaders of the Pack, Juardian regulations were clear in these matters. Regardless of rank, Joryd and Z'yenn were subject to obeying us Juardians who had command over all those who were entrusted to us to protect.

U'kristu then addressed me. I was to watch our rear, and she instructed everyone to set Kajas for auto-select. We did not know what the atmosphere contained or what creatures would be affected by what setting, so we would let the Kaja decide the yield and type of discharge.

Proceeding in the direction Laisere indicated, we treaded cautiously. I liked watching the way the Velfin moved. He ran and stalked on all fours, his heels never touching the ground. Laisere peered about, looking for more evidence in Meva's abduction, and would periodically sniff the surface and the air. Racing ahead, I questioned him about his ability to fly and why he never told me. But instead of answers, all I got was a smirk as he continued with his tracking. I returned to flanking our position.

Slithering like a snake, Avedia's lower body moved her, while her upper body remained erect. "Meva's abduction doesn't make any sense. I mean, aside from being an Animorph, she's a Wisard and more than capable of handling herself."

"That may be, but she is still missing."

"Laisere is right, Avedia, so let's concentrate on one problem at a time. First, we find our sister, and then we focus on our predicament," Z'yenn said, joining in.

"Why us? I mean, out of all those in our Pride, who could have been taken? Why us? Why not the entire Pride? Why were we selected? And by whom? And for what purpose?" Starone asked.

"When we find the ones who brought us here, we'll have our answers," Joryd stated simply.

"And remember," the Sk'tier added, "we are the visitors here, the intruders, so keep that in mind. Retreat is an acceptable option."

"Yeah, especially if our weapons have no effect on whatever creatures we may find." Torr commented.

I looked ahead to him and shouted, "Oh, you oughta stop."

The Arjai-Elphah chuckled, and turned toward the Oolong as she slithered along. "He thinks I'm kidding."

"Not now, Sivgins…check that Fonchuai trait of yours," Z'yenn commanded.

At once he followed the Tas'r's orders, and fought to control his natural urges.

"I was going to say–retreat is an acceptable option if it prevents us from harming an innocent species unnecessarily," U'kristu said, finishing her thought.

Hours passed, and the hunt had thus far been uneventful and frustrating as Meva's scent continued to dissipate, and the only creatures we ventured upon seemed more frightened of us than we were of them. Except for one, which appeared to be observing us. The creature possessed remarkable stealth, and moved like a cat, even though we were aware of its presence despite its efforts to conceal its anonymity. Since it did not bother us, we gave it the same consideration. Occasionally, we would catch a glimpse of it as it peeked out and then quickly darted back, camouflaging itself. Fanning out and keeping one another in view at all times, we made certain no harm befell each other as we widened our search parameters.

Elsewhere on the planet, aboard her Palace ship, a tall armor-clad woman of African descent entered a living room of sorts. Bending knee, she crossed her arms in front of her, and bowed waiting to be acknowledged.

"Rise, Talah," the Imperial Empress said in her native language, a mix of Swahili and Mayan. She turned to face her. "Is all ready, Captain?"

"Yes, Imperial Empress," she replied, standing.

"Good…I displaced our visitors to the Elisia forest to prevent Telus from detecting them."

"Mheria, the forest is filled with dangers."

"Nothing they cannot handle," She replied, donning her cape. "Now assemble our forces, and let's retrieve our guests before the Sorcerer discovers they are here."

"They are ready," the Captain replied, stepping to the side and allowing the Imperial Empress to lead the way. Talah followed close behind.

At the Elisia forest, I was bothered by the actions I had committed aboard Arjenadann before I was abducted. I had covertly sabotaged the Star Prysm, but now I was in a place where I could not change what I had done. I raced ahead of the Pack, stopped before them, and caused them to stop as well.

"Excuse me, Joryd. I have something important to tell you, and you're not going to like it." I took a deep breath and exhaled hard. "I committed an act of sabotage before being abducted."

"What did you do?"

"I turned the Star Prysm into a bomb that will explode should the weapon be fired.

"You did what?" Z'yenn shouted angrily.

Joryd held up a paw and silenced her. "How?"

"The energy discharge will be redirected into the system's reserve pool and slowly build up until the Prysm explodes."

"Why Va-lim? In the name of the nine gods, why?" U'kristu asked.

"To try to prevent a repeat of what happened with Asteroid Screel."

"That was not for you to say, Hawkins," Z'yenn bellowed.

"I am very disappointed with you, Marc. I wished you trusted me, trusted your family, and believed in us as we do in you." He faced the others. "Let's continue. We still need to find Meva."

"That's it?" Z'yenn replied, astonished.

"What more is there to say?" He continued to walk. "Besides, there may still be a chance to undo Marc's shortsightedness.

"How? We're here, and we don't know where we are?" the Omegah explicated.

"We find the one who brought us here and have him or her send me back," I added.

"Precisely. In the meantime, we continue searching for our sister, Meva."

What Joryd said hurt me more than anything his claws could ever have done, and the look of disappointment on U'kristu's face made the pain I was feeling–worse.

Finally…we found Meva. Having tracked our Pridesmen to a clearing, she lay on the ground, unconscious. Torr ran to her, and checked her out. Removing a small pump sprayer from his medical pouch, he squeezed off two shots, and she quickly regained consciousness–we helped her to her feet.

Before we could learn what had happened, the creature that had been playfully stalking us suddenly appeared. It was the same creature that had abducted Meva, those of us with a heightened sense of smell detected the creature's scent on her–it was strong.

Blocking our path, the creature stood a good three meters tall. It was big and hairy like a long-haired primate, and it weighed approximately 1,400 pounds. Its four arms each had hands that were tipped with claws. It had two powerful elephant-like legs. It looked formidable. When we tried to leave, it roared showing us its two rows of flat teeth and four three-inch fangs.

Uncertain of how to proceed, we stood motionless. We did not make any threatening movements or show any fear. Joryd suggested Avedia try communicating with it telepathically to inform it that we only wanted our sister back. It failed, so she employed her empathic abilities to get a sense of the creature, but that, too, was unsuccessful.

"Someone or something is blocking my abilities to connect with this creature."

"Let me try," Joryd said, cautiously moving toward it.

"Joryd, no. Let me," U'kristu said, stepping in front of him.

"Not this time, U'kristu." He moved passed her. "Protect the Pack."

"Yes, Elphah."

The Pantherus kept himself between us and the creature, demonstrating a passive-aggressive show of force. Our Elphah's movements were as non-threatening as he could possibly make them.

"Who are you?" Joryd asked.

But the strange life-form did not seem to comprehend.

With his words and body language, the Ra-Tuth tried again. "Meva is a member of our family and is staying with us."

The creature moved toward us.

"Please do not come any closer," Joryd pleaded.

He did not wish to startle the animal into taking a hostile posture, and therefore made every step as unchallenging as he could while continuing in his efforts to communicate with it.

Taking the same approach as the lion commander, the beast began circling him. Though it did not seem sentient, Joryd continued to speak to it as if it were. The creature took another step toward him.

We did not mean it harm. However, when our Elphah took a couple of steps back, the creature approached and demonstrated its continued lack of understanding.

Without warning, the life-form lunged at the Pantherus and attempted to grab him, but Joryd was fast and quickly leapt out of the way. He landed softly as members of the cat family did, then spun around as the creature started to advance toward us.

Joryd roared loudly. "Stay away my family," he shouted, narrowing his gaze.

The creature turned around, ignoring us, and faced the Pantherus, who ran and leapt passed the beast, landing between us and it. It continued its approach.

Joryd held up a paw, "Stay where you are, come no closer or I stop you."

The creature now gave our Elphah its undivided attention and charged. Quickly jumping up, Joryd drop-kicked it with all four paws and pushed it back. He landed on his feet and circled the strange life-form. Temporarily stunned, the creature shook off the effects, got to its feet, and again lunged at the Ra-Tuth. Jumping up, Joryd used both sets of his claws—front and back—on the creature's chest and stomach. It painfully cried out as he tore deep into its flesh. Before it could react, the Elphah fell back, pulling the monstrous life-form with him, rolled and flipped it over him. As it struck, the beast's massive weight cracked the large tree.

"Whoa. That was sweet," I exclaimed.

Z'yenn drew her Kaja and issued orders for us to do the same and terminate the monster, but before a single shot could be fired, the Pantherus countermanded those orders. He was not going to kill the creature over a miscommunication.

It shook off the stunning blow. It was now back on its feet and angry. Again, it charged Joryd. U'kristu at once leapt up, somersaulted through the air, and landed between her Elphah and the alien animal. Throwing her hand out as though she was physically striking the beast, her first motion stopped the mammoth monster, and it reacted as if it was physically struck in the left shoulder. Again, she repeated her maneuver with its right shoulder. Her next action darted the creature's head back, and as it brought its head forward, she used the force of her energy and propelled the beast off its feet and onto its back without having laid a finger on it.

Looking to the Juardian-Ra-tuth, I watched as she delivered a clasped hand swing, and again struck it without touching it. I never imagined U'kristu possessed such powers. I knew my Ket-sho was formidable in her fighting skills, but this went beyond that.

Lying on the ground, the creature shook its head and sported a look of bewilderment, clearly wondering what had happened. However, the stunning effect was brief, and it was soon up on its feet, and charged Joryd and U'kristu. This time. Avedia, who had maneuvered behind it during U'kristu's assault, jumped up, grabbed a thick tree branch, and lassoed the creature's neck with her snake body. Pulling hard and releasing, she slammed it even harder onto its back. The creature was barely back on its feet when the Oolong repeated her tactic and again lassoed its neck and slammed it down. When she tried roping it again, it grabbed her tail and pulled hard. That broke Avedia's hold on the branch, and the creature flung her into both Joryd and U'kristu. Dazed and down, they were helpless as the beast raced toward them.

Running to intercept, Meva morphed herself into the same creature and struck it with clasped fists. She knocked the beast back to the where it rose. With the creature stunned, the Animorph ran toward it and grabbed its ankles. She picked it up and began spinning in a circular motion, twirling herself around and around, and then she let go. The monster struck the same tree our Elphah had previously slammed it against.

Meva then turned to check the condition of the Pack, and saw Z'yenn and Torr kneeling beside the three who were down. The Arjai-Elphah examined them.

Suddenly, the creature attacked, and I shouted out a warning to Meva that came too late, and the Animorph was struck with a log. The force propelled her over us and against a large tree. Meva bounced off, laid unconscious and reverted back to her original form.

Looking to members of my Pack, the behemoth raised the log like a huge club and approached. Suddenly struck to the side of the head, the creature stumbled. Knocked off guard, the log nearly fell out of its hands. Shaking its head, it looked about.

"Leave-them-a-lone," I shouted as my Dysk returned to me.

"You heard the man," Z'yenn shouted as she too threw her Dysk at it.

It growled at us both as our Kajas boomeranged back to us. Torr formed a Gauntlet and prepared to protect our family, who were slowly recovering. Z'yenn and I again struck the creature with our Kaja-Dysks, and again it roared at us angrily.

"I said stay away from them," I shouted, and then threw the Dysk again.

It roared at Z'yenn and I and its snarling was cut short when our Dysks struck it once more. Our Kajas returned, and the creature dropped the log and turned its rage toward us. Z'yenn and I, poised for the attack, she formed a Blade and fell into a readied stance. I, not ready to kill chose a non-lethal ordinance and formed two metal batons.

Laisere flexed his wings, pushed off, and soared upward. He drew his Kaja, changed it into a studded mace, and dive-bombed the monster; striking it as he passed. The creature spun around, swatting at the air and missing the Velfin as he flew by. Roaring first at him and then at Z'yenn and I, it stopped and looked as though it had enough and would leave, but instead it suddenly raced toward us. Laisere tried to dissuade it and delivered another hard blow to its head, making it stumble. However, when the Velfin attempted to assault it again, the creature ducked his strike, spun around, grabbed one of Laisere's legs and slammed him into the ground.

I charged it, but was caught off guard by the beast's quickness. Using Laisere as a weapon, it smacked the mess out of me, and I came down a couple of meters later, and hit the ground hard. The monstrosity discarded the Velfin as though he were nothing more than an inanimate object and left our battered brother lying on the ground, draped with his own feathers. His Kaja laid in its inactive mode.

As for me, I too was disoriented and unable to focus my thoughts, as a result, my Kaja also reverted back to its neutral setting. Looking up, all I could do was watch helplessly as the monstrosity moved toward Z'yenn and Torr.

The Zahnobein joined the Fonchuai, and changing her Kaja to Gauntlet, they discontinued the auto-select, chose an energy yield and fired. The creature stopped momentarily and roared painfully. Picking up the discarded log, the monster approached them as they fired again and again, but their actions could not deter it.

The Omegah commanded, "Switch to killing force."

The creature continued its approach, raised the tree overhead, and prepared to strike. Before either the creature or the Qi-Tahh could act, a voice shouted.

"Mandegorrah, stop!"

And suspended all action.

Extreme Measures

IX

Back in our galaxy on Thada Argen, with the discovery of the Dir-nays resistance to the universal vaccine, Antonio revisited his latent thoughts from last night and called to E'Dol and E'nie, who were walking together as he approached.

They stopped and bowed. "Yes, Ra-Tuth," E'nie and E'Dol said in unison.

"E'Dol, your ability to communicate with animals and yours, E'nie, in talking to insects might work to our advantage."

"How?" the Netureal asked.

Battista explained he wanted E'Dol to go to the Priorts' cave and see if he could convince them not to help the Dir-nays, while E'nie went to the nest of the Skarbs and spoke with their Queen and explained the situation. It was doubtful either species was Influenced, so they might listen to reason.

"I will try, but there is no guarantee the Queen will fully understand me."

"I a'gre'e, An'ton'io. Th' le'ader of th' Pri'orts may n'ot en'tir'e'ly com'pre'hend me eit'her, but we w'ill try." E'Dol replied glancing to E'nie who returned a sharp nod.

"Fasbi to you both, and good luck. But proceed with caution. We do not know the extent of the King's hold on these species."

They acknowledged him, and would heed his warning. E'Dol snapped his fingers and vanished instantly, while E'nie's spanned his wings and took to the skies.

Aboard Rheeza's ship, the Arjai Prides, Nahni and her medical Pack worked together in trying to discover why Vaccine W did not work on the Dir-nays. Hours passed and still, they were no closer to finding an answer than they were before. That was when something occurred to Nahni.

"Maybe the problem is not with the Vaccine but rather with the Pygmies themselves."

"Impossible," the Zahnobein, Keelan stated.

"Keelan's right, Nahni. Vaccine W took many meads to perfect and hundreds of specialysts to make certain it would treat all species."

"Perhaps, Rheeza, but it has been my experience that once all avenues have been explored and all plausible resolutions have been exhausted, whatever remains, regardless of how improbable, must be the answer. Something in the Dir-nays' biology is rejecting the Vaccine," Nahni argued.

"All right... Let's say for the sake of argument you are correct. How do we proceed? In order to prove your findings, we would need to compare infected Dir-nay biology to uninfected DNA, and we would need samples of both from a male and a female Pygmy for comparison." Reheeza countered, telepathically.

"Hold that thought." The Arjai-Omegah replied.

Chytyck left the medical ship, and within five minutes she returned with the Pygmy family.

"Rheeza, Keelan, this is Nextus, Pisana, and Wagg—your uninfected samples of Dir-nay DNA."

"I am very pleased to meet you," the Syth doctor said, as she stooped to their level speaking their native language. Rheeza extended her vine-like arm to each of them. Looking to Nahni, she asked, *"How is this possible?"*

"They were separated from the others when the infection began."

"We need your help," Keelan said in Dir-nay as he approached.

"We know. Nahni explained it to us, and we will do all we can to help," Nextus replied.

"What can we do?" Pisana asked in laimeguage.

"We need to discover why the Vaccine does not work on your people and adjust it so that it will." The Zahnobein replied.

Far away from the Denizen Settlement and after an almost futile search, E'nie finally found the Skarbs' nest, but he did not approach too close for fear of appearing threatening. Instead he called to the Queen. She emerged guarded by many alien beetles.

"What do you want?" she asked, moving her antennas.

"My apologies for the interruption, your Highness, my name is E'nie, I am Qi-Tahh and need to speak with you on a most urgent matter."

"You carry the stench of the Eanois on you–it is offensive."

"Apologies, but as I have said, the need to speak with you is most urgent."

"Very well. You may approach, but keep it brief. If you show any sign of aggression, my colony will tear you apart."

"I understand."

The Icsiedoa approached, and though he did not show it, he was on high alert. He explained to the insect Queen that the Eanois, despite what the Skarbs had been told, presented no threat to them, and that those whom they followed were sick themselves. The Dir-nays were infected with a disease that drove them to this insurrection. Once inoculated, the Pygmies would return to normal and the fighting between them and the Eanois would end. He asked that she and her horde not participate in anymore unnecessary bloodshed.

The Queen asked, "Why should I believe you as opposed to Gutai, whom we have known for many solstices? Especially since you and your Pride have killed many of my colony."

"That was regrettable, but we had no choice. We had to save the Eanois, whom your colony were killing, and if your horde continues to aid the Dir-nays in their mad desire of eradicating the Colonists, then I am afraid many more of your Skarbs will die. Please, we do not want this." E'nie said, pleading with her.

Now angry, "Kill him," the Queen ordered, moving her antennas.

Not wanting to fight, E'nie drew his Kaja and fired at the ground between them, and created a wall of flame that held the Skarbs back long enough for him to escape.

Elsewhere in the caverns where the Priorts lived, E'Dol's encounter with the bats went just about as well as E'nie's visit, and ended pretty much along the same lines. They too did not listen, and as a result, he too was forced to retreat, and managed to teleport himself away, before he was forced to harm the Priorts.

Later that afternoon back at Denizen, E'nie joined Antonio and gave him the disappointing news.

"I would ask how it went, but the look on your face says it all," Battista remarked.

"I take it E'Dol was equally successful?" the blue man-sized grasshopper asked.

"The Priorts did not believe him, and the bats were upset that we had killed some of them." Antonio explicated.

"The Queen of the Skarbs felt the same way. I wish they believed us. I do not enjoy killing innocent species," E'nie professed.

"We may not have to, if the Arjai Prides and Packs can create a vaccine that is effective against the Dir-nay. Come with me."

Inside Rheeza's ship…

"Excuse me, Elphah Rheeza, this is our communications specialist, E'nie."

"Greetings," she said. "I just wish we could meet under different circumstances."

"As do I," E'nie replied.

"And the Zahnobein glued to his scanner is Arjai-Elphah Keelan Sopa," Nahni interjected.

"Excuse me, Elphah Battista—" Rheeza started to say telepathically.

"Antonio, please," he said as if addressing a friend.

"All right, Antonio. You are human, are you not?"

"Yes, I am."

"Forgive me, but as an Arjai, I'm interested in your species' physiology, especially in the different ways it enhances you. I find the interaction to be fascinating."

"I would enjoy discussing my physiology with you, but another time perhaps."

"Of course, I understand.

Syn'nar joined Antonio, E'nie and the other healers, and Battista inquired about their progress.

"Fasbi to Nahni, we may be onto something, and are investigating a lead," the Zahnobein Arjai explicated. "The first step is completed, but the next phase requires risk. We need two adult Dir-nays, a male and female, before we can proceed."

The Qi-Tahh Elphah tapped the micro dot behind his ear, and he had E'Dol report to him at once. Using his Wisardry, the Netureal suddenly appeared inside the vessel. Antonio explained the assignment to the Wisard apprentice, who in turn informed him that he could retrieve the two Dir-nays, but suggested having Juardians present when he did so. The Elphah looked to his Juardian bodyguard who understood the non-verbal command and acknowledged his request. She called for Talon and Te'lar.

The Scorpilyn and Maluskan, a Mollusk creature entered the medical bay. Unlike the Zonnyans who were also of the mollusk species, Te'lar's people were not grotesque-looking, or produced such an awful stench. Bluish-green, they had small black eyes, cream colored antennas, and two thin tentacles with three-finger hands that still creeped me out, and they looked mouthless until they spoke.

Conjuring up a small bottle of colored sand, E'Dol poured the sand on the floor as he spoke the language of his Sect. A picture of the Dir-nays' encampment slowly appeared in real time, and he asked for them to choose their subjects. Because it was difficult for them to distinguish between the two sexes, Pisana told them which gender was which. While holding the picture, the Wisard apprentice spoke more of his bizarre idioms and cast his spell. An instant later two Pygmies appeared—a male and a female. Apprehended and rendered unconscious before they could act, the Dir-nays were placed on divans and restrained.

"Te'lar, you are to remain here until the Juardian Pack arrives. Once relieved, report to me," Talon commanded.

"Yes Juardian-Elphah.

"Syn'nar, now that the Dir-nays know the Vaccine is useless, they will be all the more dangerous." Talon's tongue slithered out between his parted lips. "Until the Dir-nays have been inoculated, you are not to leave the Elphah's side."

"Understood. No harm will come to him." She replied, glancing to Antonio before facing Talon and bowing respectfully.

"I will be close, sister. Not to worry" the Scorpilyn added.

The Arjais ordered everyone who was not a healer or who had no business aboard the Arjai ships–out. Keelan released the Eanois who could return to their homes, and he kept those still in need of care.

Battista and the Pride worked to reinforce their defenses, while at the same time Lucan gathered the others in the great hall of their community, apart from those whom they had lost the faith in to save them. Scared, they argued about what they should do. Some wanted to leave the Settlement and go into hiding, while others were more angry than frightened that the Qi-Tahh ordered them around. Those who wanted to stay, preferred to die fighting as opposed to running away and later being hunted like prey.

Keelan, Rheeza, and Nahni continued to work on finding a solution to their vaccine dilemma, and they were still no closer to solving the mystery than they were three hours ago. They conjectured, guessed, and made suggestions about why the treatment failed, but nothing showed them how to counteract the problem. Neither the test comparisons on the infected Pygmies or unaffected parents yielded any answers, but instead the results just created new unanswerable questions.

Outside, the Elphah and Juardian-Omegah made rounds in and around the Denizen Settlement, as they checked on the Pride's progress. They were joined by E'Dol and E'nie. The Netureal told them in his broken way of speaking, that he and E'Dol may have discovered a way of nullifying the Dir-nays control over the Priorts and Skarbs.

"Explain," The Augment commanded.

Admitting that I gave them the clue, E'Dol had Antonio recall our strategym meeting when I suggested turning the creature's against the Dir-nays or perhaps even breaking their control. Based on that, the two of them have been working with this idea, and believe they have found a common link in the frequencies the Pygmies use to control the creatures.

"We believe we can block the frequency telepathically. However, there is only one among us whose mind is that powerful." E'nie added.

"Arjenadann," Antonio said.

"In theory," the blue-skinned insect started to say. "If Mother can block their control—"

"Then the bats and beetles will not assist the Dir-nays in battle," Battista conjectured.

"Or they may still, out of habit. We do not know for certain. As we have said, this is all theoretical," E'nie explained.

Then E'Dol told the Elphah about the problem that would exist. If Arjenadann is successful, the level of energy required for such a mind-block would also interfere with all other forms of telepathy as well as with communications, both on the planet and in space. That meant communications may or may not be possible. They did not know. However, they all knew what to expect if they did not try.

Antonio reminded the two Pridesmen of the danger involved. Arjenadann's mental powers were strong enough to destroy every mind on the planet.

"Unlikely. She will be using her mind to block telepathic use, not probe our thoughts," E'nie clarified.

Pausing while he considered the ramifications of this action, the Ra-Tuth gave his authorization for them to proceed and told them both that he would inform Sclee of the situation. E'Dol and E'nie both bowed to Antonio, and he and Syn'nar continued their rounds.

On board Arjenadann, the Packs continued with their mission.

"Understood?" Antonio asked over communications.

"Affirmative, Ra-Tuth. Arjenadann will contact you once she has achieved orbit," Sclee replied.

The Augment's pseudo image vanished, and the acting Elphah aboard ship informed the Xentouwish via mind-link of Antonio's orders before directing L'Pom, another Icsiedoa, to commence with the separation of ship from creature. Grayel, a Zahnobein male, readied the weapon for firing.

Back on the planet, the Scorpilyn and Maluskan arrived informed the Elphah that all was ready. Inquiring as to the whereabouts of the Colonists, Talon told Battista that they had gathered at the great hall and were ordered to remain there until the fighting had ended. Te'lar reported Antonio that she had posted six Juardians to protect the Eanois. Though he acknowledged by nodding his head and verbally dismissing them, Syn'nar could tell Antonio's mind was a million miles away. It was not necessary for her to inquire, the look on his face said it all, so instead she assumed the role of philosopher, something U'kristu would do if she were there.

"You cannot be in two places at once," Sivgons said in his native language.

"Huh, what?" he replied in Sicilian.

"Your attention is split, brother, and you need to be focused here with us if we are to win this battle, and win it we must."

"I know," he replied in his native language.

Speaking fluent Sicilian, Syn'nar reminded Antonio that Qi was a precious thing. All Qi, even the Qi of those Influenced. He knew this, but where he had a problem was what would happened if they fail to save the Eanois from the Dir-nays or fail to inoculate the Dir-nays before their insane deadline. In that event, they would be forced to destroy this world…and themselves…to save a galaxy. Who were they, Antonio asked, to decide which race had the greater right to live? Who were they to upset the delicate balance that God had made? He did not care for the equation used to remedy this problem. Syn'nar told him that he already knew the answer to all of his concerns. They are Qi-Tahh, and this was their burden to bear.

"So it would seem. Do not concern yourself, sister." He said looking down at her. "Like you, I am too well trained not to perform my duties."

Ending their Sicilian conversation, Syn'nar raised up on her tiptoes and kissed Antonio softly on both sides of his face. She smiled, and they continued their rounds without uttering another word about their discussion.

At the Coyoust Valley, Gutai gathered his people. He told them that this would be their final battle against the Offworlders and that after tonight both the Qi-Tahh and the Eanois would be dead. The Dir-nays cheered and screamed while raising their fists and weapons in agreement. Banging their drums, they commenced to dancing and chanting and praying to their God as they prepared for battle.

Night fell, and there were still no sign of the Dir-nays, though tensions were high as the Life Protectors waited for the Influenced to show. Meanwhile, aboard the Mirren and Vitalyst, the Packs worked feverishly trying to find a way of making the Vaccine viable to treat the Pygmies, as opposed to planetary termination, which was what they must do if they failed, and time was running out.

Outside, Antonio and Syn were grim. They had just received word from the Xentous posted at the Valley's outer rim. An enormous flock of Priorts just entered the Coyoust, and the Dir-nays would soon be on their way. Antonio solemnly ordered Nyrit and Saffron to return at once.

The Ra-Tuth projected a pseudo image of himself to the Pride on the planet and aboard Ship-Arjenadann, informing them that the Dir-nays and their forces were on their way, unfortunately, the Arjai specialysts have not yet come up with a vaccine.

"My Pride, this is Antonio Franco Battista, Elphah-in-charge. Unless the Arjais can discover a vaccine within the next twenty-eight hotress, I will implement Containment Protocol III. It has been an honor to fight alongside you, the best Qi-Tahh of the Supremacy. And, it was a pleasure to be a part of such a wonderful Pride. Fight well… Life Protectors." The Elphah's pseudo image faded, and he looked to his Juardian-Omegah.

"Watch yourself, Peanut." Antonio said, checking his mental control over his Kaja.

"You too, Bachew." Syn'nar replied, and did likewise, splitting her concentration, she demonstrated her accomplished level of mental discipline.

Battista informed his Juardian bodyguard that he would be at the Dir-nay family's lodge. He promised Wagg. She corrected him, and told Antonio that they would be there, because Syn'nar was not about to leave his side. He was her Charge. Nodding to her, they left to join the Augment's newly extended family.

The Xentous returned fifteen minutes later, and not long after that, the Dir-nays arrived at the Denizen Settlement. Dismounting their Priorts, King Gutai stood before the Life Protectors, fearless and angry, shouting for his people to prepare to attack.

"Now Arjenadann," the Elphah commanded telepathically.

In orbit, the Xentouwish commenced using her formidable mental powers to block the Dir-nays' connection to the Priorts and the Skarbs and worked to turn them back.

On Thada Argen, Arjenadann's efforts seemed in vain as the bats took to the sky, rising like a black expanse that hovered over the furry creatures, while the beetles moved in unison and waited like a well-trained army to begin their attack. The Dir-nay King stood with his Queen and grinned. They wanted to savor the moment before he issued the order to engage. Their grins faded.

"Attack. Kill them all!" He shouted in Dir-nay.

Gutai, Gulla and their screaming tribe of Pygmies charged the Qi-Tahh, who formed a variety of Kaja weapons, and met them. Meanwhile, neither the Priorts nor the Skarbs moved. They simply held their position. Arjenadann telepathically informed Antonio that she could not maintain the frequency block for long.

Neither the Priorts nor the Skarbs ever heard any voice inside their minds except those of the Dir-nays, and they were now confused, and continued to remain where they were. King Gutai was dismayed. Never before had the species not obeyed him.

Ordered by the Human, the Dir-nay family were to stay indoors, and not to come out until he said otherwise, and stood outside their lodging with the Kigong at his side. Syn-nar told him to stay close to her.

"Elphah, I cannot keep this up much longer." Arjenadann said, straining to continue.

"You've got to." He said, shooting four of the Influenced with plasma pulses.

Aboard ship, the Pack was rushing to complete their orders.

"Sclee, it is nearly time," Tonna said, turning to face her.

"I know our orders, but you cannot kill them," L'Pom argued.

"Do you think I want to? They are just as much my family as they are yours. When the Council said to initiate Containment Protocol III at a precise time, the Ohdens did not just pick a number out of thin air. We must. If we do not follow Kerebrol's instructions, we could be placing the entire galaxy at risk."

Denizen had become a war zone. Dispersed throughout the Settlement, the Pride fought hard not to kill the Dir-nays, while they protected the Eanois and defended themselves, but the Pygmies' savagery was making it very difficult and would soon force Battista's hand.

Aboard the Vitalyst, checking one of the slides, Nahni noticed something strange, and upon closer examination of an infected blood tissue, she excitedly began calling to the others. Gathering around her, Rheeza was next to observe her findings. Then Keelan took his turn at the slide and saw it as well. The answer had been in front of them the whole time and resided in the creatures' white S-cells. Quickly reproducing the experiment and mixing the blood tissue with a mineral base and Vaccine W, they watched as the infected cells retarded.

Immediately preparing an inoculator, Keelan approached the Influenced Dir-nays. He had two Juardians hold the male while he injected him with the modified Vaccine. Within moments the hatred in the Pygmy's eyes dissipated, and the evil within him subsided.

"What did you do to me?" he asked in his native tongue.

Keelan replied, in Dir-nay. "We treated you."

They repeated the inoculation with the female, and the results were the same.

Keelan looked to Rheeza and Nahni. "Let's begin mass production at once.

Outside, the battle had forced Antonio and Syn'nar to become separated, and after repeated use of his Kaja, the Human-Augment was exhausted. Weak, he fell to his knees and could not stand, let alone use his morphogenic device which reverted to its null setting.

Gutai and Gulla saw Battista's vulnerability and approached with spears in hand. Cautious at first, they paused, looked to each other and slowly continued toward him. Syn'nar, could not help Antonio, she was busy battling a number of Dir-nays, and was too far away.

"Ra-Tuth, I cannot hold it any longer," Arjenadann cried out in pain.

The Priorts and Skarbs were freed and moved to join the fighting.

With the approach of the two species, Antonio quickly evaluated the situation, and called Ship-Arjenadann–on intercom.

"Elphah Battista to Pride, Kileo fire." He said, watching Gutai and Gulla now running toward him. "I repeat, implement CP-III... Now." The Augment shouted.

Defenseless and too weak to protect himself, Antonio tried to stand and found even that was too strenuous, so he stayed as he was. The King and Queen were now close enough to kill the Elphah, and were about to when they were suddenly hit with darts and the evil within them vanished at once. Gutai and Gulla stopped themselves just short of running Antonio through. Confused by their actions, the Pygmies were speechless. Nahni approached and quickly explained.

In Ashanti...

To Kileo's surprise and his relief, the weapon did not discharge, but instead the unit began building up in energy. He tried again to shut it down, however the energy of the Prysm kept increasing. Kileo realized an explosion was unavoidable. Frantically, he again entered his encryption codes, but the weapon would not power down. The explosion was eminent.

"Momja, I am unable to stop the Prysm's energy buildup–explain."

"An encryption code has locked the system and initiated the overload."

"Can you break the code?"

"Affirmative, but the time required will exceed the time allowed. The Star Prysm will reach critical mass in three hotress."

Antonio's voice boomed over the communique, "Elphah to Pride, do not fire, I repeat cancel termination orders—do not fire weapon. The threat is being contained."

"I've already fired." Kileo said, strangely.

"Then were all dead." The Elphah replied.

"Not necessarily…the weapon did not fire."

"A misfire?"

"No," he again answered strangely.

On Battista's orders, the Marsupial kept the channel opened and ordered him to contact Sclee and inform her of the situation.

In Throne Pryme…

"Tonna, you are with me. L'Pom, you have the Throne," Sclee said merging with her twin. Together, they Hexagyned to Ashanti.

In Ashanti, the Twins looked at the problem.

"We need to—"

"Contact Antonio," Tonna said, finishing their thoughts.

"No need, I'm here." He replied over communications.

Appearing in Holo-Form, the Augment tried to correct the problem but failed, and was forced to take an action that could have serious consequences for him later. Disobeying the Council, he raised his LSD to its highest level of protection, knowing it would not last long, ordered his Juardian-Omegah to stay while he Ported to the ship.

In Ashanti, the Elphah exited the Hexagyn and raced to the Engineering controls where he quickly read the display. He began using his computer skills to hack the system.

"Whoever did this is smart. Maybe too smart for their own good."

"The Chamber will explode in nine et-nims," the computer relayed.

"Almost got it." He said typing fast as he could. "All most."

Momja relayed the remaining time. "Six, five, four, three, two—"

"Got it."

"Authorization code accepted. Destruct sequence terminated. Energy buildup nullified." The computer relayed.

"It had to be Marc. No one else could have done it. But why?" Kileo stated.

"I don't know, but part of me am glad he did. Unfortunately, Marc's use of extreme measures may in the end cost him dearly."

Aftermath

X

The next day on Thada Argen, the battle against the Dir-nays had ended, and Gutai and Gulla, after being inoculated, stopped the Priorts and Skarbs from attacking the Pride and Eanois. The Arjais were able to manufacture enough of the modified vaccine to inoculate enough of the Pygmies, and gave the Qi-Tahh the time needed to subdue those remaining without killing them.

Afterwards, the Healers started performing preventative vaccinations on the Eanois, and though none of them were ever Influenced, it was standard medical procedure whenever the Wehtiko touched a planet.

Antonio searching for Wagg, was told by the boy's mother, Pisana, where he might find her son, and informed him that he was not happy that he was leaving.

At the ruins, Battista found the young Dir-nay sitting among the decayed structures looking sad.

"Hey, Wagg," Antonio said, joining him.

His head was hung low as he replied, "Hi, Antonio."

"Why the sad face, buddy?" he asked in Dir-nay, taking a seat next to him. "C'mon, my little opo, what's bothering you?" he asked, placing a hand around his small shoulder.

"You are leaving."

"I know. Our assignment is over. Your people are no longer a threat to the Eanois, and they are once again the friendly neighbors they were before they were Influenced. Do you remember our secret?"

With his head still dropped, Wagg nodded, "Members of your Pride are missing."

"That's right, and we need to find them."

"I know, but I do not want you to go."

"I know–but that does not mean I cannot return to visit."

"It still hurts."

"Well, I'm not leaving for another savner or two. Why don't we play a few rounds of Bingga?"

"Really?" the child asked with glee. Wagg raised his head, smiled, and hugged Antonio.

"However, before we do, there is something I have to give you first."

"An injection," he asked.

"Yes, but do not worry. It will not hurt, and it will keep you well. Your parents already had theirs."

Before Battista could administer the treatment, the foundation of the structure gave way and collapsed. With only a moment to act, the Augment pushed the Dir-nay clear of the debris, but he was unable to escape as the structure collapsed on top of him. Pinned, with only his head, chest, and left shoulder and arm visible, Antonio could not move the debris, nor could he reach his Kaja, and the fallen structure had damaged his Holo-Com. Wagg immediately ran to his injured friend and worked to free him, but try as they may, the structure was too heavy for either of them to budge. Painfully, the Elphah instructed the young Pygmy to go back to the Settlement and bring back help.

Wagg started to run, and then suddenly and inexplicably, he slowed himself until he stopped. Standing where he was, he looked to something on the ground, stooped down, and picked it up. Uncertain as to what exactly he had found, Antonio called to Wagg, but the Dir-nay did not answer. He seemed more preoccupied with what he was holding than Battista's need for assistance. Again, he called to him, and as he slowly turned about, Antonio saw him holding a jagged piece of metal. Speaking to himself and giggling, the young Pygmy faced him, and Battista recognized the frightening change in his little friend.

Antonio slowly shook his head looking toward the sky. "Oh God in heaven no. Not him, not the boy." Battista looked to the Dir-nay, "Oh Wagg, you poor baby, I'm so sorry."

The seven-year-old had the same unmistakable look that his people had donned before their inoculation. He was no longer the same person. He was Influenced, and any goodness the child once had faded quickly with only the ancient evil remaining. Walking toward Antonio, Wagg continued to talk to himself as he played with the sharp instrument.

Back at the compound, Syn'nar approached Talon, inquiring the whereabouts of the Elphah, and were soon joined by Nahni.

"Nahni, have you seen Antonio?"

"No, Syn, not for a while. I believe he went to find his little opo to inoculate him."

"Do you know which direction he was headed?"

"No, why? What's wrong?"

"I don't know, but something does not feel right."

Pisana interjected, "I saw Antonio not too long ago. He was looking for Wagg. I told him that I last saw my son heading for the ruins not far from here." She pointed the way.

"Nahni, grab an inoculator of Vaccine W2, and join Talon and me. We're going to go find them."

She followed her instructions as Te'lar joined them and inquired, "Talon, what is it?"

"It's probably nothing. Stay here and continue overseeing the inoculations. We'll back shortly." Then the three of them left.

At the ruins Antonio painfully struggled to lift the debris off. But the strain the planet had put on him had finally taken its toll, and he was now weaker than an ordinary human.

He addressed the young Pygmy. "Wagg, it's me–Antonio."

The child knew exactly who Battista was and continued toward him while the Elphah again strained to free himself. As he struggled to lift the debris off him, he caught a glimpse of a long sharp piece of wood no larger than a pencil that laid just within his reach. Continuing to try to lift the decayed structure, the Augment struggled valiantly, but found he was much too weak to do so. In his present condition, the debris was simply too much for him.

"Wagg, I know what you're thinking, and you don't have to do this. Look on the ground. Do you see the Inoculator?" he asked, speaking Dir-nay.

Wagg stopped his approach, and for whatever reason, he began searching for it. When he found it, he picked up the ready-to-use injector and stared at it.

"Hold it against your arm and press. It will not hurt you, but it will treat you of the infection you've contracted. Please."

Looking to him, Wagg pressed the apparatus to his arm, but instead of following through, the young Pygmy glanced to Antonio, grinned evilly, and discarded it. He then continued his approach. Giggling sinisterly, he jabbered in his native tongue to himself as though he has lost his mind.

Antonio spoke calmly, "I understand. It won't let you inoculate yourself. It's all right. Go and find my Pride. They will help you. They will treat you."

Wagg climbed on top of the debris and adding his weight, pinned Battista even more securely than before.

"Don't do this. I can help you. Please let me treat you."

Giggling, the child slashed Antonio across his exposed chest and sliced open his shirt and skin. Painfully reacting to the assault, he continued to try to reason with the young Dir-nay.

"You don't have to do this."

Wagg cut Battista's face and enjoyed watching his painful reaction.

"You don't have to be like this. Please let me help you–let us treat you."

He slashed Antonio's other side of his face, and giggled.

"Please don't do this. This is not who you are, Wagg. Please I'm begging you. Let me help you. Let me treat you." Tears ran down Antonio's face as he pleaded.

Wagg slashed Antonio's chest, grabbed a handful of his long wavy black hair, and yanked his head back, hard. "This may not be who I was, but it is all that I am now." Kissing him hard on his lips, the young Dir-nay pulled Battista's head back even further and exposed his throat–he raised the jagged metal piece to strike. "Good-bye, Life Protector. Time to die."

Tears continued to run down Antonio's face. "Good-bye, Wagg. I love you."

Wagg pulled back his arm and prepared to slit his throat, when Antonio drove the sharp piece of wood he had picked up into the side of Wagg's neck, and pushed until the young Dir-nay dropped the metal instrument. Staggering back, he gasped, and angrily pulled the sharp wooden stick from his neck. Looking down at Battista with eyes of blazing hate, Wagg's eyes rolled back, and he fell away, rolling off the structure and collapsing on the ground just as Syn'nar, Talon, and Nahni arrived to witness Antonio's reluctant act.

Racing to them, Talon lifted the enormous structure off the Human-Augment with little effort, while the Gulapalae ran to the Pygmy. Antonio begged Nahni to save the boy's life.

"I am sorry, brother–he's dead," she reported.

"Nooooo," he shouted with tears streaming down his face. "Wagg," he said softly–sadly.

Talon carefully held Antonio in his arms while Syn'nar retrieved his Kaja. The Elphah told the Scorpilyn to put him down, and despite his own need for medical attention, Battista dragged his injured leg, held his hurting side, and went to the child. Syn'nar handed Talon Antonio's Kaja to hold for him until later.

"What happened?" Nahni asked softly.

Slowly, painfully, Antonio bent down grunting. Tears continued to wet his face as he gently picked Wagg up in his arms, cradling him, he ignored his own physical discomfort best he could, and held the young Dir-nay close.

"He was Influenced," he softly replied.

That was all he said as he carried the child back to the Settlement, with the others following behind in silence.

Though the Supremacy had won the war and saved most of the two sentient species, an ecosystem, and quite possibly the universe, the Wehtiko took the final victory when it claimed the most innocent life of all—that of a child.

Nextus, Wagg's father, understood and did not blame Antonio for the tragedy. He knew how much the Life Protector loved his son. However, a mother's grief was another kind of pain, and Pisana did blame Antonio for her son's death. She even forbade him from attending Wagg's burial. He could not blame Pisana for the way she felt, because Battista blamed himself as well. With heavy hearts, the Qi-Tahh left Thada Argen in search of their missing members.

Back on the dangerous and hostile planet far from our galaxy, the mighty blow of the creature, had left me hurting and somewhat disoriented, but still I found the language this woman spoke to be surprisingly familiar.

The creature lowered the log as it turned in the direction of the voice. A Caucasian woman with vibrant blue eyes walked into the clearing. She was dressed in what appeared to be a leather outfit with knee-high boots and a long cape. The beast faced her briefly and then turned back toward us, and continued its approach.

Again, the female commanded the creature, "Mandegorrah, I said stop! Now put that log down this instant!"

The creature growled at the woman while maintaining its posture, but the female was neither frightened by its rages nor intimidated by them, or its size, and continued to stand her ground.

"Don't you growl at me. I said put that log down, and I mean–now!"

She approached. Standing at 5 feet 10 inches, the three meter tall creature towered over her, but she continued to stand toe to toe with it. Roaring loudly once more, it threw the log and smashed it against a tree and cracked the thick oak. The alien female then reached toward the beast as it lowered its head for her to reach and allowed her touch. She began stroking and scratching the monstrous creature as though it were a pet.

"Good, Mande. Did they hurt you?" she asked in a mix of Swahili and Mayan.

Though stunned, I was still coherent enough to reply, "Did we hurt it?"

"You go ahead and play. I'll handle them, and we'll have fun later, okay?"

"You've got to be fucking kidding me," I exclaimed watching their interaction.

She smiled as the once ferocious creature, which was now as playful as a pup, roared at us twice more before lumbering off into the woods. As the life-form vanished, a female horde emerged and positioned themselves near us while our Pack helped one another up. Retrieving our weapons, neither our savior nor the taller females said a word–they simply watched us. Despite a pounding headache, I knew what I heard. The language she spoke was clear and unmistakable, and still, I doubted myself.

"Oh, man. Oh, man, I must've got hit harder than I realized," I said to myself as I stood shaking my head.

Regrouping, I still had trouble believing what I heard despite the fact my reply was correct. The lead woman again spoke in her native tongue and inquired why we tried to hurt her friend. As improbable as it was, as difficult as it was for me to believe, this alien female was speaking a mix of Swahili and Mayan—Earth idioms as alien and unknown to my Pack as many of their dialects were to me.

Joryd attempted to open a dialogue with her, but when I asked to let me handle it because I understood her, Z'yenn looked at me suspiciously and inquired how I could understand their language. I simply replied that I would explain later. I looked to their leader and explained our situation—our unexpected arrival here, how her "Friend" had taken one of our Pack members, and the breakdown in communications when we tried to convince it to give her back.

"Why did you not talk to her and explain? She is intelligent and would have understood. She was only playing and would not have actually harmed any of you—that is until you hurt her."

"Hold up…let me see if I understand this. You want me to talk to that big-ass, hulk-sized, long-haired spider monkey like she's a person? Who am I, Doctor Doolittle in outer space?" I looked back to the others. "Next she'll want me to be a goodwill Ambassador and negotiate that the Tukylis cease killing the inhabitants of the worlds they conquer." I looked back to her. "Really?"

Glaring at me, she shouted a word we all understood, "Amazons!"

Surrounded, her female warriors, moved toward us, their actions indicated hostility. One of them approached and stood at her side. She was of African descent dressed similar to their leader, and wore her hair thinly braided. These Amazons were sukai life-forms, and like the mythological females of old Earth, they too were made up of different ethnicities. Except for their leader, their height ranged anywhere from six to seven feet... Physically fit, they probably possessed mega strength, quickness, and agility, and I surmised that they had the same fearless courage about them. They were armed with metal hand grips capable of becoming long thick quarterstaffs precisely ten inches in diameter. Some of the warriors had already extended their staff weapons, while others did so as they approached.

"Hawkins, say something," ordered Z'yenn.

"Oh yeah, this is going to be fun," I said looking at the fifty Amazons who were taller than I.

"She meant say something useful," Joryd added, looking to me.

Speaking their language, I explained that our arrival here was against our choosing, that we did not want any conflict, and that all we wanted was to get back home. However, their leader also needed to know that we were prepared to defend ourselves if need be, and in a cautionary show of intent, I and the others placed our hands on or near our Kajas. We were ready to activate them if necessary. The Amazonian Alpha glanced down at my hand, looked to my Pridesmen, and spoke words that even I did not recognize.

She again addressed me, "Your weapons have been neutralized. Come with us."

I drew my morphogenic apparatus, but found the Kaja did not work just as she had said. I immediately informed my Pack. Regardless, they, too, tried to activate their devices and failed. Their Alpha turned, walked away, and commanded her Amazons in her native language, "Bring them."

"You're not taking us anywhere," I shouted in Zahnobein so that the Pack knew my intentions.

Quickly reaching up, I grabbed the end of the staff weapon that one Amazon had pointed at me and flung the unsuspecting female giant into two of her fellow warriors. Immediately calling out to U'kristu, I held the staff up, and the weapon suddenly switched to its null setting. Now useless as a fighting stick, I used it as a projectile and beamed one of the two Amazons charging Torr. Down she went, and at once we engaged the female warriors, while their Alpha and her second stood by and observed.

"You chose well, Mheria. These Offworlders' combat skills seem most impressive, especially the small brown female. Perhaps too much so, that one could probably take all of our sisters herself." She said, pointing to U'kristu. "They're defeating our warriors. I would have thought that to be impossible since we outnumbered them nearly five to one."

"Impossible is what we're up against, Talah, so therefore, the impossible is what we must have."

"But I thought our goal was to capture them?"

"It is. Have preparations for our guests been made?"

"As instructed," her Nubian second replied.

"Good. This should be over very soon, and then we can begin."

The battle was over quicker than the female leader thought, and we were able to defeat her warriors without seriously injuring them or killing them. We were all slightly winded, except for U'kristu whose breathing seemed normal. I did not know how she managed that, especially since she defeated half the Amazons herself. We approached the two who remained.

"Who are you?" Joryd asked angrily. "What is this place?" His heated questioning lessened a little. "What do you want with us?"

The Amazonian Alpha said nothing, but instead held up her hand as if she were being sworn in by a judge. Looking to them, for an instant they appeared out of focus, but then her hand and our bodies suddenly started to glow and ripped our strength from us. It hurt–a lot. I could barely stand. Then they physically changed–transforming into large creatures donned in red armor but stood upright like a man. We did not know what species they were, or could we have guessed, their identities were completely concealed. The more we struggled, the more savagely our strengths were sapped. On our knees we fought hard against the field that held us, refusing to yield, but eventually we had to. Laisere was first to collapse, and then Starone and Torr followed.

Their leader did not wear armor, though what it wore masked its identity, it then introduced itself in a language understood by all.

"I am Telus, Lord of all I conquer…"

Z'yenn and I fell next.

"I am a force unlike any other…"

Avedia and Meva succumbed.

"Powerful, infinite, and absolute."

U'kristu fought hard going down but she too had to join us in unconsciousness, while the Elphah continued to strain mightily against the field.

"Fall Cat!" the Sorcerer smirked, amused by Joryd's valiant struggle, he intensified the energy field around him. "Your Master commands it."

Roaring, the Pantherus finally fell and hit the ground with a heavy thud. Walking among us, Telus checked that we had all been subdued by his sorcery and grinned.

"Welcome to Ventra…Qi-Tahh." He said and laughed evilly, as if this were all a joke.

The Saga Continues with… "The Supremacy – Reign of the Sorcerer."

Glossary

Languages Used – Fonchuai (F) Sk'tier – (Sk) Zahnobein – (Z) Pantherus (P)

A

Acquil-Omegah – Deggzytepol

Acrolin (Ac Ro Lin) Apse – A plant that sprays acid.

Angela Hawkins – Human. African-American woman, average height, sexy, fit, caramel complexion, brown hair, and almond colored eyes. Marc's wife.

Anishaa Dhriti – Human-Augment Hindu female, 5'6 with an average build, long black hair and black eyes. Genius, possessing mega strength and speed, excellent eye-hand coordination, enhanced five senses, and a powerful voice. Juardian Deltah. Her name translates as "Good Heart."

Anton – Middle-aged Eanoi man.

Antonio Franco Battista – Augmented Human. Caucasian, 5'11, muscular build, approx. 205 lbs. black hair, and piercing blue eyes. Genius, possessing mega strength, excellent eye-hand coordination, enhanced senses, empathic and telepathic abilities, telekinetic and a student of both Wisardry and the Mystik Arts. Deggzytepol.

Arjai (Are Ji) – Healer

Arjai Ra-tuth – (Healer Elphah)

Arjenadann (Are Jena Dan) Xentouwish life-form, ancient space born creature, huge with greenish-grey coloring, no eyes or mouth that can be seen, hidden tendrils, empathic, telepathic and possesses great powers; can also separate from ship.

Ashanti Prism – Ship-Arjenadann's Power Source. Yellow-colored liquid energy contained within red crystallites.

Augment – To enhance or otherwise improve upon.

Avedia (A Vid ia) - Oolong. Reptilian/Sukai hybrid. Dicorp and Mystik.

B

Bah-rodft (Ba Rod Fit) – Quarantine or Off Limits (Z)

Bakorym (Bach Ko Rim) – Science Specialyst

Bashaun – on Thada Argen.

Betah – Underling

Betah-Deltah – Tux-Kahn

Bodeaco (Bo Day Co) – Sex (Z)

Broxx (Brock) – Gorilla General Simian life-form with minimal sukai traits, grey skin, black hair and eyes. Short rounded ears, snub nose and opposable thumbs on hands and feet. Aggressive, strong, agile, stocky muscular build, great sense of smell, keen eyesight, and excellent hearing.

C

Celestriel (Ce Less Tri El) - A Mystik (Mystic)

Cesuritas – Star system investigated by the Verasce Qi-Tahh.

Charge – Someone a Juardian is assigned to protect.

Clara – Large size Latina woman with long dark hair and black eyes. A member of the Council and head of her settlement.

Comini (Co Mini) Star System – Battle between the Doxini and the Melmorn.

Cougg. Cat life-form, light brown fur, small black nose, short rounded ears, orange colored eyes, short white whiskers and teeth, six legs, two paws has opposable thumbs, retractable claws and long twin tails.

Cryda – Hell (P)

Cyrivedian (Cy Riv Edian) V – Toxic, fast acting fire extinguisher.

D

Daiot (Day Ot) – Night (U)

Darr – Caucasian with dark blond hair and brown eyes. 6'3 and powerful looking.

Karoline's husband.

Deltah – Wasyn

Deltah-Omegah – Echelon

Defona (Dee Fona) – Beloved (P)

Deggzytepol (Deg Zight Pole) – Acquil-Omegah

Dicorp (Di Corp) - Pylot/Navigator

Dir-nay (Der Nay) – Thada Argen. Pygmy, half meter tall, furry and resembling the colors of the forest. Four-finger hands and feet.

Dysk (Disk) – A Kaja weapon capable of slicing through most structures, or render someone unconscious depending on the intention.

DySunn (Di Sun) – Name of Fonchuai God.

E

Eanoi (An Noy) – Sukai life-forms resembling Earthlings and consisting of a variety of ethnicities.

Echelon – Deltah-Omegah

Edat – Dir-nay Trader, Darr's friend and Magam's Mate.

E'Dol – Netureal. Male Marsupial-like species, petite with brown hair covering entire body except face, hands and feet. Anamorphic, possessing the ability to alter her form into any animal at will. He is a Wisard apprentice.

Elemental – Molecular life-form. Sukai form, head made of granite, the eyes sparkle like sapphires, with left side of torso is black as coal, the right side red like rubies, upper arms sea foam green, lower arms and hands sky blue, with his hands and feet brown like the ground. Species has ability to alter themselves into the four states of matter (Gas, liquid, solid and plasma) in any combination at will.

Elphah (Alpha) – Ra-Tuth – Leader of a Pride, Pack or section.

Enac Sus Dize (E Nak Sus Dice) – Empathic Abilities (Z)

Enac Sus Sol (E Nak Sus Sole) – Telepathic interface unit enabling non-telepaths to communicate with Arjenadann and her offsprings. (Z)

Encyllari (In Sil Lari) Pryme (Prime) – Auxiliary Throne.

E'nie – Icsiedoa. Ginsung – Communications Specialyst.

Et'nim (Et Nim) – Second (U)

F

Fasbi (Faz Bee) – Thank you or thanks.

Fonchuai (Fon Shway) – Sukai male with orange hue skin tone, brown hair, and beige color eyes. Five times stronger than humans and three as fast. High intellect and inherently sarcastic.

Frum (From) – Damn (F)

Furlonus (Fur Lon Us) – Pantherus God

G

Gaul – Insect life-form, Aphid-like, pink and green coloring, eight legs, size ranging up to four inches, with white eyes and antennas. The ship's custodians.

Gayr (Gayer) – Transporter (Z)

Gi-brey (Gi Bray) – Micro dot, telecom with hologram capability.

Ginsung (Gin Sung) - Communications Specialyst.

Grayel Unch – Zahnobein sukai and cat hybrid. Male black as night, large and the Encyllari Pryme Dicorp.

Grohn – Seague, Gibbon-like species with an olive complexion, red fur and long tails with furry ends. Walk predominantly hunched over but fast on their hands and feet. Peaceful and gentle creature.

Grumbah (Grum Bah) – Greetings (Z)

Gulapalae (Gu Lap A Lay) – Sukai with golden yellowish-brown skin tone, red hair, and green eyes with three breasts spanning across her chest. The females have three breasts spanning their chest, while the males have two penises.

Gutai (Goo Tay) – Dir-nay King.

Gy-ew (Guy Ew) – Ohden. Ancient life-form, species unknown. Large alien male brain, pewter color. Council Member.

H

Hexagyn (Hex A Gin) - A hexagon-shaped Portal that acts as a personal transporter. Appears and opens with a sound no louder than a soft whisper.

Hona (Ho Na) – Nano metallurgic dissection beam.

Hotress (Ho Tres) – Minute (Z)

Human – Any member of the Hominidae having human form or attributes opposed to animals or Divine beings.

I

Icsiedoa (Ick Si Doe A) Insect life-form man-size, dark blue skin, light blue antennas, and black eyes. Mouth divides into four parts (vertical and horizontal). Six arms (two of them are three finger hands, two are claws, and two resemble that of the praying mantis of Earth) and four large three toes feet.

J

Ja-Challah – Xentou female.

Jamonaka (Ja Mon Aka) – Please (Z)

Jhanctum (J' Ankh Tum) – Name of the galaxy.

Joryd Kenton – Pantherus. Male cat species. Large (Twice size of fully grown male lion) Rich red color mane, reddish-orange body fur, large sharp white teeth, retractable claws, five toes, with orange and green eyes, and black whiskers. Elphah

Justin – Caucasian five year-old boy with blond hair and grey eye.

Juardian (Guardian) – Security

Juardian Ra-tuth - Security Elphah

K

Kaivessh – Ohden. Ancient life-form, species unknown. Large alien female brain, rustic hue encased in transparent pentagon shape bubble. Council Member.

Kaja (Ka Ja) – Half orb-like weapon device worn in area of preference to bearer. Morphogenic weapon/tool transmutes into whatever utilities the creator thinks of.

Kahnu Aruma – Ormrindo Aquatic life-form and Arjai technician.

Karoline (Caroline) – Darr's Wife pregnant woman five-seven with sandy blond hair and dark colored eyes.

Kasauj (Ka Sau G) – Stop (Z)

Keelan Sopa – Zahnobein and Elphah of the Mirren Arjai Pride.

Kerebrol (Cerebral) – Ohden. Ancient life-form, species unknown. Large alien brain, blue color encased in transparent pentagon shaped bubble. Speaks in male and female unison and Leader of the Council of Planets.

Ket-sho (Ket Show) – Teacher (Z)

Kigong (Key Gong) - Sukai life-form with lavender skin tone, black hair and red eyes. Height and size varies. Blood related to the Fonchuais.

Kileo – Marsupial, Marten life-form and Ashanti Omegah.

Koroc (Core Oc) – Fuck (F)

Koroxsu (Ko Rox Su) – Tomorrow (Z)

Kranka – Twice the size of Alaskan Timber Wolves, dark grey fur with large white spots, six legs, five toe paws, pointed ears, and pure white eyes and six inch fangs.

Kuyo – Welcome.

L

L'Pom – Icsiedoa. Insect life-form Encyllari Tova.

Laimeguage (Lame Guage) – English spoken words.

Laisere – Velfin. Lupus-Bird hybrid. Throne Pryme Tova (Weapons Specialyst).

Life Support Device (L.S.D) – Forcefield protects user from deadly atmospheric and gravitational environments, while providing breathable air regardless the species.

Link-sys (Link Sys) – Artificial life-form, genius intellect, highly evolved, morphogenic and regenerative capabilities; self-replicating, total program reside in the smallest of their components; thus allowing them to be downloaded into a new mechanism quickly.

Lopsin (Lop Sen) – Shit (F)

Lucan – Black British bald man. Tall with a muscular thin build. Sorn's Father.

Luthium (Lu Thy Um) – Rare mineral used in Linksys experiment to asphyxiate all life in the galaxy.

Lyriss (Li Riss) III – Planetoid nearly overrun by Tukyli.

M

Magam – Dir-nay - Edat's Mate.

Maluskan - Mollusk species. Bluish-green skin tone, small black eyes, cream antennas, and two thin tentacles with three-finger hands.

Marc Hawkins – Augmented Human. African-American man, average height physically fit, chocolate brown complexion, dark brown hair and brown eyes. Possesses all of the basic prowess and abilities that all Human-Augments have. Betah.

Marsupial (Mar Sue Pee Aul) – A marten life-form, short arboreal creatures with the body of wombats, and the feet similar to kangaroos, giving them the ability to hop great distances. Their coats are usually a glossy light brown and have twin bushy tails embedded with small quills, they fire with accuracy. Each tail has a different poison, one kills and the other stuns. Brown eyes short ears, and four digits hands and feet.

Marya – Asian female Eanoi and Anton's wife.

Matsu – Older Japanese male Eanoi and Council leader of the Argenta settlement.

Mead – Year (U)

Mheria Thakien – Sukai life-form, resembling Caucasian descent, 5'10 physically fit, with piercing blue color eyes, medium length black hair and Sorceress and heir to the Throne of Ventra.

Mirrepo (Mir Re Poe) – Cousin (Z)

Momja (Mom Ja) – Computer (Z)

Mumar (Mu Mar) – Martial Arts

Mystik (Mystic) – Majikal being.

N

Nahni (Nani) Chytyck (Chai Tic) – Arjai-Omegah

Netureal (Neh Tu Rail) - Marsupial-like petite with sandy blond hair covering entire body except face, hands and feet. Have short snout, brown nose and eyes, and small five digit hands and feet with opposable thumbs and toes. They are short in height, averaging 1 ½ meters, and weighing not much over 100 lbs., and are also referred to as Animorph, for their ability to alter form into any kind of animal desired quickly and effortlessly. Species speaks in broken language.

Nextus – Dir-nay and Wagg's father.

Niya (Ni Ya) – Day (U)

Nyphomadaxel (Ny Fo Ma Dax El) – Parasitical disease that absorbs all fluid in a body, and reduce the infected to few pounds of crystallized remains.

Nyrit – Xentou male.

O

Ohden (Olden) Brain Species – Large alien brain encased in transparent pentagon shaped bubble, highly intelligent, and possesses superior mental abilities. Telekinetic, telepathy, and many powers connected with the mind.

Omegah – Tas'r

Omegus Prime – Linksys Leader. Giant Android nine feet tall and three thousand pounds.

Oolong (Ooo Long) – Reptilian/Sukai life form. Waist up, a contortionist, thin toned build with coral green scales that covered of her except for her face. Pattern and designs formed on this species. Webbed fingers with short sharp claws, eight fangs, paired in each quant rant of mouth. Sightless and no orifices, ultra-senses, fast, and strong. Covered, her patterns and designs indicate what sect her family is connected to. She is a Dicorp/Pylot and Mystik.

Opo (O Po) – Friend (Z)

Opos O Pos) – Friends (Z)

Oria (Or Ia) – Star system located at the inner rim of the of the Jhanctum galaxy.

Ormrindo (Orm Rin Doe) – Aquatic life-form, large head, slender long neck, short torso, and ten tentacles; four arms and six legs. Eight red colored eyes grouped in fours, no mouth and smooth skin.

P

Pack – A group or team of people and/or units.

Pah-fa (Pa Fa) – Joke (F)

Pantherus (Panther Us) – Cat species. Large (Twice size of full grown male lion) Rich red color mane, dark orange body fur, large sharp white teeth, retractable claws, five toes, with orange and green eyes, and black whiskers.

Pisana – Dir-nay and Wagg's mother.

Pief (Pi ef) Quino (Qui no) – Greenish-brown moss. Nature's cure for Linksys spider venom.

Priccaryan (Prick Carry an) - Bi-coexistent life-form. Twins, different color skin tone two heads, small gray thorn-like bumps covering each face, their noses long and flat against their face connected to their mouths. Small holes on both side of their heads acted as their ears, and they had four arms, and six long digits for each hand. When they spoke, one head would either start the sentence, and the other would finish, or occasionally they would speak in unison.

Pride – Family.

Priort (Pry Ort) – Bat-like creature indigenous to Thada Argen.

Pryme (Prime) – Main

Q

Qi (Chi) – Life

Qi-Tahh (Chi Tahhh) – Life Protectors.

R

Ra-Tuth (Ra Tooth) – Elphah

Rheeza – Syth and Elphah of the Vitalyst Arjai Pride.

Renn – Xentou male.

Rhetnig-Sux – Ohden. Ancient life-form, species unknown. Large alien male brain, beige color encased in transparent pentagon shape bubble, and Council Member.

Rubicund Ribbons of Diakleze – Mystik protection spell. Giant glowing red bands.

S

Satyre (Say Tar) – Repair (Z)

Savner (Sav Ner) – Hour (U)

Sclee-Tonna – Priccaryan. Bi-coexistent life-form. Throne Pryme Bakorym Specialyst.

Seague – Gibbon-like species with an olive complexion, red fur and long tails with furry ends. Walk predominantly hunched over but fast on their hands and feet. Peaceful and gentle creature.

Sercrom – Setou. Colony creature Encyllari Pryme Elphah.

Seregaia (Sear Gaia) – Seague home world on the fifth planet in the Oria star system.

Scorpilyn (Score Pi Lynn) - Biped Reptile race, walked similar to the Raptors of Earth, but far more agile. Long forked tongue, eyes black as they were cold and a long tail. Savage War-like creatures honorable, possesses mega strength, superior speed, agility, and quick reflexes. Intelligence and aggressive nature is very high.

Setou (Seh Toe) – Colony creatures resembling large gecko, especially when they add moisture to eyes with their very long tongue. They have four thin arms with four fingered webbed hands, six legs with four toes per webbed foot, and a long tail, all of which will grow back if cut off or severely damaged. Their skin is smooth like a dolphin, grey tinge with tiny red specks covering entire body. Possess ability to camouflage; matching any surroundings and giving them a great advantage. The species are revered to be as beautiful and as they are elusive.

Setsu (Set Su) – Tomorrow (Sk)

Sk'tier (Skit Tear) – Sukai, short, thin build, shapely stature, a reddish yellow tinge skin tone, long white and brown hair, with black eyes.

Skarb (Sc arb) – Beetle creatures indigenous to Thada Argen.

Sorn – Young Black Eanoi with short curly hair and Lucan's Son.

Starone Metalstorm – Elemental life-form. Sukai, head made of granite, the eyes sparkle like sapphires, with left side of torso is black as coal, the right side red like rubies, upper arms sea foam green, lower arms and hands sky blue, with his hands and feet brown like the ground. Ashanti Elphah.

Sukai (Sue Kai) – Referenced to Humans and Humanoids.

Supremacy – Mastery, Power to defeat.

Suncol (Sun Cole) – Beloved (Z)

Syn'nar Sivgons – Zigong. Sukai female of medium height, sexy build, a lavender skin tone, short black hair, and red colored eyes. Juardian Deltah and Torr's cousin.

Syth – Plant/Animal species, telepathic with parthenogenesis capabilities.

Sythean – Syth. Plant/Animal hybrid life-form, parthenogenetic capability, Red, green and blue coloring, four vine-like arms and multi-root-like legs. Telepathic. Deggzytepol.

T

Talah – Sukai life-form resembling African descent, tall, muscular, physically fit, strong, agile and fast, with green color eyes, and medium length dark brown hair braided. Amazonian Warrior, Personal Protector to Royal Family and Supreme Captain of the Amazon Forces.

Talon – Scorpilyn. Reptile species, approximately 7'0 ft. at 650 lbs. with a XXXL build and Juardian-Omegah.

Tami – Korean female Eanoi. Thin build about forty years old.

Tas'r (Taz-R) – Omegah.

Tah (Ta) – Protect or Protector

Te'lar – Maluskan. Mollusk species. Juardian-Deltah.

Torr Sivgins - Fonchuai. Sukai male, average height and build, orange color skin tone, long reddish brown hair and beige eyes. 5 times stronger than humans and twice as fast, high intellect, species inherently smart mouth. Arjai-Elphah.

Tova – Weapons Specialyst

Tux-Kahn – Betah-Deltah

U

U'kristu Rixx – Sk'tier Sukai female, short, thin build, shapely stature, a reddish yellow tinge skin tone, long white and brown hair, with black eyes. Juardian-Elphah and former member of the Vardyn Society.

Unasallo (Una Sallow) – The Qi-Tahh sent to relieve the Zahnobein Life Protectors of their post.

Underling – Betah

V

V'Hil (V Hill) – Netureal life-form, Ashanti/Engineering Deltah and Wisard apprentice.

Va-lim – Student (Sk)

Vardyn (Var Den) – A Secret Order. Reference U'kristu Rixx.

Velfin (Val Fin) - Bird-Lupus hybrid. Head, eyes, beak/nose, and chest, resembled a giant eagle, with wingspan of a giant condor hidden in his coat. Covered with fur instead of feathers, they have bushy tails, ears twice as large as timber wolves, small razor sharp teeth lining the inside of their beaks, and has optional to walk predominantly upright on the front portion of their feet. Most usually chose to run or stalk on all fours; heels never touching ground; retractable talons, paws with opposable thumbs. They are highly intelligent, strong, very maneuverable, fast in the air and quick on the ground, with keen eyesight and sense of smell.

Verasce (Vera Ask) – The Qi-Tahh sent to the Cesuritas star system and discovers the Pyrites have returned.

Verstix (Ver Stick) – Week (Z)

Virggyte (Ver Gite) – Brownish-red vulture-like creature.

W

Wagg – Dir-nay child of Nextus and Pisana.

Wahn-Jemm – Ohden. Ancient life-form, species unknown. Large alien female brain, sea foam green color, encased in transparent pentagon shape bubble. Council Member.

Wasyn (Wa Sin) – Deltah

Wehtiko (Wet Tic O) - The Wehtiko is a highly communicable contagion that began thousands of years ago. This insidious strain does not affect all who are exposed, it cannot be eradicated and once Influenced neither the host nor their planet can ever be completely cleansed of its barbarous effects. The Wehtiko is a pathogen of evil that unleashes the Influences' darkest nature.

Wurz (Wer Z) – You and You're (Z)

X

Xentouwish (Zen Towel Wish) – Name of the sentient life-form, ancient space born creature, huge with greenish-grey coloring, no eyes or mouth, hidden tendrils, empathic, telepathic and possesses great powers; joined to ship.

Xentous (Zen Towels) Offsprings have same color complexion as their mother and is empathic, telepathic, and possesses great powers.

Z

Zahnobein (Za No Be In) – Cat/sukai hybrid, black as night, smaller than the male of her species, tall when standing upright, athletic build with dark yellow claws, whiskers and markings, as well as greenish yellow eyes, possesses strength, speed, agility, and other senses, but lacking the same advantages as a pure feline creature.

Zinkeel (Zen Kill) – Ranks.

Ra-Tuth	Elphah
Tas'r	Omegah
Deggzytepol	sub-Omegah
Acquil	Omega-Deltah
Wasyn	Deltah
Tux-Kahn	Deltah-Betah

Underling	Betah

Zonnyan – Grotesque looking, soft and shapeless like large mollusks out of their shell, and pus oozed out from ports in their bodies.

Z'yenn Kaira – Zahnobein female sukai and cat hybrid. Omegah/Tas'r.

APPENDIX

Lord Telus

Inside the Palace converted Fortress, far from the Elisia forest, a large simian creature with strong gorilla-like traits, walked upright like a man and marched heavily down the long stone hallway carrying his red helmet tucked under his buffed arm. He soon reached a pair of heavy doors which opened automatically and proceeded inside.

Walking to the foot of several long steps, he ascended to the first platform and knelt. Bowing his head, he brought his left fist and pinned it to his right chest.

"Lord Telus, General Broxx reporting as ordered." The grey skinned, black haired man-ape remained in his respectful position until a voice commanded otherwise.

"Rise," The Mandrake life-form ordered, standing with his arms behind him and his back to Broxx.

Lifting his head, the General stood facing his Master.

"Tonight when it is certain the Amazons are asleep, you will lead two attack regiments to Thakien's supposedly hidden Throne ship." Telus turned and faced Broxx, narrowing his red eyes. "There, you will slaughter all of her sisters and deliver the Sorceress to me. I will then force her to watch as I execute her would-be saviors. It is time the Empress learned who is Master."

Next Installment

The Supremacy

Reign of The Sorcerer

Marc Hawkins is the latest human recruited by the Ohdens, the Governing Council Authority of the Jhanctum galaxy, to fight in a war that has been waging for thousands of years, and who reluctantly had joined their Supremacy. Placed with an assortment of creatures who consider themselves family, they educate Hawkins in what it means to belong to a Pride, while his training teaches him what it means to be Qi-Tahh. However, unbeknownst to Marc, he will soon be forced to put aside the conflicts he has with his new family, with his responsibilities as a Life Protector, and with his Zonnyan assignment after he, Joryd and seven Pridesmen were whisked away from ship and planet during a skirmish with the Dir-nays on Thada Argen.

Transported to the dangerous and hostile planet Ventra, the Pack were captured and sentenced to death by Telus, a powerful, sadistic Sorcerer, and barely managed to escape captivity with the aid of Thakien and her Amazons. Later, the Qi-Tahh learn the young Sorceress was responsible for their being brought to her planet, and must overcome their personal conflicts with the Imperial Empress and her female warriors, in order to help restore the status quo to Ventra.

The Life Protectors, Mheria and her Amazons must win the no-holds-barred, winner-take-all, fight-to-the-finish against a creature whose powers rival that of an Ohden. However, their mission is jeopardized when an unforeseen betrayal Influenced by the Wehtiko, endangers them all, as well as their objective. Fail to stop Telus, and it will cost them their lives, and give him the means he needs to become omnipotent.

CPSIA information can be obtained
at www.ICGtesting.com
Printed in the USA
LVOW07s0326210417
531608LV00001B/9/P

9 781524 624811